D

Just as dusk wa⋯
the old men hear⋯
hung in the still⋯
a tone that was so⋯
itself harshly to⋯
slowly, almost li⋯ ⋯veral
seconds in betwee⋯ ⋯en peal. Yet it was as
though the first note never really died away,
hanging in the air, waiting for the subsequent
ones, amalgamating into a sound that grew
and grew . . . and grew until the listeners
clutched their hands to their ears in a vain
attempt to shut out the noise.

But the noise went on and on, growing in
magnitude, pounding against the interior of
the skull with all the force of a steel clapper.

DEATHBELL

GUY N. SMITH

Hamlyn Paperbacks

A Hamlyn Paperback
Published by Arrow Books Limited
17-21 Conway Street, London W1P 6JD

A division of the Hutchinson Publishing Group

London Melbourne Sydney Auckland
Johannesburg and agencies throughout
the world

First published in Great Britain by
Hamlyn Paperbacks 1980
Reprinted 1980, 1981 and 1984

Printed and bound in Great Britain by
Anchor Brendon Limited, Tiptree, Essex

ISBN 0 09 938230 X

1

THE WATCHERS

The leaden winter sky darkened perceptibly and spat a flurry of snowflakes, the strong easterly wind swirling them across the tree covered mountain slopes. Dusk was already starting to blend into darkness and before morning the whole of this rugged landscape would be covered by a thick fall of snow.

The half-dozen or so villagers who huddled together on the narrow lane at the foot of the hillside glanced at one another. Old men, all of them, the last of a generation that dressed in ankle-length navy blue overcoats, faded mufflers tied in a knot at the throat and peaked caps pulled well down to shield their faces from the lashing gale. Pipe-smokers, with short stemmed Seadog briars, the bowls burned black and uneven, thick black twist glowing like braziers in the wind. A sense of comradeship, an instinctive joining of forces against the younger breed and their way of life. Several of their comrades had their names engraved on the war memorial inside the church. The advancing years had claimed others. Now only these few remained in living contempt of those who openly despoiled everything for which they had lived and fought.

Their eyes never left the scene on the opposite side of the road. The large grey stone house with mullioned windows, many of the panes cracked or missing, the walls almost totally covered by ivy, incorporated an air of dereliction from the broken slates on the roof down to the crumbling wide front steps. In summer the grassy

1

banks which surrounded it were cushioned with mauve aubretia, and the stunted orchard at the rear was a carpet of snowdrops and yellow daffodils in spring. The stream beyond rushed on relentlessly, oblivious of the passing of time, widening out into a deep still pool, its surface a mass of water-lilies and blanket weed. The rambling overgrown grounds were bounded by a crumbling eight-foot stone wall, built at the time of the thriving mill which had once stood on the stream and was now a heap of debris beneath the spreading briars. It had been a prominent landmark for the traveller and a means of livelihood for the villagers.

This was the place that had once been known as Sodom, a terrible name for such remote tranquillity and beauty, in the days of the mill-owner, a tyrant who had driven his two daughters to suicide and murdered his wife before turning the knife blade upon his own heart. Sodom it had once been, now it was Caelogy Hall. But a change of name could not erase the memory of its past. Few, apart from the stoic watchers in the wintry dusk, recalled the old days, yet the place had lain empty since before the outbreak of World War II, the elements eating away the stonework, dashing the slates from the roof, and the glass out of the windows in the house and the old chapel with its ornate belfry. Time eroded and none cared, least of all the villagers. Nobody went through the rusting gates. Until now.

A large furniture van was parked in the drive. Men in overalls struggled with large crates and items of furniture, carrying them down the tailboard, across the mossy fore-court and into the house. Back and forth, an air of urgency about them as though they wished to be away from this place before darkness fell.

This was the third van to unload today. The previous two had already departed. Parked nearby was a white Mercedes with tinted windows, silent and out of place in these derelict surroundings.

'I dinna like it,' the stooped man with the drooping

2

white moustache clenched his teeth hard on the stem of his pipe as he voiced his opinion. 'I dinna like it at all.'

'Me, neither,' the one immediately behind him muttered. ''Tain't right. The place should've bin burned to the ground in the days when it was known as . . .'

'Dinna ye mention that name,' Tom Williamson snarled. 'Not no more. Blasphemy, that's what it is. That's why all them folks died. The old man was a disciple o' the devil hisself, set up in 'is own palace of evil. It shoulda' bin demolished. And who are these folks to come and live here, I ask you? What right have they?'

'Aye,' a chorus of agreement.

The men strained their eyes but the light was failing and it was possible only to see the shapes of the removal men in silhouette against the yellow square of light from the big doorway.

'That chapel was an abomination in the sight o' the Lord,' Williamson puffed out clouds of rank-smelling tobacco, 'I remember the bell callin' the family to worship on Sundays when I was a boy. Worship,' he spat, removing his pipe from his mouth for a second, 'it weren't no worship. No man who is a Christian would murder 'is family. No, they were makin' pacts with the devil. Arkwright was, anyway. 'E traded in 'is wife and daughters, and then when 'e realised what 'e'd done, 'e killed 'isself.'

'You was too young to remember, Tom.'

'Mebbe. And mebbe not. But I knows. Everybody knows. And no good will come of this new lot movin' into Caelogy, you mark my words.'

The men were still there when the big van reversed into the road and drove away. They made no move to disperse. Their curiosity was greater than their physical discomfort.

There was a movement in the lighted doorway of Caelogy Hall and they stepped back into the hedge as though fearing to be seen. They strained their eyes, drawing heavily on their pipes. A man appeared on the steps, tall and lean, moving with a purposeful step, walking out on to the drive and heading in the direction of the gates. The watchers shrank back still further, closing their ranks as though seeking safety in numbers.

The stranger came right up to the gateway and stopped, looking to the right and left of him, not once peering out across the road. He saw the rusted gates, noticed that they were still intact and began to exert his strength, pulling them forcibly from the trailing briars and weeds entwined around the ornamental wrought iron. They creaked, protesting loudly at this disturbance after forty years, but yielded in the end. Within a few minutes both were closed, and the catch was forced down into place.

Something clinked metallically. A small chain glistened. A sharp snap. A key turned and was withdrawn from the large padlock. The man retraced his steps with long strides.

'I told you,' Williamson whispered hoarsely. 'They're up to no good. 'E's locked the gates. There's sommat they don't want nobody to see. Sommat . . . *evil*!'

The men remained there, smoking and staring at the steel chain wrapped around the rusty ironwork. The wind strengthened to gale force, bringing with it larger flakes of snow. But they made no move to leave.

'What's that?' one of them spoke sharply, fearfully, pointing with a gnarled finger.

'What's what?'

'Over there. In them bushes. Sommat moved.'

Seconds later they all saw it, a huge slinking shape, tongue lolling from fearsome jaws, pausing suddenly as the wind wafted their scent in its direction. The pointed head went up and back, and it let forth a low growl, the hackles on its back rising.

'It's as big as . . . as a wolf!'

'It's a dog,' Tom Williamson's reply was a hoarse whisper. 'One o' them alsatians. Half wolf, and as savage. Now what the devil do they want a dog like that loose in the grounds for?'

'To keep people out.'

4

'Aye, because they're up to no good. Never thought I'd see the day anybody came to live in Caelogy.'

The group moved away, heads low, collars turned up in a futile attempt to protect their faces from the tearing wind. Sparks flew from their pipes as the tobacco was fanned into a dull red glow.

They were beyond the church and nearly at the row of small neat white-washed cottages when they heard the sound of human laughter. It was no sound of mirth but rather an inarticulate bellow that rose to a high pitch and then died slowly away. One of them started involuntarily and clutched at his companion.

'What the . . .'

'Easy on, Alf,' the other chuckled, 'nothin' to worry about. That's only Donald Hughes.'

'Aye, course it is,' there was a distinct note of relief in the first man's voice. 'Fooled me for a second. Didn't expect 'im to be about on a night like this.'

'You should know Donald better than that,' Tom Williamson cut in. 'He's as crazy as they come, but he'll harm nobody. I'd sooner meet 'im on any dark night than that lot who've bought the Hall. Deaf and sorta dumb, that's all. All 'e can do is grin and make that noise that's supposed to be laughter. If more people were like Donald there'd be a lot less trouble in this world.'

'All the same, 'e gives you the creeps if 'e's around when you ain't expectin' 'im.'

They hurried on, eager to seek shelter in the warmth of their respective cottages. Not one of them noticed the figure crouching motionless beneath a spreading holly bush, clad only in a rough working shirt, open at the neck, and trousers that did not meet his frayed working boots. The features were broad and mongoloid in appearance, the eyes wide and staring, missing nothing. Outsize upper teeth touched the lower lip.

Donald Hughes, the simpleton of Turbury village, chuckled, a noise that began and ended in his throat for he understood that silence was imperative if he was not to be seen. He was happy. It was a wild night and he could travel where his fancy took him without interference from anybody. That was the most important thing in life to him. Freedom!

Donald Hughes did not hurry. He had all the time in the world. All night. His folks wouldn't worry about his absence. A few years ago they would have come searching for him. But not now. He was eighteen. Old enough to look after himself. Sod 'em.

He left the road and struck off into the woods. It was pitch black but that didn't worry him. He didn't need to see. He knew every track, every tree and bush. Even the driving snow which was already beginning to settle did not disturb him.

He came to a fork and took the left path. Along here somewhere . . . ah! He sensed the movement rather than saw the rabbit pulling and struggling in the snare. A low grunt escaped his lips. That was lucky. He'd only set the wire the previous night. Mr Walsh, the butcher, would be pleased. He'd give him ten pence for the coney. It was good money. He ought to set a few more snares.

As he reached for the rabbit it pulled back to the full extent of the thin strand of wire. It squealed as Donald's thick fingers grasped it but the youth did not hear the creature's cry of terror. Holding it firmly around the flanks he loosened the noose and slipped it over its head with his other hand. The rabbit quivered but did not squeal again. Its eyes rolled but it had already resigned itself to its fate.

Donald was reaching for the knife in his belt when a sudden thought occurred to him. Mr Walsh had said not to cut the throats of rabbits he caught. It spoiled the look of them when they were hung up outside the shop. That was a pity. It was so easy, so satisfying to watch the scarlet fluid spurting from the animal's jugular vein as its struggles grew weaker and weaker until they finally ceased altogether. But ten pence was ten pence . . .

6

He held the creature by its back legs, and with his left hand gripped its neck, straightened it out, took the strain. Then he was staggering back, cursing in his own language as head and body parted, warm blood splattering all over him. He stood there, slowly licking some of the blood which was running down his nose and dripping on to his lips. It was sort of tangy.

He wondered about the rabbit. It would be a sheer waste to throw it away. Perhaps if he explained to the butcher, Mr Walsh would give him something for it. He walked on, carrying the rabbit's body in one hand, its head in the other, leaving a trail of scarlet spots in the snow to mark his progress.

Sometime later he arrived at a high stone wall. He knew that it marked the boundary of the grounds of Caelogy Hall. He could have scaled it but there was no point. A hundred yards or so further on were the main gates, left permanently open. He would enter there, mooch around, climb in through one of the broken windows. Just mooch. It was warm inside the big house, like a kind of home where there was nobody to ridicule him, to push him around. Always his ramblings ended there.

He began to walk in a northerly direction, following the wall, clambering through a thick bed of briars in one place, not bothering to skirt them. The brambles scratched his hands but he hardly noticed the discomfort, still clutching the dismembered rabbit. The wind howled, driving the snow into his face, once causing him to turn his head away to gasp for breath. It was a wild night. It would get even wilder, but it would be nice and snug inside the Hall.

He lumbered forward, his instinct telling him where the gateway was, his head bowed against the blizzard. Then, without warning, he bumped into something solid. He grunted, almost slipped on the carpet of snow beneath his feet and gazed in amazement. Immediately in front of him, their ornate criss-cross pattern shown up by the

7

light which filtered from the downstairs windows of Caelogy Hall, he saw that the big gates were closed.

Donald stood there perplexed. Slowly his bewilderment
turned to anger. The gates were never shut. They had no
right to be. They were kept open for *him*! This was his
very own stronghold, his outlaw hideout like the bandits
in the western films on television had.

He fumbled with the heavy rusted latch. It yielded, but
the gates moved only a few inches, checked by the steel
chain which encircled them. He stepped back. Nobody
was going to prevent him going in there. Not even the
intruders who were occupying the house. He could scale
the wall easily enough, but he would be cautious. See
without being seen; find out what was going on.

He moved away from the gates and found a section of
wall in which the stonework had crumbled and broken.
The decay offered ample footholds. His hands hooked
over the top and he heaved his fifteen stone upwards with
surprising ease.

He sat there straddling the wall, his fury mounting until
his whole body trembled. He still held the rabbit. Not for
one moment had he thought of discarding it.

He jumped down on the other side, his landing softened
by a thick rhododendron bush, the brittle branches snapping under his weight. The fall knocked the breath from
his body and for some moments he lay there gasping and
wheezing.

A movement a few yards away attracted his attention.
Against the whiteness of the snowy background he saw
the dog moving stealthily, seeing him, standing with its
jaws open, uncertain. For some seconds the youth and
the alsatian regarded each other. Donald felt no fear,
only curiosity. He did not recognise this animal, and yet
he was familiar with every dog in the village of Turbury.
What was it doing in here? To whom did it belong?

With one deft movement he tossed the rabbit's head in
its direction. The dog lowered its head, sniffed at the ball
of bloody fur, and then its teeth crunched on the bone.

Donald grinned. The dog was hungry. Maybe it hadn't eaten for days and was starving. He threw it the rest of the rabbit. Mr Walsh wouldn't give him much for it, anyway.

Donald watched whilst the alsatian finished its meal. Only then did it stare at him again, but this time there was no malevolence in its expression. The upright hairs on its back were flat once more, and the tail moved slowly from side to side. They were friends.

The youth stood up and began to walk in the direction of the Hall. The dog came forward and sniffed at him. He patted it. Its rough tongue licked at his fingers, gently removing the traces of dried rabbit blood.

He moved slowly, instinctively keeping to the narrow belt of trees which fringed the wall, determined to find out who was inside the house without being seen. The dog followed him for a few yards, then, sensing that there was no more fresh rabbit meat to be had, slunk away into the shadows.

Donald crossed a patch of open ground to where some laurels, their boughs already bending under the weight of the falling snow, stood immediately opposite the front door. The windows were lighted up. There were no curtains and he could see inside.

A tall grey-haired man, a slim cigar between his lips, stood with his back to a blazing log fire. Seated in an armchair, her chin resting in her hands, a woman regarded him steadily. Her finely moulded features bore the stamp of worry. More than that. Anguish. Donald could sense that they were unhappy.

The door opened and a girl came inside, twisting her fingers together, anxious . . . afraid. Donald stared at her. She was beautiful but she was unlike any other girl he had ever seen. She was dressed in a green trouser suit that showed her petite figure off to perfection, but it was the colour of her skin which astounded him. It was yellow, and her eyes were narrow and slanted. Long black hair fell below her shoulders. She said something, but the man gestured impatiently and she withdrew from the room, closing the door behind her.

The man was talking excitedly now, gesticulating wildly, pointing towards the window. Donald shrank back, fearing for a moment that he had been seen, but nobody came outside. The couple continued talking. Something had happened which had upset them. The woman was crying, huddling in her chair.

Donald could not understand what it was all about. His anger had subsided. Now he experienced another sensation. Fear! Seldom was he afraid of anything. He could not determine what it was that was frightening him now. Nobody knew he was here. These people were not exactly hostile. They were . . . he didn't know the word for it, but they engendered an atmosphere that made him wish that he had not scaled the wall. Sinister.

He chewed on his well-bitten fingernails. Decisions never came easily to him. Should he make tracks now and leave this place? But if he did, then he would never discover what was going on. He always had problems understanding anything outside his normal way of life, and this was way above him.

Suddenly he was aware that the man was no longer in the room. The woman was on her own, brushing long strands of hair back from her attractive tear-stained face. She wrung her hands together in obvious despair. The door opened again and the girl with the yellow skin entered. The two of them were conversing, shaking their heads.

Donald emerged from his hiding place in the laurels and crept on to the drive, his gaze centred on the two women inside the house. If he got closer, maybe he could lip-read. His vocabulary wasn't very good but he might be able to glean something from their conversation.

He stopped within a couple of yards of the big bow window, staring inside. From here he could see the formation of their lips but the words meant nothing to him. Gibberish. They were talking rubbish, jabbering incessantly, pointing up towards the ceiling. They were mad, he concluded. They couldn't make themselves understood any better than he could when he tried to converse with some of the villagers.

So intent was Donald Hughes on trying to make something out of the conversation between the two women inside the house that he had not spotted the crouching figure which advanced upon him from out of the shadows, the tall man with grey hair, his handsome features contorted into a mask of rage, fists clenched, cigar clamped firmly between rows of even white teeth.

'You scoundrel!' strong fingers dug into Donald's shoulders and spun him round, 'what's the game, eh? How did you get in here?'

'Uh-uh-um,' Donald grunted, his eyes widening, shrinking back.

'Come on, speak up, boy, before I fetch the police or set the dog on you.'

Donald stared dumbly at the man who held him. There was no point in saying anything. He wouldn't be understood, anyway.

A shape materialised out of the snow-covered shrubbery at the rear. The alsatian. It sniffed, trotted forward, and came right up to the two men. Its tongue flicked out and licked Donald's hand.

The tall man stared in amazement.

'Sheba,' he called. 'Sheba . . . what the devil's got into you?'

The dog slunk back and stopped a couple of yards from its master, belly touching the ground.

'Come on, you bastard,' the new owner of Caelogy Hall shook his captive roughly, 'I want to know what you're doing here?'

Donald mouthed his inarticulate reply, shrinking back. Fear gripped him. He sensed evil, something he could not explain. Then he heard a woman's voice behind them and turned his head. It was the older of the two who had been

11

conversing in the room. She was standing framed in the front doorway, peering out into the blizzard.

'Martyn,' she called, 'is it . . . is it?'

'No, it isn't,' he answered her abruptly. 'I don't know who the hell it is. I caught him staring in through the window.'

'Shall I call the police?'

'*No!*' It was almost a scream. 'I'd let Sheba deal with him if she would, but the bitch has gone all stupid. He's an idiot of some sort, the local imbecile at a guess. I'm going to throw him out, and if he ever comes in here again something very unpleasant will surely happen to him!'

Donald felt himself being propelled towards the main gates, held firmly with one hand whilst the man called Martyn fished a key from his pocket and with some difficulty unlocked the padlock one-handed. The gates screeched their protest at being dragged back, and then the youth found himself on the outside.

'Now just listen to me,' a forefinger was shaken, school-master-fashion, before the broad ugly features of the Turbury simpleton, 'just let me catch you inside these grounds once more and you won't be walking home. You'll be crawling. Understand? And the same will happen to anybody else who goes prowling about in here.'

Donald walked away feeling physically weakened and frightened at the way his night's ramble had turned out. He wasn't going back to Caelogy Hall. But somehow he would have his revenge on these strange people who dared to take over his nocturnal hideout.

The landowner walked quickly back towards the house, his bushy eyebrows knitting together and giving him a hawk-like appearance. The woman still stood at the top of the steps, watching him anxiously.

'Go back inside, Sylvia,' he snapped. 'It's nothing to worry about. Just a simpleton. I don't think he'll come back.'

Once inside, the front door closed behind nim, his features softened and he smiled wanly.

'Is . . . is everything all right now?'

'Yes,' she sighed, 'thanks to Karamaneh. She . . .'

'Good. We must be more careful in future.'

'But it's difficult without . . .'

'I know,' he slipped an arm around her, and kissed her forehead tenderly, 'but it won't be for long. The bell should be arriving any day. It should have been here a week ago, but you know what these shipping firms are. Next week will do. I'll ring them first thing in the morning and play hell. We won't be able to relax until we've got the bell.'

2

THE BELL

'Well, Mr Reubens, how long will it take you to fit the bell?'

Fred Reubens tipped his frayed working cap on to the back of his head and scratched his thick mop of iron-grey hair. His wide freckled forehead crinkled into a frown and he fidgeted with the slide-rule which protruded from the pocket of his capacious brown overalls. A well-built man in his mid-fifties, a jobbing builder by trade, he had come to live in Turbury just over a year ago. He had intended the move as a step towards retirement but somehow he had become busier than when he was living in the city. One job followed another, and just when he was looking forward to a rest whilst the worst of the winter passed, Martyn Hamilton had summoned him to Caelogy Hall to install this ornate bell in the crumbling belfry.

'I dunno,' he muttered, and peered closer at the intricate design on the huge bell, the handiwork of craftsmen in some foreign country, a perfect pattern on the copper and tin. One emblem entwined with another to form an overall picture like some eastern tapestry.

'What do you mean, you don't know?' There was a note of annoyance in Hamilton's voice. 'There's nothing complicated. It just has to be installed in the belfry. I'm not asking you to *make* a bell for me.'

'It's the weather.' Reubens felt uneasy and dropped his gaze.

14

'What's the weather got to do with it?'

'Well, that tower needs some work doing to it, otherwise this bell could come crashing down. There's some bricks and woodwork that needs replacing before we think about hoisting this thing up there. Now if you could wait until the summer . . .'

'I can't,' Martyn Hamilton snapped irritably. 'There's enough work about the Hall to occupy you for the summer if you want it, Mr Reubens, but the bell is a priority.'

'I wouldn't've thought it mattered that much . . .'

'Well, it does. My wife and I are very religious. We shall be holding our own services in this chapel, and we want to start as soon as possible. Now, Mr Reubens, how long will it take you?'

The builder glanced about him. Three inches of snow lay upon the ground and the belfry tower. He did not relish the task, but he realised that he was dealing with a wealthy eccentric man. People in the village said that Hamilton was a millionaire. Made his money out of a business abroad. Tibet, or somewhere. There could be a good screw in this if he kept on the right side of him. Regular work, payment over the odds.

'Three weeks, maybe a month,' Fred mused, 'depending on the weather. If there's any more snow I'll have to leave off. And there's always the danger that the mortar in the brickwork will get the frost in it.'

'I'm willing to take that risk.'

'Okay. That's your pigeon, Mr Hamilton. I could start Monday. First job is to renovate the belfry. Can't really say what's involved until I make a start. I'll do my best, anyway.'

'Thank you, Mr Reubens,' Hamilton smiled. 'Oh, and by the way, I like the main gates kept locked. So if you will let us know in the house whenever you wish to leave the grounds, either my wife, myself or our Chinese servant girl will come and unlock the gates for you.'

'Blimey, it's like working for Securicor,' Fred grunted.

15

'Sure you aren't going to issue me with a pass and identity card?'

Martyn Hamilton turned away. He did not appreciate the remark.

The following Monday morning was sunny and very cold. The sky was a deep blue as Fred Reubens drove his battered old pick-up truck from his bungalow in the village down to the gates of Caelogy Hall. The snow was holding off. Frost was the danger. Not only was the lane a sheet of solid ice, but up in the belfry tower each movement would be precarious, fingers numbed as they worked. The weathermen forecast that this ridge of high pressure centred over Great Britain would remain for the next few days; sunshine by day, cruel frost by night.

'Pity it didn't bleedin' well snow and keep this job waitin' until the spring at least.' Fred Reubens spoke aloud as he sat before the locked entrance gates, his engine ticking over. There was nobody about. He blew the horn, softly at first, then louder when still no one showed up. Hamilton wasn't the kind of man to be hurried by a klaxon, but you couldn't sit there all day.

Then he saw the Chinese servant for the first time. She emerged from the back of the building, clad in a duffle coat, unbuttoned, the hood thrown back and displaying her long black hair. Fur-lined boots came up to her calves, just high enough to stop the powdery snow from spilling inside. In her hand she carried a key.

'Nice bit o' stuff.' Reubens waved to her through the windscreen and then drove forward slowly as she pulled the gates wide enough for him to pass through. She regarded him steadily with dark eyes that showed no hint of a smile. Her expression was stoic, a robot obeying a command and carrying it out to the letter, efficient and emotionless.

He drove down the narrow snow-covered track, a wall of ten-foot-high rhododendrons on either side until he reached the chapel on the west side of the Hall. The doors were open, and through them he could see Hamilton standing looking down at the bell as though it held some secret fascination for him.

'Barmy bugger,' Fred muttered as he got out, 'like a bloody Christmas present that he can't wait to get working.' Aloud, he called, 'Morning, Mr Hamilton.'

'Mornin', Reubens.' Hamilton turned away from the object of his scrutiny. 'A magnificent specimen.'

'What's its country of origin?'

'Tibet, of course.' Hamilton raised an eyebrow. 'Look at the copper workings. You don't find that type of craftsmanship anywhere else in the world, Reubens.'

'Oh, I see, sir.' Daft bleeder. Does 'e think I'm a ruddy expert on bells? 'I'm going to make a start renewing the brickwork. That'll take a day or two. Then we'll see what new timber we need.'

'Very good.' Martyn Hamilton moved towards the door, 'I'll leave you to it then, Reubens. Oh, and by the way, if you want anything, just knock on the tradesmen's door. Karamaneh will see to you.'

Fred stared after the departing owner of Caelogy Hall, noting the bowed head and stooped shoulders. A man with a lot on his mind, he decided. Worried. Anxious. Snapping at everybody. Good natured beneath it all, perhaps. Likes to let you know who's bloody boss. If you want anything, Reubens, use the tradesmen's door. And don't get poking about on your bloody own outside this chapel, that was what he really meant. Like he'd got sommat to hide.

The builder surveyed the chapel. It was small, just room enough for four small rows of pews on either side of the narrow aisle. It was built to accommodate the previous owners of the Hall and their servants, with room for one or two friends or guests. The altar was a simple wooden structure on a raised platform at the far end. There was even a pulpit and a lectern. A stained glass window, miraculously still intact, depicted a crucifixion scene. No detail had been spared by the builders, possibly

17

a century and a half ago. In effect, it was a miniature church. Only the belfry spoiled its otherwise sedate appearance. It was clumsy, as though constructed as an afterthought on the instructions of an owner like Martyn Hamilton. A sudden whim. Build me a belfry. Spare no cost or effort. A big one. As big as the chapel.

Fred stood staring up into the tower. It was almost as wide as the one in Turbury Church. At one time it had housed a set of bells. But Hamilton wanted just one. His Tibetan bell. It was too flamboyant. Too overpowering. The gaze of any future worshippers would be elevated. They wouldn't be able to take their eyes off it. It put the altar into second place.

Blasphemy, almost, Fred decided as he began to climb the fixed ladder up into the tower, testing each rung before putting his full weight upon it. It was almost as though the bell itself was to be a symbol of worship.

He stood on the platform looking around. Sunlight filtered through a series of apertures. It was bitterly cold up here.

The rafters showed traces of woodworm. He tested them. Ordinarily they would have been adequate, but the weight of the single bell was somewhere in the region of three hundredweight. The woodwork would have to be renewed. He removed several birds' nests and dropped them down to the floor below. House-martins. They would be disappointed when they returned in a few weeks' time. The larger structure of dried twigs and moss was the handiwork of either a jackdaw or a rook. It followed in the wake of the others.

He tested the mortar between the stonework. It powdered as he scraped a nail along it. Hard luck, Mr Hamilton, this is going to take longer than a month, I reckon.

It was towards mid-morning that Fred Reubens heard the shouting. The sounds were muffled, coming from the east wing of Caelogy Hall. He paused, masonry hammer raised for another devastating blow, and listened. Gut-

18

teral voices. Unintelligible. High-pitched yelling in a foreign tongue. That would be the Chinese girl jabbering in her native language. Then Hamilton's voice. Angry, commanding, dominating. All went silent. Fred shook his head in bewilderment and continued knocking out the masonry.

As the day wore on he became increasingly uneasy. The noise of his hammering echoed in the confines of the belfry before it escaped through the small slits into the open air. The sound was like sacrilege, the silence the invisible fury of pagan gods. The chapel should have been a sanctuary, a haven of tranquillity. Fred Reubens experienced the opposite effect. The atmosphere was cloying, sinister. And outside there was not a sound to be heard. The dense shrubberies blanketed any noise that might otherwise have drifted across from the village. Apart from that one outburst of shouting in the Hall, there were no voices to be heard, no movement. Frozen snow lay deep on the ground. Any crunching footfall could not have gone unnoticed. But there were none.

Towards mid-afternoon the light inside the belfry began to fail and with a sigh of relief Fred Reubens climbed down and began to tidy up his tools. It was creepy enough in there during the daytime. He certainly wasn't going to work into the dusk. He shivered, pulled on his jacket and made his way outside. Use the tradesmen's entrance, Mr Reubens.

He made his way round to the rear of the building and found the small door bearing a faded sign that read 'tradesmen'. He rapped on it with his knuckles and stood back. Nobody came in answer to his knock. He lit a cigarette, waited and knocked again. Still no reply.

He was angry. Never before in his working life had he been imprisoned on any premises. He was his own boss, almost retired, and he wasn't going to stand for it. If nobody could be bothered to attend to his welfare then he would go and find somebody. He tried the latch. The door creaked open and he stared down a long gloomy

19

corridor. There was another door at the far end. He licked his lips nervously, shrugged and stepped inside, the nails in the soles of his heavy working boots scraping on the stone floor.

Beyond the second door were the kitchens, extensive rooms with numerous cupboards and working surfaces, and a solid-fuel Rayburn, which was heating a stew of some sort. There was nobody about.

He crossed to the nearest door. It led out into the hall, polished mahogany blocks and a wide oak staircase. Impressive, but it needed some work. The picture-rails needed replacing. His practised eye was subconsciously renovating the interior of the building as he continued his search for the occupants or their servant.

Voices again. From upstairs. The same ones that he had heard that morning from his elevated position in the chapel belfry. Animal-like grunts, the jabbering of the Oriental. Rising to a crescendo. Then he heard hurried footsteps across the landing immediately above where he stood, a door being opened and closed. More shouting. Hamilton, without a doubt, but the owner of Caelogy Hall was not speaking in English! Fred listened. Martyn Hamilton was angry and his outburst seemed to have a quietening effect upon whoever he was talking to. Within seconds silence reigned. The door was opened again and the footsteps came back across the landing, turned and headed for the stairs.

Fred Reubens stood there in the hall, his heart beating quickly. A feeling of guilt crept over him. He shouldn't have been here. He was trespassing. Oh, sod it, why should this crazy lot piss him about?

'Reubens!' Martyn Hamilton stood at the top of the staircase, clad in grey flannel trousers and a tweed sports jacket. In his hand he held a riding crop. His face was flushed and angry, his lips compressed into a thin bloodless line. 'Reubens, what in the name of God are you doing in my house?'

Fred swallowed. He wanted to be angry but there was

20

something about this man which overpowered. No matter what the situation, however just you felt your cause, you were always relegated to the status of under-dog.

'I . . . er, I was looking for somebody to open the gates to let me out,' he replied meekly.

'*You have no right inside the Hall.*'

'I knocked, sir, but nobody came, so I thought . . .'

'My servant was called away to another task. You are an impatient fellow, Reubens.'

'I'm sorry, sir.' Fred hated himself for apologising but he was unable to check it.

'All right,' Hamilton sighed loudly and began to descend the stairs. 'You chose an unfortunate time to knock off. I would have thought that you could've worked another half hour or so yet. Never mind, I'll come and let you out myself.'

Fred followed the other out through the front door and down the steps to where his truck was parked. As he climbed in behind the wheel he was aware that he was sweating, and his fingers shook as he turned the ignition. As he drove back down the drive he noticed the alsatian dog chained up by its kennel. There were rumours in the village that the animal was allowed to roam the grounds freely after dark. He quite believed them. There were some strange things going on at Caelogy Hall, and the sooner he finished that job on the belfry, the better. No way was he going to undertake the renovations to the house. He never left a job unfinished, but once that bell was up in the tower Fred Reubens wasn't going to set foot inside the Hall or its grounds again.

'That's it, Mr Hamilton, sir.' Fred Reubens stood back and looked up at the bell which hung suspended above the platform in the chapel belfry. It glinted in the rays of the late afternoon sun coming through the exterior slits in the tower. Three hundredweight of latent power, waiting silently to be tolled, seeming to mock the two men standing beneath it.

21

'Excellent,' Martyn Hamilton smiled appreciatively, 'excellent. You underestimate your own capabilities, Mr Reubens. A month you said. You've finished it in three weeks to the day.'

Because I worked so bloody fast so that I could get away from this place, Fred thought. And don't ask me to do anything else.

'Hadn't we ought to check to see that it rings all right?' Fred stepped forward, hand outstretched to grasp the bell-rope.

'*Don't!*' Hamilton snarled. 'Don't you dare ring that bell!'

'Oh . . . I'm . . . I'm sorry, sir. I just thought . . .'

'It's all right.' The other man relaxed. 'It will be all right, I can tell. But there's no need to ring it now. The . . . the villagers might wonder what was happening and we don't want to alarm the good people of Turbury, do we, Mr Reubens?'

The builder nodded.

'If there's anything wrong with it I'll get you to come up and put it right,' Hamilton smiled. 'Now, I'd better pay you. I think I can give you a little bonus on such an excellent job.'

It was with a feeling of relief that Fred Reubens climbed into his pick-up truck for what he promised himself would be the last time at Caelogy Hall. The gates had already been opened in readiness for his departure but as he passed by the large grey stone building a movement caught his eye from one of the third-storey windows. He eased his foot off the accelerator and glanced upwards.

A face was pressed against the dusty stained pane of glass. It was a woman. Not the Chinese girl. An older person, a European, strikingly good-looking. He knew instinctively that it was Hamilton's wife. It had to be. She wasn't looking down at him. Indeed, it was probable that she was totally unaware of his presence or even knew that he had been working in the chapel these past three weeks. It was as though she was being deliberately hidden away by her husband for some purpose.

Now she stared fixedly ahead of her, above the tops of the Caelogy trees and out towards the range of mountains on the western horizon.

But it was the expression on her features which caused Fred Reubens to stare. There was more than just anguish on her face. It went deeper than that. Her very soul was in torment.

There was a hint of spring in the air. Over the past few days the snow lying in the village and in the hills beyond had begun to thaw rapidly, melted by a sun that had warmth in its rays, and the nocturnal frosts were nowhere as severe as they had been.

The group of elderly men had gathered on the church steps, a favourite meeting place for the remnants of a dying generation, as though they were preparing themselves for the long journey into the life hereafter which they would begin from the graveyard on the other side of the wall. They smoked their pipes in silence, watching the coming of spring. There was nothing to say which had not been said before.

The sun, a glowing orange ball, disappeared slowly behind the distant range of peaks and the evening shadows began to creep across the sky. The air turned cooler and the men pulled up their overcoat collars. Tom Williamson meticulously cut two thin slices of black twist from the roll in his pocket and began rubbing them between his gnarled rheumatic hands. It was a deliberate process, not to be hurried, one that gave him as much pleasure as filling and lighting his pipe. Indeed, it was ten minutes before he was drawing on the tobacco and puffing out fragrant clouds of smoke into the still, windless atmosphere.

'Them folks is still at the 'all,' Frank Garfield grunted. 'All winter. Never seed 'em outside. Not once 'as they bin to the village.'

'Fred Reubens 'as bin there every day fixin' a bell in the chapel tower.'

'They're 'eathens, you mark my word. What do they want a bell for?'

The question went unanswered because nobody could answer it. The group fell into silent rumination once again. Darkness approached and they all remembered that night when they had stood and observed the new owners moving into Caelogy Hall. The alsatian still prowled the grounds after dark. Donald Hughes didn't play games of make-believe up there any longer. That wasn't any wonder, but something had happened to the boy. He was no longer his cheerful idiotic self. He had become morose and furtive, shunning company, keeping clear of the village altogether. Aye, everybody agreed, he'd been up there one night. And seen something. And whatever he'd seen had played on his mind, scared the life out of him. Strangers had no right to do that sort of thing, encroaching on the lives of the locals. Now everybody avoided Caelogy Hall and its grounds. Let the Hamiltons shut themselves away. It was the best thing. The less they were seen, the better.

Just as dusk was turning to deep darkness the old men heard the bell. Its first clear note hung in the still atmosphere, reverberating, a tone that was soft to the ear yet transmitted itself harshly to the brain. The bell tolled slowly, almost like a funeral bell, several seconds in between each peal. Yet it was as though the first note never really died away, hanging in the air, waiting for the subsequent ones, amalgamating into a sound that grew and grew . . . and grew until the listeners clutched their hands to their ears in a vain attempt to shut out the noise.

Six men stared at each other, eyes rolling, lips moving soundlessly. Afraid. They knew whence the sound came but not why. Two minutes that seemed an eternity, and then it ceased. But the noise went on and on, growing in magnitude, pounding against the interior of the skull with all the force of a steel clapper.

Six men staggered down the church steps and out into the road, hands clutched over their ears, their senses numbed, unable to reason, screaming their terror.

A tall white-haired man emerged from the church. His angular, kindly features were contorted, his bony fingers pressed into his large ears. His black overcoat was unbuttoned, displaying beneath it the robes of a clergyman. He attempted to control his own fear, stumbling in the direction of those long-established devout members of his congregation.

'Gentlemen, please,' the Reverend Rawsthorne shouted, but he knew they could not hear him. 'Gentlemen. Do not fear. It is merely a bell. Like our own bells. It . . .'

It was no good trying to explain it. The tone, the frequency defied explanation. It tortured the brain with its mounting decibels. There was no escape from it. Long after it had ceased to toll, the vicar of Turbury and his aged parishioners were still reeling from its effects.

Finally, with ears buzzing, the vicar managed to communicate with the others. He supported himself against the wall with one hand, and turned breathlessly to Tom Williamson.

'It is the work of the devil,' he gasped, *'a bell of evil meant to destroy our sanity.'*

'Aye.' Williamson's pipe fell from his mouth and rolled into the gutter. 'And the devil has taken up residence in Caelogy Hall.'

'We must fight against it.' Rawsthorne drew himself up. 'I shall go and see this man Hamilton personally, and I shall demand to know what is behind all this. I . . .'

He broke off as a shambling figure appeared at the bend in the road. All of them stared in disbelief. The ungainly shape was all too familiar, rolling from side to side, grotesque in every aspect, the head turned this way and that at an unnatural angle, the tongue protruding from beneath a row of mis-shapen upper teeth. Seldom did the full horror of Donald Hughes make its impact

25

upon them. It was an everyday scene which they had come to accept. But now . . .

'Look,' Rawsthorne's hand shook uncontrollably as he pointed to the simpleton, 'do you see? The boy's hands are clasped to his ears in an attempt to shut out this noise. Yet he is deaf and dumb. May the Lord have mercy upon us. *Even the deaf cannot escape from the sound of the bell! He has heard it even in his deafness. His simple brain has been tortured just as ours have. Oh, merciful God!'*

3

LOCKED GATES

'How's your head this morning, love?' Fred Reubens came back into the bedroom carrying two cups of tea, placed them on the bedside table and drew the curtains. Bright sunlight flooded into the room.

'Ooh!' Jane Reubens groaned and struggled up into a sitting position. A small, plump, red-faced woman in her mid-fifties, she had suffered with blood pressure for the past decade. 'I can still feel it throbbin'. Just like them migraines I used to get years ago. Thought me 'ead was goin' to burst. It was that damned bell, all right. From the moment it started I couldn't shut it out. Not even ear-plugs would've stopped that damned row. I could even 'ear it in me sleep. If I ever did really get to sleep, that is. Fred, I've cussed you a thousand times for puttin' it up for those people.'

'If I hadn't put it up,' Fred took a sip of tea and began to dress, 'somebody else would have. This Hamilton bloke wouldn't let a little thing like my refusal stop him. He'd've got a firm of builders over from the city if I hadn't obliged him.'

'I suppose so,' Jane sighed, and reached out for her cup. 'And I don't suppose we've 'eard the last of it. I wonder what they rung it for last night.'

'Search me. Maybe they were just testing it. We haven't heard it since I fitted it, and when I was going to give the rope a pull, Hamilton went fair barmy. Did his nut. "Don't

27

you dare touch that, Reubens." Anybody would've thought there was a charge of gelignite strapped to the clapper.'

'I reckon they're some sort of religious fanatics. Like Buddhists. They came from Tibet, didn't they? So it figures. I was saying the same thing to Mrs Davis only yesterday. So long as they don't start performin' human sacrifices or anything like that.'

'Just you mind what you get saying round the village,' Fred regarded her steadily. 'Like I always say. Hear all, see all, but say nowt.'

'Why should I? *I'm* not scared of 'em, even if you are.'

'I'm not.'

'Yes you are. You was bloomin' scared stiff when you came in from workin' up at the 'all. Made sure you knocked off before it got dark, didn't you?'

'It was just that it was creepy in there.'

'Huh. Well, the question is, 'ow are we goin' to stop 'em ringin' the damned thing?'

'We can't. It's their bell. It's not like they were runnin' a disco and making so much noise that . . .'

'But they *are* makin' a noise that's upsettin' everybody. You ask the "Church Steps Brigade". You know, them old fogies who spend all their time 'angin' around the church, smokin' their pipes and discussin' 'ow things ain't what they used to be. They were almost rollin' in the road in agony, 'oldin' their ears. It's a wonder some of 'em didn't 'ave an 'eart attack. Then the vicar come on the scene, 'e said it was the work o' the devil and somethin' 'ad to be done about it.'

'Well, just leave it to the vicar. Maybe he'll do something. There's not much we can do.'

'Always the same, ain't you, Fred?' There was contempt in Jane's tone. 'Always frightened o' gettin' on the wrong side o' folks. Well, I'll tell you this. If they keep on ringin' that bell up at the 'all, then I ain't stayin' in Turbury, or anywhere roundabout where you can 'ear it. I wish to God I'd never let you talk me into comin' to live in the country.

28

Well, any more sessions like last night and I'm off back to the city, with or without you!'

The vicar looked pale and ill at ease as he left the vicarage and walked along the main street of Turbury. He nodded, smiled, raised his black homburg to all the ladies, but everybody knew that he was not his usual self. The ruddy complexion had paled, the jaunty gait had slowed. His movements resembled a stupefied stagger, his eyes deep sunken, glazed over, reflected despair. People huddled together in groups, subdued, talking in lowered voices, casting furtive glances in all directions. There was no mistaking the atmosphere of terror which prevailed in Turbury.

'Vicar!'

Rawsthorne pulled up, stiffening. The whiplash tone of the man who had spoken seemed to cut into his brain. He turned around slowly, apprehensively.

'Oh . . . Good morning, Mr Hughes.'

The other man was stocky and sunburned, his skin tanned a dark red by the elements. The short body was thick and powerful, the eyes narrow, giving a somewhat sly expression. Rawsthorne knew the man by sight, the father of Donald the simpleton, a forestry worker who spent most of his leisure hours in the Buffalo. As far as the vicar knew he had never set foot inside the church.

'Vicar, what the hell is going on?'

'I'm . . . I'm afraid I don't understand you, Mr Hughes.'

'The bell, man. What's behind it all?'

'At the moment I'm afraid I'm as puzzled as you are. I'm on my way now to see the Hamiltons in an attempt to unravel the mystery.'

'You know what it's done to my boy, don't you?'

'I saw him yesterday evening, whilst the bell was tolling. He appeared to be able to . . .'

'Yes.' Rafe Hughes leaned forward, his tiny eyes glinting angrily. 'He *heard* it, vicar. He's deaf, but he heard it, all right.'

'Then . . . then perhaps the bell has done some good after all.'

'Like hell! It hasn't done Donald any good. He's scared to death. Last night he got *under* the bed, and nothing me nor the missus could do would persuade him to come out. He was gibbering with terror. He knows more about that bloody bell than either you or I. The trouble is he can't tell us.'

'Perhaps he should see a doctor.'

'We finished taking him to see doctors and specialists years ago. Nothin' they can do for him. His whole personality has changed since last night. He doesn't grin and laugh any more. He's got a frightened look on his face, and he skulks when folks are around. He's gone off into the woods now, like he does most days, slinking off like a fox with the terriers on its trail. God knows where he's gone . . . or if he'll ever come back!'

Rawsthorne stroked his chin. His lower lip was trembling slightly.

'I'll go and see the Hamiltons.' There was a tremor in his voice. 'And then, if Donald doesn't come back tonight, we'll have to go and look for him. Come and see me at the vicarage, Mr Hughes.'

Rafe Hughes turned on his heel impatiently. He had no time for vicars or churches. Wait and see was their policy. Have faith. Faith! You needed a lot more than faith to sort this lot out.

Rawsthorne reached the gates to Caelogy Hall and stared in dismay. It was quite evident that they were locked. The padlock glinted, taunting him as it reflected the bright sunlight. Beyond the overgrown bushes which bordered the drive he could see the building itself, huge and gaunt. Unfriendly. No smoke came from the tall chimneys, and for all he knew it was deserted.

He stood there undecided, rubbing his hands together nervously, something he always did during the last verse of the hymn which preceded his sermon, gazing at the sea of faces below the pulpit and wondering if he would be

30

able to get his message over to them. This was a thousand times worse. The stage was empty. He was the only actor in a grim drama which was rapidly slipping beyond his comprehension. He was unsure of his own part. He glanced around. There was no bell, nothing by which to attract attention. He coughed, and cleared his throat as loudly as he could.

'I say,' he called out, 'is anybody at home?'

Nothing moved. There was no sign of human occupation on the other side of the gates.

'Is anybody there?' Louder this time, rattling the gates as he shouted. 'Hey!'

He was just about to turn away when he heard footsteps to the rear of the Hall, beyond his range of vision. Coming towards him. He waited nervously, going through the motions of lathering his hands with invisible soap again.

It was a girl. The Chinese servant some of the villagers had spoken about. She wore a long flowing orange dress and her hair was tied up in a bun on the top of her head. Her eyes regarded him steadily as she approached and stood about a yard from the wrought iron structure.

'Er,' the vicar coughed, and forgot the opening speech which he had carefully rehearsed. 'Is . . . is Mr Hamilton at home?'

'Can I help for you, thank you?' The words were scarcely audible, spoken slowly with a conscious effort, the girl struggling to remember the rudiments of the English language which her employer's wife had attempted to teach her.

'Mr Hamilton. I wish to speak with him.'

'No,' she shook her head, 'not today, thank you.'

'But is he at home?' The clergyman was becoming agitated and impatient.

'Not today, please.'

'I must see him. It is important. Will you kindly go and fetch him?'

She regarded the vicar closely, then, as if she had come to a sudden decision, she turned abruptly and walked back

31

towards Caelogy Hall. Rawsthorne stood watching her, perplexed. He was sure that Martyn Hamilton was in the building, but was this servant going to fetch her boss or had she merely tired of the difficult conversation and abandoned it? He didn't know, but he was determined to wait for a few more minutes. He could, of course, return to the vicarage and telephone Hamilton, but that wasn't like a personal encounter. Over the phone a man could stall and lie. One couldn't determine his true reaction by his expression. A telephone call, he decided, was a last resort if all else failed.

Five minutes passed. Rawsthorne had almost decided to leave when he heard a door opening somewhere, and footsteps again. Heavier ones this time, crunching on the loose stones, walking quickly, impatiently.

Martyn Hamilton was dressed in a windcheater and corduroy trousers, hands thrust deep into his pockets. His attitude was one of arrogance, scowling at the man who had dared to persist in spite of his servant's efforts to get rid of unwelcome visitors.

'What's the trouble?' he snapped, making no attempt to introduce himself.

'Ah, Mr Hamilton, I presume.' The vicar adopted an attitude of humility. Indeed, it came naturally when faced with such a forceful personality. 'I wanted to have a word with you about . . . about your bell, if you could spare me a few moments.'

'What about it?'

'Well . . . it seems to have caused an awful lot of distress in the village.'

'I was not aware of the fact. What is the trouble?'

'The people were . . . deafened, many had headaches, some migraines, and a youth who has been deaf since birth has been frightened out of his wits.'

'What utter nonsense!' Hamilton threw back his head and laughed mirthlessly, a sound that made the watching Rawsthorne shudder. 'So the deaf can hear my bell? You surely don't expect me to believe such rubbish, vicar? Any

32

complaints, I suspect, are derived from a sense of jealousy because I have bought Caelogy Hall and installed a new bell. They are quite unfounded. Childish, in fact.'

'I assure you, Mr Hamilton . . .'

'Tell me, vicar,' Hamilton's eyes narrowed, 'you rang your church bells for communion, matins, and evensong last Sunday, didn't you?'

'Indeed, I did.'

'And how many complaints did *you* have from the villagers?'

'None. But . . .'

'Precisely. That answers my question. And yours, I think. You are the Church, so you have a divine right to the sole bell-ringing in the village of Turbury. Furthermore, you have a number of bells. I have just one.'

'But the tone . . .'

'Mine is softer than yours. Much softer. I listened to yours as I stood in the grounds last Sunday evening. They were harsh. Clanging, for want of a better expression.'

'Yours is so *vibrant*.' Rawsthorne reddened at the reference to his church bells, the pride of Turbury. 'One can hear it in one's head long after it has ceased to ring.'

'Really, vicar, this is preposterous.' Hamilton drew himself up haughtily. 'You have wasted my time over a most stupid discussion and I must bid you good-day. If there are any more complaints about my bell then I suggest you put forward some concrete evidence that it is causing a nuisance. Oh, and in future, if you wish to see me will you kindly telephone and make an appointment!'

Rawsthorne watched the tall man striding angrily away. The vicar sighed. It was a humiliating defeat, and he had achieved absolutely nothing. He began to retrace his steps wearily, but when he came to the fork in the road he took the turning to the right instead of continuing directly through the village. Doubtless, word had already circulated in Turbury that he had gone forth to do battle with the 'ogre at the Hall'. He had no wish at present to discuss

33

the outcome of that encounter with an irate throng of parishioners.

It took him twenty minutes to reach the vicarage, a black and white timbered residence that stood in an acre of ground behind the church. He entered by the rear gate, passing through the overgrown orchard, but as he stepped on to the drive his attention was drawn to an egg-shell blue Mini van which was parked there, luminous lettering on the doors – POLICE. Rawsthorne felt their impact like a physical blow. A law-abiding man, he had no fear of the constabulary, yet their infrequent visits seldom heralded good news. He knew that on this occasion they would not be the bearers of glad tidings. He sighed. It was all getting too much for him.

'PC Lewis is waiting in the study,' his housekeeper, Mrs Brisbane, a frail timid woman in her seventies, whispered to him as he paused in the hall to hang up his hat and coat.

'Thank you, Mrs Brisbane,' he nodded, and went through into the large book-lined room. 'Good morning, officer. And to what do I owe this visit? Not a parking offence, I hope?'

'No, sir,' the young constable smiled and self-consciously stroked his slim dark moustache, a recent growth intended to add to his authority. His transfer from the city force a few months ago was proving more difficult than he had anticipated. These villagers were a close-knit community. They did not accept a total stranger readily.

'It's about this bell, the one at Caelogy Hall,' the policeman began. 'It seems to have caused no small amount of concern and I was wondering if you might be able to throw some light on it.'

'Unfortunately, no.' The clergyman dropped his gaze to the frayed carpet. 'I have just made an attempt to see Mr Hamilton. After some difficulty I managed to get him to come to the gate. He was abrupt, to put it mildly. The church ring their bells, so why shouldn't he ring his? You have to admit that he's got a point there.'

34

'Yes,' the constable pursed his lips, 'but did *you* hear it last night, vicar?'

'Indeed, I did.' Rawsthorne winced as he remembered the peals, the deafening clarity inside his skull, the physical pounding which his brain had suffered. 'It was like . . . like having the clapper swinging inside your head.'

'Precisely. I was in the van at the time, trying to take a message on the radio. I couldn't hear anything for about five minutes afterwards, and then this bloomin' headache started up. Aspirins wouldn't shift it. It's gone now, but I can't get it out of my mind. Like a tune that nearly drives you daft. But *why*? What kind of bell is it that can do that to you? I've spoken to Fred Reubens who fitted the thing. It's some kind of Tibetan bell, but why should it be any different from the ones that ring in thousands of churches every Sunday?'

'I wish I could explain it,' Rawsthorne smiled ruefully, 'because then we might be able to combat it some way. Sure enough, Hamilton will ring it again. Nevertheless, something has got to be done. Perhaps a visit from the law might have more effect than one from such a humble body as the Church.'

'I'll go up and see him now.' John Lewis twirled his flat cap thoughtfully on the end of his forefinger. 'Though right now I don't see as I can do much. All I can seek at this stage is his co-operation. If I don't get that then we'll have to take other steps.'

'Such as?'

'A meeting will have to be called amongst the residents. Unfortunately, I can't take part in that as a member of the force. I suggest you might organise something, vicar. A petition. Call in the Noise Abatement Society and get them to monitor the decibels. There's plenty of things that can be done. But it takes time. I remember a pub once that persisted in running a disco without the proper acoustics. It took a year to get the noise cut down.'

'By which time serious harm could have befallen many of my parishioners.' Rawsthorne shook his head slowly.

'It isn't a pleasant prospect. Anyway, go and see what you can do, constable, there's a good fellow.'

Locked gates presented only minor problems to PC John Lewis. He drew the Mini up close to them, regarded the deserted landscape beyond for a few seconds, and then switched on his siren.

Bee-bor-bee-bor-bee-bor. The blue light flashed its authoritative demands for entry.

Within a minute the Chinese servant girl was to be seen hurrying towards the gates. Lewis switched off the siren but left the light flashing. A half-smile flickered around his mouth as he got out of the vehicle.

'Come on,' he snapped. 'Open up.'

She hesitated, watching him carefully, her eyes slitted so that they appeared to be almost closed. But she made no move to obey.

'Unless you open these gates I shall get a warrant,' Lewis said. 'Now, why not be sensible about it?'

'Wait,' she turned away, 'Mr Hamilton. Wait there.'

Lewis waited. A few minutes later Martyn Hamilton appeared. There was no sign of the girl. The owner of Caelogy Hall was scowling. It was only an hour or so since he had sent the old clergyman on his way. But the police had to be handled a little more carefully.

'And what can I do for you, officer?' he asked.

'I'd be glad if you would open these gates and let me through, sir.' Lewis was determined not to be overawed by those hooded eyes which seemed to bore into him with hidden malevolence.

'We can talk here.'

'No, sir. I'd prefer to talk inside. Also, I must remind you that by law you are required to provide a caller with access to your front door by daytime. You may only lock your gates after sunset.'

'Is that so? I must telephone my solicitor to check on that.'

'That's up to you, sir. But in the meantime would you please let me in?'

Slowly, with great deliberation, Martyn Hamilton produced the key to the padlock. The constable climbed back behind the wheel and edged the vehicle forward as the gates were dragged back. He drove up to the front of the house, parked and stood by the front door awaiting Hamilton's return.

'Come in, please.' Hamilton spoke coldly and mounted the stone steps, Lewis following behind him.

They went into the first room on the right. The policeman noted its bareness – one or two items of furniture, a table and three chairs. There was no carpet.

'Now, what's the trouble?' The owner of Caelogy Hall did not offer the other man a chair. His attitude was that this was an enforced meeting and the sooner the business was terminated, the better.

'There have been some complaints in the village about your bell, sir.'

'So I believe.' Hamilton smiled faintly, placed a small cigar in his mouth and took his time lighting it. 'As you doubtless know, the vicar came to see me a short while ago. It's all a load of rubbish. Petty jealousy on the part of the villagers. The church bells can be rung but I mustn't ring mine. Is that it?'

'I heard your bell myself, sir.' Lewis fought valiantly against a wave of nervousness which was threatening to sweep over him. 'And, quite honestly, I must agree with what people say. It . . . it takes over your brain. Nearly drives you daft, for want of a better expression.'

'What an absolutely unfounded idiotic remark to make.' Twin red spots appeared on Hamilton's cheeks. 'My dear fellow, I was right beneath it in the chapel when it was being tolled. And I never suffered any discomfort.'

'I note that you wear a hearing aid, sir.' Lewis suddenly spotted the minute plastic earpiece which rested behind the other's lobe.

37

'Indeed, I do. But I can't see what difference that makes.'

'I'd like to have a look at this bell if I may, sir.'

Hamilton hesitated, watching the officer carefully as he drew hard on his cigar, eyes narrowing, expression inscrutable. Finally he spoke, the words scarcely audible, vibrating with an anger which he was attempting to control. 'All right. But we'll have to be quick. I have an urgent appointment in the city for which I must leave in a few minutes.'

John Lewis felt decidedly uneasy as he followed the tall man outside and across to the chapel. He experienced a sensation of being watched, hostile eyes boring into his back from the upper windows of Caelogy Hall; a sixth sense that had saved his life on one occasion when he might have had a knife in his ribs. He knew that it did not fail him now. His every move was under observation.

'There you are.' Martyn Hamilton flung open the door of the chapel and pointed up into the belfry. 'There it is, the infamous Caelogy bell. Quite harmless, rather unique in design but nothing to worry about.'

John Lewis walked forward and stood beneath the tower. He saw the clapper, motionless now, and some traces of what appeared to be rust on the interior of the bell. As Hamilton had said, it was perfectly harmless . . . until it was rung!

'D'you think we could just listen to it?' he asked.

'*No!*' Hamilton moved a pace forward, standing between the policeman and the bell rope. 'On no account am I going to allow it to be rung now.'

'I'd just like to . . .'

'Well, you can't. I've conceded to your requests and co-operated to the very limits of my patience, but I will not have my chapel bell rung on the strength of a pure whim. Now, I must hurry if I'm not to be late for my appointment so I should be grateful if . . .'

'Very good, sir.' Lewis stepped outside into the dazzling

sunlight. 'I must admit it all seems very straightforward and ordinary.'

'Of course it is. Nothing to worry about at all.'

'One more question, sir. Why is the bell rung? I mean, I know it's used to mark religious ceremonies but in a small private chapel . . .'

'That, officer,' Hamilton's eyes blazed and no longer was he able to check his mounting fury, 'is entirely *my* business. I have to account to nobody for that. Now, I shall be glad if you will kindly vacate my premises.'

'Very good, sir. I'm on my way.'

'And, officer . . .'

'Yes, sir?'

'For your information, not that it's anything to do with you, I shall, in all probability, be holding a service in this chapel for my family tonight. And that means that I shall be ringing the bell. I merely warn you because these stupid locals seem to be under the impression that it is harming them. You have now seen it for yourself. Tonight you will hear it again. Please, I beg of you, don't try to disturb us in the midst of our worship!'

'And that's the position.' John Lewis eased himself out of the armchair in the vicar's study and looked across at the elderly clergyman. 'Hamilton's going to ring his bell again some time tonight, and there's nothing whatsoever we can do to stop him. I shall make out my report, but there's nothing I can recommend except that he's made to comply with the law and stop locking his entrance gates. I suggest that you might try and warn your parishioners about tonight.'

'Thank you, officer.' Rawsthorne extended his hand. 'You have done everything that could reasonably be expected of you. I will now do the only thing that is left to me. *I shall pray to God that our sanity may be spared this night when that terrible bell begins to toll!*'

4

DEATH!

Word had travelled around the small village situated at the foot of the mountain slopes that the bell was going to ring again that night. The vicar had spread the evil tidings, and now, his duty to his parishioners completed, he had retired to the church. A few of his devout congregation were already kneeling in the pews before the altar when he arrived.

'We shall pray together,' he smiled, 'but first, I think a little practical remedy might not come amiss in these circumstances. I have here a roll of soft cotton wool, more than enough for us to plug our ears, and plenty left over for any others who may decide to join us before the bell tolls.'

Rawsthorne knelt alongside the others, their heads bowed, each muttering private prayers for salvation. Up above them the church clock chimed six times. The daylight was fading rapidly, but nobody bothered to switch on the lights.

Time passed slowly. They prayed and rested, and counted the muffled striking of the hours, only just audible through their improvised ear-plugs. Seven o'clock . . . eight o'clock . . . nine . . .

It was shortly before ten o'clock that the first note of the Caelogy bell was heard. It hung in the air, soft and yet loud, sweet but harsh, penetrating, escalating in volume like a mountain echo, building up to a peak and searching

40

out its listeners indiscriminately, pounding into their brains with unbelievable intensity.

Those in the Turbury church clutched at their ears, moaning aloud at the pain from within their skulls, writhing in agony, praying, pleading with their Maker to spare them.

Others, seeking refuge in their homes, turned up the volume of radio and television. Record-players were played at full blast. But it was to no avail. The music was swamped like seaweed beneath an incoming tide, and within minutes the bell had dominated a whole community. People groaned, and tensed in readiness for the next peal, the last one still reverberating inside their brains.

A mile or so outside the village, Donald Hughes crouched in the darkness of a dense larch plantation, hands pressed tightly over his ears. He felt every nerve in his obese body responding, torturing him, a current of electricity circuiting without being able to go to earth, angrily taking its revenge out on him.

He screamed, a gibbering sound that was constricted in his throat. He scrambled to his feet and began to run blindly. All sense of direction had left him. No longer did the winding deer tracks and rabbit runs mean anything to him. He blundered on. Several times he crashed into the trunk of a tree and was sent staggering back. He tasted blood in his mouth. He knew, also, that his ears were bleeding, but it did not halt his shambling flight.

He was out of the wood, grass beneath his feet, going uphill, labouring for breath, a vicious pain in his lungs. He fell again, his foot twisting in a rabbit hole. He tried to rise, but his injured ankle would not bear his weight.

He lay there writhing as the bell in the village continued to peal, the noise drifting upwards on the wind. Then it died away gradually. Yet his brain was like a tape-recorder playing back all that had gone before. The volume was still at full pitch.

The stars in the sky above him became blurred, pin-points, receding. The universe was tinged with red as

41

though the morning sun were embarking upon a nocturnal trip across the heavens. Donald Hughes groaned, and then everything went black. Mercifully he was even spared the continued peals of the Caelogy bell.

'Blimey, it's actually stopped.' Fred Reubens grunted and turned to where his wife was sprawled on the couch, a thick woollen scarf wound around her head, covering her ears.

'What did you say, Fred?' she mouthed at him hoarsely.

'I said the bloody thing's stopped,' he yelled.

Jane began to unwind her muffler, closing her eyes and shaking her head from side to side.

'I can still 'ear it,' she groaned, 'but not *quite* so loud. Just in me 'ead. I'm goin' to 'ave another migraine, that's for sure.'

'This'll have to be stopped,' Fred muttered. 'Can't have this nonsense every night. I'll see a solicitor tomorrow. Failing that we'll have to move and go and live somewhere else.'

'Why should we?'

'Precisely. But we can't put up with this. Now, you lie still and I'll get you some aspirin. Then I think we'd better turn in. What we need is an early night.'

It was half-past ten when the Reubens climbed into their twin beds and Fred switched off the light. His head throbbed. He could still hear the bell as plainly as though it were still pealing out its chimes from the chapel belfry. He ought to have taken an aspirin himself, but it was something he never did. The days of illness in his life could be counted on the fingers of one hand. Anyway, there was no point in disturbing Jane now. She was breathing steadily, regularly. She might even be asleep already.

He dozed. The bell. It chimed spasmodically bringing with it uneasy dreams; of Hamilton, the Chinese girl; trapped inside the grounds; being hunted by that alsatian; trying to scale the wall; being pulled back. Falling . . . falling . . . *crash!*

42

Fred jerked into wakefulness, his body jarred by the imaginary fall, his head still throbbing wildly from the vibrations of the bell. He stared into the darkness of the room. Something was wrong. He sensed it. And even as his hand was reaching up for the light-pull, he heard a low groan from close by.

The room was flooded with dazzling light that seared his eyeballs and increased the pulsing of his temples. He stared through slitted lids at the bed opposite his own. It was empty, sheets thrown back, the pillow crumpled and spotted with scarlet. Another moan, one of pain and despair.

'My God!'

He was leaping out of bed, kneeling by the huddled figure on the floor. Jane was scarcely recognisable. Her features were contorted into a mask of agony, and from her ears seeped thick rivulets of blood. Her neck and mouth were smeared with it. Her eyes were glassy, consciousness threatening to slip away any second.

'My head,' she whimpered. 'Oh, my head. The bell . . .'

He felt her sag limply in his arms and he laid her gently back on the floor. As he straightened up he saw the state of the pillow and knew that she had been haemorrhaging for some time.

He rushed out into the hall and even as he put the telephone receiver to his ear he heard the bell again. Three peals. They might have been the echoes of his imagination, but he knew they were not. For some inexplicable reason the Hamiltons had tolled their Tibetan bell again. The clock on the wall said 3.20 a.m.

He dialled 999. It was quicker than trying to look up the number of Dr Jones in the village, and it might have taken some time to rouse him. Right now time was at a premium.

He told them his name and address, and explained that his wife had had a bad haemorrhage.

He replaced the receiver and drew a deep breath. It needed courage to go back into that room. He had to force himself to walk forward, push open the door and look down upon the middle-aged woman who lay there without moving, her pallid face streaked with crimson.

Fred Reubens knew that his wife was dead. He had felt her go when she had slumped back in his arms. He'd tried to kid himself that she had just fainted. Hanging on to a shred of hope for no other reason than that he could not bring himself to put it into words over the telephone. The ambulancemen would find out when they arrived.

He did not panic. Neither did he submit to grief. It hit him hard, but not like it had on the night when his first wife had died. There was a difference. Gwen he had loved. She had been a part of him; still was, if he really thought about it. Jane had been a companion. They had agreed upon a marriage of convenience. She had lost her husband, Fred had lost his wife. Both of them needed somebody. It was as simple as that.

He found a packet of cigarettes, shook one out and lit it. His head ached abominably. He would have to phone Julian Dane, his stepson, but there was no point in doing that yet. Wait until a respectable hour. The younger man would be faced with a two hundred-mile journey. Let him get his quota of sleep first.

His thoughts turned to Martyn Hamilton. The bell. He looked again at Jane's ears. They were full of congealed blood. It *could* just have been a brain haemorrhage. It was the most feasible explanation. No, he decided, as agonising as the sound of the bell was, it couldn't have done . . . *that!* No way could it kill. It was just a bloody nuisance.

Then he heard the ambulance drawing up in the road outside.

Julian Dane looked out of place in a dark suit and black tie, his muscular body and sun-tanned complexion giving the impression of being imprisoned inside the expensive cloth against its will. The collar was ill-fitting and the shoes seemed a size too small.

His features were grim and his eyes were black-rimmed and sunken as he sat alongside Fred Reubens in Turbury church, staring fixedly at the coffin in front of the altar. His mother. It was unbelievable. A nightmare that was gradually becoming reality and making its impact on him.

The vicar droned on. None of the dozen people in the pews were really listening. At the rear sat the 'Church Steps Brigade', hunched forward, faces hidden behind gloved hands, their everyday solemn attire in keeping with the funeral. Tom Williamson glanced up from time to time, his eyes wide and staring.

Suddenly, a low metallic sound impinged itself upon each and every one of them, a single note that hung in the air, vibrating, causing the candlesticks on the altar to rattle. Heads were raised, expressions turned to alarm, fear. Just the one note, its echo dying away to a drone like an insect up in the rafters.

The vicar faltered in his address, clutching the lectern until his knuckles became white and bloodless. It was a tremendous effort for him to carry on.

'This our beloved sister . . . snatched from our midst . . .'

Killed by the bell . . . killed by the bell . . . the Caelogy bell . . . the death-bell.

Dane shook his head. It felt muzzy, stupefied, like the nagging ache which one sometimes awoke with in the morning and which became progressively worse as the day wore on. He glanced at Fred Reubens. His stepfather's expression was stoic, the lines deeper, more pronounced.

Abide with Me. The congregation mumbled the words, some mouthing them soundlessly. The organist increased the volume. He usually had to at funerals, otherwise the hymns were a farce. Nobody really sang.

They filed outside. Rawsthorne in the lead, head bowed, stumbling along. The undertaker and his assistant wheeled the coffin on its bier. Fred and Julian, white-faced and shaken, glancing apprehensively in the direction of Caelogy Hall. But the bell remained silent.

The others brought up the rear, keeping their distance, shuffling along, huddled together. The grave yawned deep

45

and symmetrical, a hungry void that awaited the remains of human flesh and bone.

Everybody clustered around. The undertakers struggled to lower the coffin, the ropes slipping and tilting its weight. Somehow they righted it with efficiency and dignity. It grated on the bottom and settled, a shower of loose earth spilling on to the varnished elm.

'Ashes to ashes, dust to dust.' Rawsthorne was gazing skywards as though offering up a prayer of his own, a silent plea for salvation.

Fred and Julian stepped forward, picked up a handful of loose soil from the mound and dropped it into the grave, listening to the faint thudding, a grim sound of finality. The end.

Then the Caelogy bell rang again. A soft chord that seemed to grow in the breeze, homing in on the group of mourners, striking them with the harshness of a physical blow. Again and yet again, at lengthy intervals, a slow melancholy rhythm.

The old men standing back beneath the elms were clutching at their ears, their faces masks of anguish. One had sunk to his knees, mumbling, praying.

Rawsthorne turned to Fred, shouting, trying to make himself heard, 'They do not mean even to let the dead rest.'

The undertakers backed away, the task of filling in the grave forgotten. They glanced towards the road where the grey hearse stood and had decided on flight, when the bell suddenly stopped.

Almost silent. Just the vibrations in the atmosphere and in the brains of those who had heard the slow, metronome-like clanging.

'God!' Julian breathed. 'How awful. I see what you mean, Fred.'

'Yes,' the builder grunted, 'that was what happened on the night your mother died. Only it was louder, more persistent then. This was like . . . well, like a funeral bell. As though it was rung deliberately to coincide with . . .'

'They're not going to get away with this,' Dane muttered. 'I'm going to have a word with this Hamilton guy and . . .'

'It's already been done,' Reubens sighed, 'to no avail. The next step is a meeting in the village hall on Friday night. A petition first. Then the Noise Abatement Society will be called in. Christ, if they can't stop it, then God help the people of Turbury!'

An hour later Fred and Julian were back in the small bungalow. Fred made a cup of tea and passed his stepson the aspirin bottle.

'How's your head?' he grimaced.

'Thumping like an old traction engine,' Julian tried to smile. 'Look, Fred, is it okay with you if I stay on for a few days?'

'Of course. You know you're more than welcome, but what's behind it? You're not going to stir up trouble are you? Because I can assure you you're backing a loser. You won't get anywhere with the Hamiltons.'

'I'd like to poke around and make a few enquiries.' The younger man pulled out a packet of cigarettes and passed one to Fred. 'For a start I'm not happy about the post-mortem.'

'The coroner said it was a cerebral haemorrhage.'

'Exactly. And as a neurologist I'd agree with him, but everybody is content to pass it off as that. Death from natural causes. But there are factors which can bring on a haemorrhage in an otherwise healthy person, and cause death, whereas, without that factor, they might have lived for another ten or twenty years. A severe blow is the most common, a jarring of the brain cells. Now a noise which caused vibration to the extreme could have the same effect.'

'You mean the bell?'

'Exactly. You know yourself how it jars the brain. I feel like I've just come out of the boxing ring after taking a damned good pounding. Mother would be less resistant to the decibels, obviously. And there are bound to be others like her in the village. How long will it be before somebody

47

else dies? From "natural causes". Jesus, this Hamilton guy could wipe out half the population of Turbury without anybody being able to pin anything on him, though God knows what he'd stand to gain by that. Unless, of course, he's a maniac.'

'There's something else behind it. They're a funny lot, and I'm sure they're steeped in some kind of weird religion. That bell isn't just to call them to chapel.'

'This youth you were telling me about, the village idiot. Now, he'd been deaf from birth yet he can hear the bell. I made a study of deafness when I was at University. The ear is a complicated arrangement of very fine tubes embedded in the bone and containing watery fluid. Part is concerned with balance, part with hearing. The latter, the cochlea, is shaped like a snail's shell, the tube being coiled up to make it more compact. The auditory nerve ends are along the inside of the tube. By a very delicate vibration detector the nerve ends are stimulated, individual nerve fibres carrying currents for individual pitches of sound. Low pitch sounds are detected at one end of the tube and high pitch at the other, rather like a piano keyboard. The fibres leave the cochlea and are bunched together as the auditory nerve and pass the sounds on to the brain, where they are heard and understood.'

'It's a bit above me,' Fred Reubens grunted.

'Look at it this way,' Julian continued. 'The ear is made to receive certain pitches. But anything outside those that it is made for will have a variety of reactions. Soldiers in wartime were deafened by shell blasts and bombs bursting too close. But take a normal sound but with such a frequency that the ear cannot cope ... like the Caelogy bell. It reverberates inside the head like a firework exploding in an empty tin can. There's no knowing what damage will result. Each ear, like its owner, is an individual. Some can stand more than others. No two will react alike. Do you see what I'm getting at?'

'Vaguely.' Fred wasn't entirely convinced. 'You mean that this bell could affect everybody in a different way?'

48

'Precisely. Deafness in some cases, whilst someone who has always been deaf, having a damaged ear-drum, is able to hear this particular noise. Terrifying, if you've never ever heard anything before. *And it can also cause death!*'

They smoked in silence for some time.

'I'd like to have a look at this bell.' Julian stubbed out his cigarette in the ash-tray.

'Hmm,' Fred shook his head slowly. 'Not much chance of that, I'm afraid. Hamilton won't let you on the premises. John Lewis, the local bobby, told him he'd got to keep his gates open as a means of access but I noticed yesterday that the padlock and chain was still around them. He's a tough nut, and he's going to take some cracking.'

'Maybe I could go at night,' Julian mused. 'It'd be worth the risk just to have a look at it.'

'There's a half-wild alsatian prowling the grounds. You'd be torn to pieces.'

'I'll find a way.' Julian stood up. 'Seeing the bell is more important than having a set-to with our sinister friend from Tibet. I'll find a way.'

The village hall was crowded. Every available chair was filled, and those who had arrived too late to get a seat stood around the sides of the large oblong-shaped room. People talked amongst themselves in low whispers, angrily giving their own versions of why the bell had been installed at the Hall.

'Ladies and gentlemen.' The vicar had to shout to make himself heard. His voice was a husky croak and he leaned his full weight upon the back of the chair on the raised platform. 'I am delighted to see so many of you here tonight at such short notice. As you are all aware, the purpose of this meeting is to discuss a problem which has been thrust upon us. Each and every one of you has heard this bell, a sound which defies description and leaves us with a feeling of weakness, headaches, migraines and . . .'

'*And it killed Mrs Reubens!*' A woman wearing a headscarf and a shabby coat, seated at the rear, called out.

'We have no proof of that,' Rawsthorne answered her.

'We don't need it. We all know. And we know what it's done to Donald Hughes. The boy is living in terror of it, hiding out in the woods for most of the day and sleeping *under* his bed at night.'

'We must do something positive.' The vicar attempted to quell a feeling of mass hysteria which threatened to ripple through his audience. 'Indeed, we have already made a very useful start. Today, our willing volunteers have visited every house in Turbury, and out of a population of seven hundred and ninety we have obtained a full complement of signatures to our petition. One hundred per cent,' he smiled, dwelling on the achievement for a few seconds. 'Everybody is with us. Now it only remains for me to forward these signatures to the Noise Abatement Society.'

'And how long will it take before we get some action?' It was the same rebellious-natured woman again, spilling cigarette ash down her coat as she shouted. 'How much longer have we got to endure this bell before something is done about it?'

'I shall personally press for immediate action.' Rawsthorne had visions of an irate mob with blazing torches converging on Caelogy Hall. 'In the meantime, I suggest that you take advantage of any protective hearing equipment which you can lay your hands on. Stereo headphones . . .'

'Bloody useless,' a lanky youth wearing denims called out. 'I tried 'em last time. You could hear the bell as plainly as if you were standing right next to it.'

'Be patient.' Rawsthorne held up his hands. 'Rome wasn't built in a day.'

'But Turbury could be destroyed in a night.'

The meeting broke up, people hurrying back to their homes, glancing apprehensively in the direction of Caelogy Hall, expecting to hear the peals of the death bell at any second. But the night air remained silent. Yet in some ways the silence was even more terrible. As though the bell was waiting patiently, choosing its time to strike again

50

when its victims were at their weakest, when they were least expecting it. Gradually, it was wearing them down, preparing for the kill.

Rawsthorne remained behind in the village hall after everybody had gone. He sat at the trestle-table and sank his aching head into his hands. Sheer exhaustion threatened to swamp him. It would have been all too easy to slump forward and let sleep claim him.

With an effort he pulled himself together. These people were depending upon him. He owed it to them. Simply to preach the Word was not enough. God helped those who helped themselves, and it was his duty to bring back peace and tranquillity to Turbury again.

Something else troubled him. He had not seen old Tom Williamson since the funeral the day before. Usually the village stalwart was to be seen every day with his cronies on the church steps whiling away the hours. 'The Brigade' had been there today, but there had been no sign of Williamson. It was uncanny. He had meant to ask after the old boy but a visit to Rafe Hughes and his wife had seemed more urgent. Poor Donald. It was only a matter of time before he had to go away. He was in a terrible state, a nervous wreck.

Rawsthorne's concern for Tom Williamson mounted. The old man had looked positively ill in the churchyard. He lived alone, with a home help calling twice a week to do his cleaning. Yes, the vicar decided, it would be prudent to go and see if Tom was all right. His cottage was on the other side of the village, a walk of twenty minutes or so, but it was a fine night. He stood up and reached for his coat. The fresh air would do him good. Maybe even clear his muzzy head.

Tom Williamson's cottage was on the end of the row of six solidly constructed pre-World War I dwellings. The vicar stood on the opposite side of the road looking at it. No lights showed. It was difficult. The old chap might have

51

turned in for an early night. Then again, he might be ill and in need of help.

Rawsthorne crossed the road and knocked on the door. He waited. There was no response. He knocked again. Nothing. The breeze stirred some dead leaves around his feet. Otherwise there was silence.

Somewhat hesitantly he tried the handle. It turned, and the ill-fitting wooden door creaked open a few inches. A smell of stale cooking came out of the stygian darkness and caused him to wrinkle his nose.

'Is anybody at home?' he called. 'Tom. Tom, are you there?'

No answer. An ice-cold trickle began to inch its way up the clergyman's spine. He sensed that something was wrong. Very wrong. For one more moment he hesitated, and then he pushed the door wide, stepped over the threshold and groped for the light switch.

The front room bore all the untidiness of an elderly bachelor. Cartons of kindling wood were stacked on the couch. Unwashed clothing that smelled of all that old men smell of was draped or piled on the two dilapidated armchairs. The fireplace was a heap of dead ashes.

In the second room he found Williamson. The man lay fully-clothed on the single bed, his body rigid, twisted at an unnatural angle, legs drawn up as though his last moments had been of terrible pain. The head was turned, puppet-like, in the direction of the door, eyes wide and bulging. Death had preserved the terror-stricken expression.

It was the ears, though, which caused Rawsthorne to step back involuntarily. They were scarcely recognisable. The blood seeping from them had congealed and filled them, like scarlet sealing-wax which has cooled and solidified. Some of it had soaked into the cushion which served as a pillow, and dried.

The blood-filled ears and staring eyes told their own story. The physical agony, the mental anguish, terminating in a cerebral attack. Rawsthorne felt the bile rising in his

52

throat, his stomach turning over. He had witnessed death in many forms. Mutilation in the trenches in France and Belgium; more recently, a motorway pile-up whilst holidaying by coach. But this was far more terrible. Inexplicable, defying logic.

As he doubled up and vomited he knew only too well that the Caelogy bell had claimed another victim. And at any second its sound waves might again be scouring the village on a mission of madness and murder.

5

THE DEAF HEAR

The mini-bus pulled up on the green at Turbury sometime after mid-day. The driver turned off the engine, stretched, yawned and turned to the woman who was seated directly behind him.

'Might as well make a break here, Miss Towler,' he said. 'Nice quiet place to give the kids a walk. We can have our sandwiches and be back at school for about three-thirty.'

'Good idea, George.' The robust middle-aged woman turned to the children, who were clamouring and pushing behind her. 'Now, children, steady on. Have you all got your hearing-aids turned on?'

A combined reply in various frequencies of the juvenile vocal chords affirmed that all hearing-aids were switched on. The ages of the children varied from seven to eleven. They jabbered excitedly amongst themselves, pointing out the various types of trees and wild flowers which they could see through the windows, the subject of the previous day's lessons in class two of the Partially-Hearing Unit.

'All right, children.' Miss Towler was firm and yet kind, a lifetime's experience in this often-neglected branch of education enabling her to control her over-active pupils, 'we are now going to see how many different types of flowers we can find in this place. Ten minutes,' she held up the fingers of both hands, 'and then we shall return to the bus to eat our lunch.'

They spilled out on to the half-acre of green grass, in the centre of which a century-old oak tree was just beginning to sprout its new growth of foliage. Beyond the green they could see the tower of the Norman church, where some jackdaws were busily milling together on a crumbling ledge.

Miss Towler could not afford to relax for one moment. 'Rachel, I said don't pick the flowers. Yes, that daisy *is* a flower. Paul, don't throw sticks. Now, come on, somebody tell me what this flower is. Yes, you're right, David. It's a dandelion.'

George Arkwright, the driver, remained behind the wheel of his vehicle. It was warm and he felt sleepy. The constant yapping of the kids had got on his nerves. It was a relief to get them outside for a few minutes. He decided that he would go and stretch his legs when they returned. Give himself another welcome break. His head sagged forward and his eyelids drooped. Just a quick forty winks.

No sooner had his eyes closed than they were jerked open again. A resonant clang seemed to jar every nerve in his body. His ears popped, the way they did when he drove high up into mountainous regions, only in a different way. As if somebody had twanged an elastic band right on the drum. It hurt like hell.

He sat bolt upright. For a moment his vision was blurred. The sunlight blinded him, burning his eyes. His skull hummed and buzzed.

Clang . . . clang.

Like a double shotgun blast came the metallic sound again, almost throwing him back in the seat. He gripped the steering wheel, sweat pouring down his face.

'George!' Miss Towler's voice, high-pitched. A scream.

'What the fuck . . !' He scrambled out of the door and almost fell to the ground.

Clang.

Somebody was ringing a bloody bell. Each note was like a xylophone being played inside his head, the hammer banging on the tenderest part of his brain.

'George! Help me. The children!'

The children were a priority. He broke into a run, his

55

blurred vision focusing with difficulty. The kids were running amok. Yelling. Holding their heads, beating the air as though a swarm of angry wasps were pursuing them. Miss Towler had hold of two of them, infant girls. They were trying to drag themselves from her grasp.

'George. That bell. It's doing something to the children!'

They were scattering in all directions, running blindly. A nine-year-old boy had fallen and cut himself on a sharp stone. Blood oozed from a gash on his cheek. George Arkwright grabbed him, lifted him up. The youngster was crying, kicking, struggling.

'Hold still. Take it easy.' George pinioned the arms of his captive and stood there, looking to the teacher for instruction.

Miss Towler was attempting to drag the two children back towards the vehicle. They were protesting loudly, trying to escape.

Then, as suddenly as it had begun, the bell ceased. Gradually, the moment of panic subsided. The frightened pupils calmed and began to sob.

'It was that bell that did it.' Miss Towler, white and shaken, succeeded in getting the two children back into the mini-bus. George joined her a few seconds later, dabbing at the boy's gashed cheek with a handkerchief.

'I'll get the first-aid box,' he grunted.

'No, leave that to me.' Miss Towler reached out for the boy. 'Get the others together, George. Round them up. For God's sake make sure that we've got them all.'

George turned back to the green. Fourteen kids. Three in the vehicle. Another eleven had to be accounted for.

'Come on, children,' he shouted. 'Who's for sandwiches? And cakes.'

Faces turned in his direction. Faces he knew. Daphne, Margaret, Kevin, Peter, Adrian. Five. The two new ones. He couldn't recall their names. That made seven. Three crouching by the oak tree. Ten. Gavin, lying on the ground as though he was having another of his tantrums. One to go. Jesus! He stood there looking round, and experiencing

56

a feeling of panic as he failed to see the missing child. Count 'em again. Ten, sure enough. Oh, fucking hell!

Only then did he realise that there was something wrong with the children on the green. Normally they would have come running at the mention of something to eat. Instead they just stood and stared at him with blank expressions on their faces. Glassy-eyed, mouths open wide, hands clasped over their ears or poking inside with their fingers as though trying to dislodge a wedge of stubborn wax.

He walked towards the nearest one, Adrian.

'Come on, Adrian.' He stretched out a hand.

At the last second the boy darted away, springing clear of George's outstretched hand, running as fast as he could in the opposite direction.

'Hey, come back!'

Two others joined Adrian in his flight. George pursued them for about twenty yards, then pulled up abruptly. His head was hurting, he couldn't think properly and his lungs were almost bursting after the sudden exertion. The problem was whether to go after the three runaways or round up the others first. He just stood there helplessly.

'Are you all right? Can I help you?'

He had not seen the tall man approaching. By his clothing George assumed that he was a clergyman, even though he wore an ordinary collar and tie. He had the bearing, the mannerisms, rubbing his hands together as though cleansing them.

'The children,' George Arkwright gasped. 'They ... they've gone crazy. The bell frightened 'em. They're deaf, you see.'

'Oh, dear!' Rawsthorne's expression changed to one of alarm. 'Let me help you.'

'There's three gone off over there, towards the church.'

'I'll try and find them.' The vicar moved off at a shambling urgent gait, calling back over his shoulder, 'You see to the others.'

Rawsthorne knew that the missing children had gone

57

into the church. He had shut both doors when he had left ten minutes earlier. Now one was open.

He paused to get his breath. His temples throbbed and he could still hear the bell inside his head. *Clang. Clang.* He winced. It was driving him mad. No doubt about that. It was driving everybody mad. But first he had to find the children.

The cool of the church was a relief after the brilliant sunshine outside. Rest a second. Get your wind again. Maybe your head will stop whirling.

Then, through the resonant bell sounds in his brain he heard whimpering. Not crying. Whimpering like an animal in distress. He peered around him. At first he saw nothing. It must have been his imagination. No! It was real enough. A pair of legs protruding from beneath the altar cloth. Boy's legs, torn white socks and scuffed shoes.

He advanced slowly up the altar steps, bowed out of habit, then reached down and lifted up the tapestry. Shrill cries of fear greeted him. Three children, two boys and a girl, pressed themselves back in an attempt to evade his reaching hands.

'Don't be afraid.' He spoke softly, kindly, smiling. 'I'm not going to hurt you. The bell has stopped ringing now.'

Or has it?

Their hands were clapped over their ears. Their eyes reflected their terror. And then, as if at a prearranged signal, all three burst into a fit of hysteria. They were screaming, crying, pointing. Their fingers stabbed the air, denoting some place beyond where Rawsthorne stood, a stone passageway that led out to the vestry.

He turned and stared. Dark shadows that held a host of unmentionable fears for children, a curtained doorway, the material moving slightly. Draughts. The building was plagued by them. All churches were. That was why the fuel bill was so high during the winter months.

'You're quite safe.' He stroked the face of the girl, feeling the dampness of her tears on his fingers. 'There's

58

nothing there. I assure you.' *At least I think there's nothing there!*

He shivered. Never before had he felt a desire to get out of his own church, to run blindly into the open sunlit countryside where there were no shadows. No place for . . . for *things* to hide.

'Vicar.'

He started involuntarily, whirling round. The woman who had been trying to placate the other children stood in the aisle, a worried expression on her face.

'Yes?' his voice was weak, guilty, as though he had been surprised in some unnatural act with the children, snatching his hand away quickly.

'Are they all right?'

'Yes . . . well, no. Not really,' he stammered. 'I . . . I don't know. They're very frightened. They seem to think that . . . that there's . . . *something* . . . hiding in the vestry corridor.'

She came forward and stooped down, gently grasping the children, pulling them out one by one. They were sobbing, clinging to her.

'I think we'd better get back to the bus,' she said. 'I can manage these two if you would like to carry Adrian.'

He followed, the boy cradled in his arms, tiny hands clutching tightly at his clothing. The boy was sobbing. The other two were talking to Miss Towler, jabbering, pointing back into the church. Something had really terrified them . . . apart from the bell!

They were nearly back at the mini-bus when the woman slowed so that he caught her up. She licked her lips and looked at him steadily.

'They've had a bad time,' she said. 'A kind of nightmare. They appear to have seen something in there which has given them a bad fright.'

'I assure you, madam,' Rawsthorne tried to sound indignant but his voice quavered. 'There is nothing in my church to frighten anybody. Not even children.'

'Maybe it was one of the scenes on the stained-glass

59

window, the sunlight reflecting it like a slide projector. They say there were some men in robes, and beneath their hoods they had shaven heads . . . and no ears. *Their ears had been cut off!* That sort of thing frightens deaf children.'

'Madam!' Rawsthorne stared, almost speechless. 'I . . . I promise you there is no such horrific scene depicted on any of my stained-glass windows.'

'They probably imagined it,' she shrugged. 'You know what children are. Deaf children are twice as perceptive. By the way, that bell of yours . . .'

'It was not *my* bell,' the clergyman snapped irritably. 'That bell, madam, belongs to Caelogy Hall. The people of this village are doing everything within their power to get it banned. You heard it for yourself. You understand what I am talking about?'

'Yes.' She rubbed her ears as she set the two children down. 'I certainly do. We've all had a bad fright, and I've changed my mind about stopping here for our lunch. Thank you for your help, vicar. And now I'll try and convince these children that they didn't see anything in your church. I'm afraid that's going to be quite a problem!'

'I shouldn't really be here,' the girl said.

She looked nervously at the young man who sat beside her on the grass. Long greasy hair fell to his shoulders. His jeans were torn and stained, his hands dirt-grimed. Yet in spite of all this he excited her. There was a kind of basic sex-appeal about him, an animal attraction. Rich had been in and out of trouble since his schooldays. Petty thieving, a string of motorbike offences, assault. He'd assaulted the Turbury policeman, John Lewis' predecessor. That had resulted in a spell in a remand home. Now, much to the villagers' consternation, he was back in Turbury.

Emma was already having second thoughts about coming out to the woods with Rich. If her father got to know about it . . . Dr Jones was one of the old school. No matter what the modern generation tried to make out, there *was* a social scale. It was unfortunate, but it was a fact of life,

60

he was constantly impressing upon his daughter. There were no 'in betweens'. What was it that Mark Twain had said? 'East is east, and west is west, and ne'er the twain shall meet.' That was going a bit far, she decided. There wasn't really a lot of choice regarding boyfriends in Turbury, and when a girl reached eighteen she found herself desperately in need of male company.

It was silly, she admitted to herself, to agree to go for a stroll with the likes of Richie Martin. There were lots of rumours about him and his various girlfriends. He hadn't brought her out here in the gathering spring dusk just to sit and hold hands and talk about all sorts of things that didn't really matter. She had already noticed the protrusion in the front of his jeans, the way he was eyeing her up. Her body had been crying out for its first sexual experience for a long time now, and she'd had fantasies about situations such as this. But when it came to the crunch she was frightened. No way was he going to have her.

'Why worry yourself about a big fat slob like your dad?' he leered and rested a hand on her thigh. 'You can't let him rule your life.'

'He isn't a big fat slob,' she retorted hotly. 'He's very nice really. He just has a few funny old-fashioned ways.'

'Like believing that because a guy hasn't had a good start in life he's no good and will never make it?'

'Well, you haven't exactly endeared yourself to society, have you?'

'Fuck society!'

'I . . . beg your pardon?'

'I said fuck society. Look how they've treated me. From the time I started school they'd made up their mind that I wasn't going to be any good. You have to be born in the right cradle to make it, and there's sod all anybody can do about that. It's the law of the jungle. The rich trample on the poor and make sure that they keep 'em down. Don't give 'em a chance to get up and fight back. Except me. I stood up for myself and they don't like me for it.'

'But you can't go around stealing and . . .'

61

'Look, the folks I stole from wouldn't miss what I took, and . . .'

'Robin Hood, eh? But I bet you didn't give your loot to the poor.'

He looked at her steadily and his eyes narrowed. Stuck-up little bitch. Well, the upper class was about to be taught another lesson. He withdrew his hand from her thigh, lit a cigarette and blew the smoke arrogantly in her face. She recoiled, coughing.

'I think we ought to be getting back.' There was a trace of nervousness in Emma's voice. 'You never know, they might decide to ring that bell at the Hall again.'

'Fuck the bell!'

'I wish you wouldn't swear, Rich.'

'I'll swear if I want to. The upper class don't like that either, do they? So they say. But I'll tell you something. I've heard 'em fucking and blinding as good as the next man, and I'd bet a tenner that your old man does when you're not around.'

'Daddy doesn't say those sort of things.'

'You'll be telling me next that he doesn't fuck, and then I'll really call you a liar, because your mother had *you*. Unless, of course,' his lips curled in a sneer, 'some other bloke was screwing her!'

'How dare you!' her hand went back and her palm caught him across the face in a stinging slap.

'Jesus Christ!' he guffawed. 'I'd never've believed it! Quite a little hellcat, aren't you? Why, there's even a chance that you just *might* not be a virgin!'

'I wouldn't tell you whether I was or not,' she snapped, cheeks flushed, tears of rage welling up in her eyes.

'I'm goin' to find out, anyway.' He moved closer, grabbing her by the wrists, pinioning them with one huge hand and pushing her back on to the ground with the other.

'Let go of me. Don't you dare touch me!'

'Stop playing the little innocent, Miss Goodie.' He kissed her neck as she turned her head away. 'You're nothing but a stupid little prick-teaser. "Oh, yes, Rich, I'd love to go for a walk in the woods with you." You stupid cow. What did you think we was going to do? Pick flowers?'

Emma began to struggle desperately, but the youth's strength was too great for her. He held her helpless with his left hand whilst his right groped up beneath her skirt, the thick fingers hooking into the elastic of her pants. She closed her thighs tightly, pressing them together. He tugged hard. She felt the elastic snap then heard the material ripping. He laughed coarsely and began to force his hand in between her compressed limbs, opening her up. She screamed and writhed as he groped, cruelly oblivious of the pain he was causing her.

'Rich,' she was sobbing, pleading. 'Don't. Oh, for God's sake stop it. *Please!*'

'If you didn't struggle and make such a fuss you might enjoy it,' he poked a finger right inside her, felt something give and winced as she yelled at the top of her voice.

'You could go to prison for this!' she gritted her teeth, attempting to conquer her panic. 'It's rape!'

'Don't be bloody stupid, girl! I ain't done anythin' like that. I've just . . . just 'elped meself to . . . to a feel.' There was a note of disquiet in his voice, a sudden realisation that perhaps he had gone too far. Emma Jones was not one of the girls who hung round the village bikers, only too willing to drop 'em.

'Look,' she choked on her words, 'you've assaulted me. You've . . . hurt me.'

He released her, and for the first time for many years he felt fear creeping over him.

'I'm sorry,' he wiped his mouth with the back of his hand. 'I didn't mean to. I got carried away. I thought you was willin'. Look . . . er . . . can't we just be friends and forget all about this?'

She looked at him, sensing safety, victory. Just play your cards right until you get back to the village. Then you can decide what to do. Tell Dad. Tell the police. Get the book

63

thrown at him. In the meantime, keep it low key, enjoy his apologies. Make him crawl.

'I don't know.' She straightened her clothing and sat up. 'It all depends. I didn't like what you did to me. And it hurts like hell.' That was true, anyway. Her lower regions were throbbing like bad period pains, as if a length of barbed steel had been thrust up her vagina. She knew she was bleeding, too. She'd have to let a doctor see her. Not Daddy, though.

'I was right, wasn't I?' he muttered. 'You were a virgin.'

'I still am. You only did it with your finger.'

'Okay, you're still a virgin and I'm sorry.'

They looked at each other steadily. She could not hide the contempt, the hate which smouldered in her eyes. This was a night she would remember for the rest of her life.

Then, without warning, a vibrant metallic sound rolled across the countryside, a force that destroyed the soughing of the breeze in the trees and the late evening birdsongs. Dominant. Painful to the ears. Obliterating the tranquillity.

'Oh, God! *No!*' She stiffened and clutched at her companion. '*The bell!*'

'Fucking Christ Almighty!' He winced as the second note hit him, biting his lower lip until the blood flowed freely.

Clang. Clang. The momentum was speeding up, the bell tolling faster than ever it had done before, the noise gathering like a series of tidal waves hitting a sea-wall. Roosting woodpigeons were taking to the wing, flying crazily in the dusk in an attempt to seek sanctuary. Grazing cattle in the adjoining field huddled together, pawed the ground and then broke into a mad stampede, crashing through a hawthorn hedge, bulldozing their way into a stretch of winter wheat.

Emma Jones clasped her head and closed her eyes. A steel pendulum was crashing against her skull, knocking it first one way, then the other. She clutched at Rich Martin, burying her face against his chest. She needed protection, and he was the only man around.

Martin's brain was numbed. The first few notes had pounded him like hammer blows. The others came fast and furious but they didn't hurt any more. Just the noise. It made him angry. A lot of things were making him angry. This wench, for a start, with all her bloody prudish ways. He looked down at her through a shimmering red haze. No fucking virgin was going to get the better of Richie Martin. No sir!

His fury escalated and his lust returned, his hardness pushing and pulsing again. Roughly he pushed her from him, throwing her back on to the soft grass, laughing, kneeling over her. Her eyes flickered open.

'Rich,' she groaned. 'Oh, my head. The bell . . .'

'Fuck the bell.' He unzipped himself, and her eyes widened in horror as she saw the outline of solid vibrant flesh in the half-light, the bell-shaped tip a menacing symbol of danger.

'No!' she screamed and tried to struggle up, but a clenched fist caught her in the face, throwing her back down again. There was a blaze of coloured lights before her eyes and she felt the warm blood gushing from her nose. He was shouting something, but she couldn't catch the words above the noise of the bell.

His fingers tore at her clothing with almost superhuman strength, shredding her blouse, her bra snapping to bare her breasts. The nipples were crushed, pulled and then bitten as he came on top of her. She felt her skirt pulled from her, the remnants of her tattered underwear following them into the undergrowth. Naked and totally helpless, she wanted to die before this fiend had his way. He had been nasty with his lust before. Now he was a monster, spittle forming on his lips and spraying over her as he frothed his blasphemy and curses.

He entered her, causing excruciating pain every inch of the way, his barbs tearing her as he thrust faster and faster, almost as though he was using the bell as a metronome. Every part of her body cried out for relief. Once she thought she was going to faint, but oblivion cruelly eluded her. Then he was grunting and gasping, his alcoholic breath fetid in her face, his tongue demanding entry to her mouth. He was shuddering, clutching at her, his fingernails scraping her tender flesh.

Finally, he was lying still on top of her, his breath rasping, swallowing. Totally spent. Only the bell continued with its torture of mind and body.

'You bastard!' she hissed, and derived satisfaction from her first-ever use of the word. 'You bastard!'

'Well, you're certainly not a virgin now, whichever way you look at it,' he sneered. 'You can tell your Mummy and Daddy that you've been fucked good and proper!'

'I shall tell the police,' she snapped as her anger began flooding back. 'You're right, you went the whole way. Against my will. That's rape. And you'll go to prison for it, make no mistake about that, Rich. But I don't suppose you'll mind because you've already been to a remand centre. It must be like home to you.'

He stiffened and licked his lips, hesitating as though trying to come to a decision.

'So you're going to tell the cops, are you?' he hissed.

'I am. Make no mistake about that.'

'You won't be telling anybody.' He moved his hands slowly, deliberately, from where they had been cupping her breasts, sliding them up until they encircled her neck. 'Nobody at all. You bitch!'

Her scream ended in a gurgle as his fingers tightened over her throat. She flailed her arms, beat at his head with her fists, but it made no impact on him.

Her head was back, her eyes bulging. She couldn't breathe. The blows she was raining on her attacker became weaker and weaker. The blood throbbed in her temples . . . or was it the bell? She could still hear it, louder than before. The death-knell. Oh, God, she wanted to die. Now. Quickly. It was the only answer.

Her prayers were heard. She felt consciousness slipping

66

away from her. The pain had gone. Just the bell. It was still ringing but it didn't hurt any more, getting slower and slower . . . and slower. Then it was silent.

Richie Martin shook her by the neck. Her head lolled to one side, eyes staring up at him in the darkness. She seemed to be smiling. Mocking him.

'Fuck you!' He drove his fist down with all his strength into her bloody face, felt the crunch of bone. Again. And again. The smirking hussy! No guy would want to screw her after this.

He eased up, gasping for breath, sagging forward on to his hands. He wasn't finished with her yet. He had enjoyed every minute of it, not just the copulation. The blood pulsed hotly in his veins and he still had an erection. Sod her, opting out on him just when . . .

He shook his head. Silence. It was like a hammer blow, forceful, awakening his senses as if a bucket of ice-cold water had been thrown over him. His flesh goosepimpled, and his stomach muscles began to contract. He backed away, shuffling like a crab, unable to take his eyes off the bloody twisted naked body. The features were unrecognisable. The legs were lewdly spread, the hair between a matt of congealing blood. Oh, Jesus Christ!

He shook his head, trying to clear it, closed his eyes and opened them again. Emma Jones was still there. Dead! Raped and murdered by Richie Martin!

He rose to his feet, swaying unsteadily. A wind had got up, freshening, cooling him, making him shudder. Grim reality, no getting away from it. No excuses. *Murderer!*

He broke into a run, fleeing blindly, his sobs whipped away by the night wind. A protruding root caught his foot and he sprawled headlong. He hit the ground and lay there, the breath knocked from his body. Murderer!

He began to pick himself up. He was still trembling but the fall had dispelled some of his panic. He rubbed his head. It ached abominably, throbbing as though the clapper of a bell was swinging gently from side to side inside his skull. The bell! Jesus, it had really hit him this time. Last time when it had started to ring he had picked a quarrel with Sid Beddoes in the Buffalo. He'd've killed the sod if some of Sid's mates hadn't ganged up on him and thrown him out. He hadn't realised at the time, but that *had* to be the reason . . . *the bell!* It had turned him into a killer.

He felt sorry for Emma Jones. Sure he'd meant to screw her, but he wouldn't have hurt her. It was the Caelogy bell that had killed her. But when the day of reckoning came they wouldn't come looking for the bell, or Martyn Hamilton. They'd clap the handcuffs on Richie Martin and put him away somewhere for a long time. For life!

He was calmer now. He remembered where he had left his bike, on the outskirts of the village. Nobody had seen him with Emma. They'd have to find her first, then work out who'd killed her, before they came after him. He had time on his side. Time to get away, to make tracks . . . before the bell rang again.

He walked on quickly into the darkness.

A few rabbits crept out to feed after the bell stopped, timid creatures, ears pricked up, ready to dart back to their burrows at the first sound of danger. The wind had dropped again to a gentle breeze, and the silence rolled softly backwards.

A movement, the cracking of a dead branch. The coneys scurried towards the wood, white tails bobbing like ghostly will-o'-the-wisps in the darkness.

A figure emerged from a clump of silver birch trees, ambling forward, long arms dangling ape-like, head twisting from side to side as though he feared a hidden lurker waiting to pounce on him. His breathing was stentorian, phlegm rattling in his lungs. Large ears that were normally dead buzzed incessantly, and the brain within the huge skull vibrated to the sound of the Caelogy bell, which had ceased more than two hours ago.

Donald Hughes stood and looked down upon the lifeless body of Emma Jones. Compassion at first brought tears to his eyes. Then curiosity. He had always wondered about the opposite sex, what they were like beneath their scant clothing. Once he had lain and watched a courting couple on the edge of a cornfield. Kissing he could understand. But they had done other things. Or rather, the man had. He had been insistent on removing the girl's tights and pants, and as they had been peeled off Donald had moved closer in an attempt to see what lay beneath them. But the fellow had screened his view, lying in between the female thighs and entering her with his . . . it didn't make sense, although Donald was only too well aware of the pleasurable sensations which he was able to bring about by finger movements on that same part of his own body. He had often wondered about it, but now it seemed that the mystery was solved. Partially, anyway. That chap had really enjoyed himself. They had gasped and rolled over, convulsing as though they were having a fit. Then they had got dressed and gone off, arm-in-arm.

Donald wanted to try it with a woman. But what girl was going to let him do things like that? Not even old Florrie who often admitted men into her cottage in the village after darkness.

All these thoughts came back to him, and with them a familiar sensation in his lower regions as he stared at the still form of Emma Jones, her thighs spread stiffly and invitingly. He knelt down and fingered her softly, exploring her mysteries, grunting to himself. He understood what had excited that lover in the cornfield.

Clumsily, his fingers trembling with excitement, he positioned himself in between her open legs. It was too good a chance to miss. And he didn't care if the Caelogy bell did start to ring again.

6

BLOOD OR RUST?

The telephone rang just as Fred Reubens and Julian Dane were finishing their breakfast.

'I'll get it.' Fred got up from the table, pausing to swallow a mouthful of toast. 'It'll probably be old Chorlton. Wants a bit of work doing on the guttering around his cottage.'

Julian could hear Fred's side of the conversation through the half-open door. 'Yes. Of course. All right, sir, I'll be up about ten. Yes, that's fine . . .'

'A day on the guttering?' Julian looked up as his stepfather entered.

'No,' Fred grimaced, 'that bloody bell at the Hall. The setting has slipped a bit. I thought it might, but I hoped it wouldn't because it means taking the sodding thing off again. Hamilton's in quite a tizz about it. It's ringing too fast, apparently. Anyway, I'm going up to have a look at it. Let's hope that nobody sees me, otherwise I'll be labelled as aiding and abetting. You know what these villagers are like. Maybe I ought to have refused altogether, told him I'd got some other work on, but he said it was worth fifty quid to me to put it right. Fifty quid for a day's work, maybe less! Perhaps I ought to sabotage it whilst I'm at it.'

'I'm coming with you,' Julian said.

'What! Don't be bloody daft, man.'

'I told you I wanted an opportunity to look at that bell. What better chance?'

'Hamilton won't let you inside the gates.'

'He will if I'm your assistant. It needs two of you to take the bell down and put it up again. Either he lets me help you or you don't do the job. If he's that concerned about the thing he won't raise too many objections.'

'I suppose there's no harm in it.' Fred stroked his chin thoughtfully. 'But I don't like it.'

'Well, I do.' Julian began piling the dirty crockery into the sink. 'Fate is really on our side, Fred.'

It was five minutes to ten when Fred Reubens drove up to the gates of Caelogy Hall. Julian Dane sat beside him wearing a borrowed boiler-suit which was a size too small, but by leaving the front unbuttoned he was able to move about reasonably freely. Karamaneh appeared on the scene, opened the gates, and as the pick-up drove slowly through, her eyes met Julian's. For a few fleeting seconds the couple stared at each other. The slanting eyes flickered briefly, a hint of an expression that died away almost instantly. Hope? Fear? It was impossible to tell.

'So that's the oriental beauty I've been hearing about,' the neurologist murmured. 'A nice bit of stuff, eh, Fred?'

'Aye,' Fred grunted. 'She certainly doesn't fit in with this bloody household, though. I wonder if they pay her a wage, or is it slave labour?'

Martyn Hamilton was waiting by the chapel. His expression hardened as he watched Julian getting out of the truck.

'Who's this, Reubens?' he snapped. 'I thought I made it quite clear that you alone were working for me and . . .'

'My stepson, sir.' Fred glanced apprehensively at the owner of Caelogy Hall. 'He's learning the trade. Going to work with me for a while.'

'Not here, he isn't.' Hamilton took a step forward, almost a threatening gesture. 'You'd better take him back home, Reubens.'

'I'm sorry, sir.' Fred shifted his weight from one foot to the other. 'But humping that bell about is too much for me on my own. If I can't have a mate with me I'm

71

afraid I'll have to ask you to get somebody else to do the job!'

Hamilton stared at him, tight-lipped. The colour drained from his features as his anger mounted, but with a visible effort he controlled himself.

'All right,' he snapped, and turned away abruptly. 'Just get on with the job and get it done as quickly as possible!'

The two men moved into the chapel. Julian looked up, saw the bell and whistled.

'Phew!' he breathed. 'Some bell! Must weigh half a ton.'

'No.' Fred began climbing the ladder. 'It's much lighter than it looks. About three hundredweight at a guess. You can see how it's slipped to one side where that one joist has come out. We'd better take it down first and rest it on the platform whilst I put some new woodwork in there.'

It took them less than quarter of an hour to remove the bell from its position. Whilst Fred busied himself sawing a new length of timber, Julian began a minute examination of the large object. He studied the design and shook his head in bewilderment.

'Beats me how those old craftsmen had the time to engrave a thing like this. Attention to every detail. Must've taken years. Hey, what's this on the inside?'

'Rust,' Fred grunted, a couple of nails held between his teeth. 'I thought about cleaning it up, but you can never tell with a bloke like Hamilton. He might actually *like* it rusty. My motto is "do what you're asked to do and no more." You can't go wrong then.'

'Just a minute. Look at this!' Julian was scraping at the brown coating, flaking bits off with his nail and scrutinising them in the palm of his hand.

'What's the matter?' Fred was busily trying to fit a length of wood.

'*This isn't rust. It's dried blood!*'

'What!' the older man looked down, dropping one of the nails as he did so.

'Right enough.' Julian's voice was low. 'It's blood, all right. How old, I don't know. Could be centuries old. But how the hell did blood get inside here?'

'Nowt to do with us, anyway. Maybe the Tibetans used to kill a fatted goat and spray its blood on the bell to improve the tone.'

'There's a lot of funny things going on around here. Look, Fred, I'm going to take a mooch around outside. I don't know what I'm expecting to find, but I'd just like a peek at the set-up.'

'You bloody well stay where you are. If Hamilton catches you poking your nose into his business . . .'

'There's not much he can do about it, except kick us off the premises, and then he won't get his bell mended. This isn't the Middle Ages. He can't throw us in the dungeons.'

'All right.' Fred Reubens was fully aware that once his stepson's mind was made up, nothing would dissuade him. 'But just you be careful. And don't be long about it.'

Julian Dane emerged from the chapel and walked quickly across to a clump of bushes. From there he could see the Hall plainly, and there was sufficient cover to screen him from anyone watching from any of the windows. He stood there, trying to come to a decision. There really wasn't much to see. If only he could get inside the building. The tradesmen's entrance was only twenty yards or so away. That was where Fred had explored the day he'd overheard the shouting in foreign tongues, the banging. It was worth a try. If he bumped into Hamilton then he could claim to be searching for the kitchens to get some hot water to make a cup of tea. Fred was an inveterate tea-drinker. It sounded plausible, anyway.

He crossed the open space and tried the door. It was unlocked. He breathed a sigh of relief as he closed it behind him. His heart was thumping and his forehead was damp. God, he didn't think that he'd be as nervy as this.

The kitchens were deserted. A pile of unwashed plates

and bowls stood by the sink, and there was a sharp spicy odour hanging in the room. Garlic-flavoured something-or-other for breakfast, he heaved at the thought.

Then suddenly the door immediately in front of him was opening. He tensed, glanced around, but there was nowhere to hide. He swallowed. So much for his reconnaissance trip. Trapped at the first hurdle. He'd never make a detective.

It was Karamaneh, dressed in a long flowing orange dress, her black hair neatly tied in a pony-tail. She started when she saw him and her narrow eyes widened in what could only be interpreted as terror. Not surprise or annoyance, Dane decided. Fear! She closed the door quietly and moved towards him.

'You . . . must not be here.' She struggled with her words, forming them slowly.

'Maybe, but I am,' Dane smiled, his eyes travelling over her petite figure, noting its perfection. 'I was looking for hot water to make some tea.'

'You do not . . . speak truth.' Her eyes scanned him, but there was no hint of reprimand in her expression, only concern. Nervousness. She glanced over her shoulder, listening.

'You're right. It's not the truth. I just wanted to have a look round.'

'Why?' She was watching him closely.

'I wanted to find out about the bell. Why it is being rung. Why it does strange things. *Kills people!*'

'*No!*' A hand went to her mouth in horror. 'It has not killed. Has it?'

'Yes.' His expression hardened. 'It killed my mother.'

'Oh!' Her eyes closed momentarily, then opened again. 'It is indeed terrible. I never knew . . .'

'What's your name?' he asked suddenly, tenderly.

'Karamaneh.' She pronounced it slowly.

'Mine's Julian. Julian Dane. I'm staying in the village with my stepfather. That's the man who is mending the bell.'

'Ju . . . lian.' She let the name roll off her tongue and smiled for the first time. 'But you must not stay here. It is . . .' she searched for the word, 'dangerous!'

'Why?'

'We are having troubled times.'

'You can say that again. Tell me, why do they keep ringing the bell?'

'I cannot tell you.'

'You mean you won't!'

'I cannot. I dare not. But go from here quickly and forget all about it.'

'That isn't easy. Not when it deafens you and gives you a thumping headache every night.'

'It is an accident. They do not mean to harm you or the people of this place. It is just . . . unfortunate.'

'I'll say it is. Come on, tell me what's going on here.'

'*No!*' She recoiled a pace. 'I have told you . . . *listen, someone comes!*'

Dane heard the footsteps in the passage and stiffened. Whoever was coming would be in the kitchens in a matter of seconds. It was too late to flee or hide. Karamaneh turned towards the door, cowering. It burst open, and Martyn Hamilton stood there, an expression of surprise and anger on his angular face, the veins on his receding forehead beginning to knot and stand out. In his hand he held a riding-crop.

'What's going on?' His expression flicked over the Chinese girl and came to rest on Julian Dane. 'What the hell are you doing in here?'

'I came to ask for some water to make some tea,' Julian replied, meeting the other's gaze and trying not to shrink before it. 'Is that a crime?'

'You're a liar!' Hamilton spat the accusation out angrily. 'You're snooping. Trespassing in my house like a common burglar.'

'I happened to be asking your servant for some water.' Dane felt his own anger rising. His huge fists clenched.

75

God, he'd like to hit the bastard! 'So I'm not trespassing, am I?'

Hamilton whirled on Karamaneh. 'Go to your room. How many times have I told you that strangers are not to be admitted to the Hall?'

She flinched as though she expected him to strike her with the crop, turned and hastened from the room. As the door closed behind her, Hamilton turned to Julian.

'You've been questioning my servant,' he snarled.

'You've got something to hide, then?'

'I am entitled to my privacy. That's why I retired here from Tibet. To be left in peace. And you damned villagers are determined that I'm not going to get any.'

'I don't happen to be a villager,' Dane rapped, 'and as for peace and tranquillity, you're not giving the folks around here any with that bloody bell of yours.'

'The stories about the bell are grossly exaggerated. The vicar rings his church bell. I ring mine. There is no difference.'

'Except that his is musical and yours either deafens . . . or kills!'

'Don't you dare say that! What proof have you?'

'My mother died as a result of your bell.'

'That's a lie. Impossible. Prove it!'

'I'm in the process of doing that.' Julian's voice was low and menacing. 'And when I succeed, Mr Hamilton, then you're going to go to prison for a very long time!'

'Get out!' The other man's mounting fury suddenly erupted and he stepped forward, the crop raised threateningly. 'Get out before I hit you.'

'Go on, hit me,' Julian taunted. 'And then the law will really have something on you.'

With a supreme effort Martyn Hamilton brought his temper under control. His nostrils flared as he breathed deeply. 'Go back and finish your work,' he snapped. 'And then get out. And don't try coming back. If you do, it will be on your own head. I must remind you that a guard-dog is loose in these grounds between the hours of sunset and sunrise.'

'Which goes to prove that you've something to hide.' Julian turned and walked back towards the door. He felt Hamilton's malevolent stare spraying him like twin searchlights. He grinned to himself. He hadn't achieved much. In fact, his reconnaissance trip had proved a total failure. But he had certainly thrown the gauntlet down at the feet of the owner of Caelogy Hall. Now both of them knew where they stood. The games of cat and mouse were over.

'What kept you?' Fred looked down as Julian walked back into the chapel. 'You've been gone so long I thought they'd invited you to stay for elevenses.'

'That's one way of putting it,' Julian laughed. 'I have been entertained. By Miss Karamaneh and then by the laird of Caelogy himself. I've got a message from him for both of us. Hurry up, and fuck off.'

'Jesus!' Reubens looked worried. 'You haven't been causing trouble, have you?'

'I haven't. Hamilton has. And if we had any doubts before, we haven't now. Something decidedly sinister is going on here. That Chinese girl is absolutely terrified of him. She's virtually a prisoner here. Well, there'll be no more snooping around today. More than likely the bastard's sitting in the window watching this place to make sure we don't try anything else. How much longer are you going to be, Fred?'

'No thanks to you,' Reubens muttered. 'I'm virtually finished. Even hauled the bloody thing back up myself.'

'Good work.' Julian stood back as his stepfather began to descend the ladder. 'Just hold your hands over your ears, Fred.'

'What the hell for?'

'I'm going to ring the bell. Just once. To make sure we've done our work properly!'

'For Christ's sake!' The older man jumped the last

three rungs and reached out to stop Julian. 'Don't do that. The bugger'll go berserk!'

But he was too late. Julian Dane leaned back, taking the full weight of the bell-pull in his hands. The clapper struck the bell. Slowly. Just enough momentum. *Dong!*

Fred and Julian staggered back under the force of the impact in the confined space. The building vibrated, holding the sound, slowly releasing it through the door and belfry windows.

Seconds later they heard running footsteps on the mossy flagstones outside and Hamilton, beside himself with fury, stood framed in the doorway. He was panting, gulping, for a moment unable to speak articulately.

'What the . . . you . . . you did that deliberately!' he grunted. 'Nobody shall ring that bell except the . . . except me!' he yelled. 'How dare you! How dare you!'

'We were just testing it,' Julian shrugged nonchalantly. Fred Reubens shuffled his feet and wished that there was somewhere he could hide.

'You could have done untold harm!' Hamilton raved.

'That's interesting. Like what?'

'Get out. Get out, the pair of you. Immediately!'

Fred Reubens picked up his tool bag and Julian followed him out to the pick-up.

'You bloody fool,' Fred muttered as they drove off. 'Look at the trouble you've caused now.'

'The trouble with you, Fred, is you're too . . . hey, slow up a minute!'

His stepfather eased his foot off the accelerator. Julian was craning his neck, looking up towards the third storey windows. A face was pressed against the glass, the features those of a woman in her early fifties, perhaps younger, beautiful, yet cruelly stamped with the marks of anguish. Eyes that watched the disappearing vehicle as though she longed to be a passenger aboard it. Then, suddenly, she was gone, vanishing as though she had never existed.

'What's up now?' Reubens grunted irritably, and began to accelerate again.

'That, I presume,' his stepson replied, 'was Mrs Hamilton. And she looked as scared as Karamaneh did earlier.'

'Huh!' the builder was glad to pass through the wrought iron gates, experiencing a sense of sudden freedom.

'That Karamaneh.' Julian Dane drummed his fingers on his knee. 'She's quite a girl. Extremely beautiful, but very, very frightened. For a number of reasons I'm going to try and see her again. As soon as possible.'

7

MOB LAW

Three men moved quietly through the dusk, threading their way through the maze of gravestones in the Turbury churchyard. None spoke, all communication was made by gestures and an occasional grunt. They carried suitcases from which protruded an assortment of wires, and the man bringing up the rear had a folded tripod with a microphone attachment.

They looked around, picked their spot and began to unpack their equipment. Lengths of flex were looped over tombstones and connected to the standing tripod. The suitcases were opened, the lids thrown back to reveal complicated tape-recorders with numerous dials and switches.

The men worked diligently, silently, and by the time darkness had fallen they were ready, crouching apprehensively over their apparatus.

'God blimey, George!' the tallest of the three muttered, 'it's like ruddy ghost-hunting. This place gives me the creeps.'

'Can't say I'm struck on it,' the one called George replied in a hoarse whisper. 'I've been to some rum places since I've been working for the Society, but this one beats the lot. I ask you, a bloody bell. 'Ow can a bell cause a nuisance. These folks must be round the twist. But I hope the bleedin' thing rings tonight otherwise we'll be creepin' about 'ere tomorrow night and the night after that. Might be 'ere the whole bloomin' week.'

'Don't say that.' The third man struck a match and held it between cupped hands whilst he lit a cigarette. 'Bloody remote out-of-the-way hole like this. You'd think they'd welcome a bit o' noise to liven things up.'

The men fell silent. Time passed slowly, the church clock chiming the hours and the quarters. It was warm for April. And calm, too. Their raincoats had been left behind in the vicarage.

'Bit of a nutter, that vicar, if you ask me. All flustered, wanting to come with us. Bloody hell, you couldn't have an old geezer like that sitting with you for half the night. You'd end up like him, yourself.'

They all laughed.

'How long are we going to give it, George?'

'The vicar said that if the bell hadn't rung by midnight . . .'

The sentence went unfinished as a deep resonant clang shattered the stillness. All three men jumped, wincing.

One reached forward and flicked a switch on the machine nearest to him. There was a humming sound. It could have been the vibration that hung in the atmosphere like electric waves.

'Jesus! I see what they mean. Break all records this one will. My bloody ears!'

Clang.

They cowered in the darkness, anticipating the next ring, still reeling from the impact of the last one. A green light flashed on the recording device, dials clicked and revolved.

Five terrible minutes that seemed an eternity, and then the noise ceased. The silence struggled to fight its way back.

'Come on.' One of the men was starting to dismantle the machinery, working feverishly, eager to be away from this place. 'That'll do. We'll check it back at the vicarage. Blimey, it's a wonder it didn't bust the instruments. Shouldn't have any trouble proving this one is over the limit!'

Rawsthorne was standing on the vicarage steps, an

81

agonised expression on his face, peering into the darkness. He was white and shaken.

'Ah, there you are.' Relief in his voice. 'Well, you heard it for yourselves. You know now that I wasn't exaggerating.'

'Too right, vicar.' They crowded into the hall and set their suitcases down on the floor. 'Crikey, we didn't expect that. My head's ringing, can hardly hear a thing.'

'Well, what are your findings?'

'Hang on. Got to take some readings first.'

'Come on into the study.' There was excitement, agitation in the old clergyman's movements as he led the way. 'Here, use this table.'

He watched as the men busied themselves, lifting one of the recording devices on to the table, and setting the spools moving in reverse. A gentle humming sound, or was it the vibrations inside their heads? A dial clicked, figures revolved, slowed, stopped. The man called George peered closely at the reading.

'Jesus Christ!'

'What is it?' Rawsthorne snapped. 'What's it show?'

'Impossible.' George turned to the others, a look of amazement on his face. 'I wouldn't believe it. I'd say the machine had had a brainstorm if I didn't know it better. *The decibels are well below those of an ordinary peal of church bells!*'

'Never!'

'Look for yourselves if you don't believe me.'

The others stared in disbelief at the figures on the dial. It was as George had said.

'How . . . how do you account for that?' Rawsthorne asked weakly.

'I can't.' George spread his hands. 'But the facts are there for all to see. If you want a second testing you can ask for one, but I'm damned if I'm going anywhere near that bell again. The noise, quite obviously, isn't as loud as it seems. Something to do with the *tone*, I'd say, the way the bell is made. It reacts on the ear, makes you think it's louder than it is. Something like a silent dog-whistle. It isn't the sound, it's how you hear it. Frequency.'

'But ... but ...' the vicar stammered, 'if that's the case ... how do we go about getting the noise stopped?'

'You can't, mate.' George began packing the equipment back into the cases. 'Nothing you can do about it. *This* is the proof, this dial. As I say, you can ask for a second reading, but you'd be wasting your time. The reading wouldn't be any different. That guy, whoever he is, can ring his ruddy bell all day long if he wants to, and there isn't a thing you can do to stop him!'

After the Noise Abatement Society officials had left, Rawsthorne sat slumped in the chair in his study, his head in his hands. Tomorrow he would have the task of telling his parish councillors, the people. He knew how prime ministers felt when they had the odious duty of conveying bad tidings to the nation. You were the target man. They blamed you because you had not told them what they wanted to hear.

He shuddered. There was nothing more they could do. He feared for the safety of the villagers. They faced madness and death at the hands of Martyn Hamilton and his sinister, inexplicable bell.

Vicki Mason had been headmistress of Turbury School for three years. It was a post she had relished, dreamed about during her years at training college. The ideal situation. Tall and dark-haired, her large glasses gave her an added attraction, sex appeal blending perfectly with studiousness. She had had her admirers over the years. Plenty of them. One affair led to another. The idea of marriage did not appeal to her. At twenty-nine she had a lot more living and loving to do before she settled down. If she ever did. She was only too well aware of her own shortcomings. Six months was a lengthy relationship with a man for her. New horizons always beckoned. Even when her lover was the suave, good-looking, wealthy Hedley Chesterton, estate agent and a lot of other things besides – things he didn't talk about, preferring to leave that to the gossips. So long as his bank account showed a healthy increase from month to month it didn't matter what folks said about him. His wife wouldn't leave him. She knew when she was well off; a home port which he returned to every so often when his romantic buccaneering took him into rough seas.

He lay on the bed looking appreciatively at the tall naked girl beside him. Vicki Mason had her attractions. She was the kind of girl he could have married. The sort who was worth all the trouble of getting a divorce for. Only she wasn't the marrying kind. Too much like himself. A rover. Determined. Knew what she wanted and generally got it.

Things hadn't been going right between them lately. Nothing that you could really put your finger on. It was a question of attitudes really. Well, her attitude. That lessening in response, barely noticeable except to an expert lover. And Hedley reckoned he was all of that.

But tonight had been a catastrophe. For once he couldn't blame his partner. Both of them had been in the mood; a mutual seduction, coitus timed to perfection. Two well-oiled machines had worked in perfect unison, a steel piston plunging into a soft rubber valve, the level of passion rising steadily. Then, without warning, the bell had rung. Two or three minutes of brain-searing chimes had ruined everything.

Now they lay side by side, each trying to recapture the desire. But it had gone. Their bodies ached from the strain, restless almost to the point where they would have welcomed the opportunity to dress and go downstairs for some coffee. Somebody had to make the suggestion, though, and neither was willing to capitulate. So they just lay there.

'Something went wrong.' Hedley Chesterton closed his eyes to shut out his embarrassment. He knew that she was gazing at his limpness. That was fine after he'd made it, but her stare was almost an insult after the way things had

84

turned out. 'It was that bell that did it. Kind of knocks the stuffing out of you.'

'It won't be ringing for much longer.' She transferred her gaze to the ceiling. 'Not after tonight when the Noise Abatement Society work out a few figures. Hamilton will have his chimes cut off.'

'That's a bit drastic.'

'Siding with your friend again? I wonder you don't take a self-contained flat up at the Hall. You'd be away from that nagging wife of yours who doesn't understand you, and you'd be able to screw that Chinese wench. Or is Hamilton already doing that?'

'Who said he was a friend of mine?' Chesterton snapped.

'Most people say so. You can't deny that you conducted the sale of the Hall. Or that you've been up there to dinner. You're about the only outsider who's been welcomed there.'

'It was a business deal, that's all.'

'I've no doubt.' Her lips curled. 'A classic case of gazzumping.'

'That's slander.'

'Going to sue your mistress now, eh?' She laughed harshly. 'Come off it, Hedley. You took a backhander there. I know it and you know it.'

'Look,' he spoke sharply, 'my business affairs are my own business. This whole village is witch-hunting. A lot of malicious rumours have started because one perfectly ordinary guy, who made his pile abroad and decided to retire to England, bought a country mansion and doesn't want to get involved in village life. Just because he chose to rig up a unique bell everybody's got the idea that something sinister is going on. I've been up there. I know him. He's okay. Hell, it's mass hysteria, nothing else. And if it goes on this place is going to become a second Salem Town.'

'Maybe it already is.' She sat up and reached for her clothes. 'Sorry, Hedley, but my head's thumping like hell,

85

and that isn't the conventional housewife's excuse to get out of screwing. I need an early night.'

'All right.' He swung his legs to the floor. 'I guess I'll just wander home and see how wifey is.'

'Better luck with her.'

'No chance. She went off sex years ago. Just not the sexy type.'

She lay there after she heard his car pull away from the school house. She felt a depression coming on. They always hit her when an affair was nearing its end. As far as this one was concerned she knew it was over. It had just ended. The bell had gone for the end of the last round. Possibly she could have gone on longer, but there was no point. She wouldn't see any of Hedley Chesterton's money, anyway, and when he had tired of her he would ditch her. Far better to throw him overboard first. At least it gave her some satisfaction. She had gone off him rapidly. All that talk about his relationship with the Hamiltons. It stank. And if word got around the village that Hedley was her lover she'd surely get the sack. A Church of England school didn't expect its headmistress to engage in adultery. And when the other party happened to be on the side of the common enemy, that made it worse.

It was over between them. Finished. Hedley would ring her tomorrow. She'd spell it out for him then. She wondered how he'd take it, if he'd ever been jilted before. God, her head hurt. She could still hear that bell. Sleep wasn't going to be easy.

Rawsthorne stared at the blurred sea of faces, heard the angry mutterings, some curses from the back of the hall. He stood there, supporting himself against the flimsy table on the stage, feeling totally helpless.

'What are we going to do now, vicar?'

'How are we going to stop the bell?'

He had no answer to the many questions. No one had. Perhaps there was none. The initial anger was bubbling to a peak. It worried him. Mass hysteria. There were some

86

of the villagers who might rashly take the law into their own hands and regret it later.

'I beg you to be patient.' He struggled to make himself heard above the noise.

'We've been patient long enough. If nobody else is going to sort this out, we will!'

His worst fears were confirmed. Some of the hotheads would be going to try something themselves. There would be trouble. The law would be brought in. And the bell would continue to sound. Those visions came back to him, the mob, a Middle Ages gathering, flaming torches, shouting abuse. Some of them were leaving already. Nothing he could say would stop them.

The village hall emptied. Rawsthorne sank down at the table. Only a handful of people remained. Vicki Mason was chatting to that newcomer, the chap who was staying with Fred Reubens. He couldn't remember the young man's name. The trouble with Miss Mason was that she was always getting involved with men. Possibly she thought it hadn't come to his ears. It was just that he lacked the moral fibre to speak to her about it. People were talking. It was getting the school and the village a bad name. If only she would settle down with some nice young man, it would solve a lot of problems. This might be it, though. Rawsthorne didn't know if the big fellow was married. He hoped that he wasn't. He'd make a few discreet enquiries. In the meantime, there were more pressing matters.

The double doors swung open and a man in dark uniform, wearing a flat peaked cap, walked quickly inside. PC John Lewis. The vicar experienced a sudden sense of foreboding. The expression on the other man's face was tight-lipped, worried.

'Vicar.'

'Yes? What's the trouble, officer?'

'Dr Jones has reported his daughter missing. She was seen at the disco at the Buffalo but left early. She hasn't arrived home.'

'Oh, dear. Perhaps she's visiting some friends.'

'I've checked. Also Donald Hughes hasn't been seen since yesterday evening.'

'I don't think she's the type to . . .'

'She isn't. But you know how that youth's been acting lately. Frankly, I'm worried. I want to organise a search for the girl. Both of them, in fact. Maybe a few of the villagers . . .'

'They're in an ugly mood. Some of them, anyway. I'm . . . I'm afraid a bunch of them are bound for Caelogy Hall!'

'Oh, Christ!'

'I don't know what to suggest, constable. I really don't.'

John Lewis stroked his chin thoughtfully. Too much was happening all at once. He couldn't be in two places at the same time. The Jones girl might well have gone off into the fields with a lad. There was nothing wrong in that. It didn't necessarily have to tie up with the village simpleton. But if he didn't go and look for her Dr Jones would be telephoning the chief constable. And if the mob stormed the Hall, Hamilton would certainly be demanding help. First things first, he decided. He'd had no official summons to Caelogy Hall, and if he was elsewhere on legitimate business, then that couldn't be helped. It might be a good thing.

'I'm going to look for the girl.' He turned briskly away. 'If the police are needed for anything else, then Sergeant Price at Bryncalid will have to be called out.'

Lewis went outside. The night was dark and silent. He was uneasy. Far rather would he have heard shouts of derision and anger borne on the soft breeze. It was as though all was well, just an ordinary remote village, contented, no problems. He knew otherwise. This was the lull before the storm of hate and violence broke.

A dozen men spanned the narrow road, walking briskly. None spoke. Each was busy with his own thoughts, his own level of anger simmering silently inside him. Once past the vicarage, they converged into a tightly-packed group, instinctively seeking safety, looking furtively at one another. Electric torches showed them the way, picking out the straggling hedges on either side, the gaunt elm which had died two years ago and nobody had bothered to fell. This was the trouble with Turbury. Nobody bothered . . . until it was too late.

Fear drove them on. Their courage stemmed from their numbers. As they approached Caelogy Hall some of them began to converse in low tones.

'What're we goin' to do?'

'Dunno, really. See this Hamilton guy, I suppose. Tell 'im to stop ringin' 'is bell.'

Their footsteps slowed. Uncertainty, their own weakness prevailed. The tall red-bearded man in the lead turned and looked back at them, flashing his torch over them, seeing their fearful expressions and sneering openly his contempt for them.

'Anybody who wants to chicken out better do it right now,' he grunted.

'Are you sure we're doin' the right thing, Tom?' somebody asked.

'You got any better ideas, Fred Willis?' Tom Blakely had worked on the council roads all his life. He savoured his lowly status now, addressing the Turbury foreman, seeing him wince visibly.

'No, but . . . well, this ain't really legal is it?'

'To hell with that. Neither is this bell, but nobody's willing to do anything about it. If the law won't act, then we will. It's either that or sitting around like scared rabbits until we're driven into the asylum.'

They moved forward again, their minds made up as one. There was safety in numbers, someone to protect you. Martyn Hamilton was just one man. He wouldn't be able to stand up to them.

They saw the gates, the padlock and chain glinting in the light from the torches.

'The gates are locked. We won't be able to . . .'

Tom Blakely laughed loudly and drew a small pair of

bolt-cutters from the pocket of his raincoat. 'You didn't think I hadn't thought of that, did you?'

They watched as the big man stepped forward, heard the metallic snap, the chain buckling and falling to the ground – a snake that had suddenly had its life snuffed out, no longer a danger to its enemies.

Blakely was already pushing the gates open. His followers hung back, bunching together. Beyond was total blackness. Desolation. Not a single light showed from the huge grey stone building with mullioned windows. Caelogy Hall was as it had been for decades. Deserted.

'There doesn't appear to be anyone at home.' Fred Willis would eagerly have turned back, grasping at a convenient sop to satisfy his conscience. They could return and face their womenfolk, the other villagers, tell them they had tried their best but Hamilton was not there, so they couldn't do any more.

'Too bad,' Blakely laughed. 'Makes our task easier. We'll take the fucking bell. Put an end to it once and for all!'

The others gasped. They hadn't bargained on going to such extremes. Just a talk with Hamilton, to put their own point of view as forcibly as possible.

'That's stealing.'

'What's that when weighed against *murder*? That's what these folks are. *Murderers!* They killed Jane Reubens and Tom Williamson, didn't they? Come on, what are we waiting for?'

Anger overcame fear and they surged forward, following the big man. A few yards further on they pulled up sharply as Tom Blakely's torch picked out a shape on the edge of the bushes which lined the drive – a crouching animal, its eyes glinting green, its jaws wide and slavering, a low growl rumbling in its throat.

'It's the dog. The alsatian! Christ, you forgot all about him, Tom. Now what the fuck are we going to do?'

The alsatian made no move to attack, lurking there in

90

the shadows, growling, its hackles rising until they stood up vertically. The men began backing away.

Suddenly from the darkness beyond the big house the bell began to ring, peals of metallic thunder rolling deafeningly like some angry psychic force. Somebody screamed. A torch was dropped, its glass shattering, the beam extinguished immediately. The alsatian was forgotten. Flight was uppermost in their minds, but cohesion between brain and body was severed. They stood there, unable to move, lips forming soundless screams and curses.

The bell was ringing fast. Faster than it had ever done before. Viciously, as though its anger had been aroused and it sought vengeance. Preventing the flight of its enemies, holding them, battering their brains with an invisible cudgel.

Five minutes. Ten. It could have been an hour. Then it ceased, the echoes dying away gradually over the mountains beyond.

Twelve men shuffled back through the gates. Their torches gone, they groped blindly in the darkness holding on to each other, all sense of direction gone. They wandered aimlessly in the roadway, some going to the right, others to the left, mumbling incoherently.

The alsatian did not move from the bushes until the last of them had passed through the gates. It cringed and whined, scratching at its ears with its paws as though trying to remove some unwelcome guest. It sensed rather than heard its master's approach.

'Good dog, Sheba.' Hamilton's voice came out of the darkness.

The alsatian came to him, rubbing herself against his legs. He shone a torch briefly, picking out the items which had been dropped by the men from the village. He gave a grunt of satisfaction and shone the beam round in a circle to make sure that there was nothing else left. He gathered up the torches and the padlock, his eyes glinting angrily as he saw where the bolt-cutters had severed the chain.

'For once, Sheba' – he looked down at the dog – 'we

shall comply with the request of that turnip-headed policeman and leave the gates unfettered. I have every faith in
your capability to repel nocturnal intruders.'

The alsatian whined, sensing praise in her master's tone,
and slunk away into the darkness. She knew just what was
expected of her. Only the bell had saved those who had
dared to trespass within her domain.

Sergeant Price drove the pale blue police Allegro hard all
the way from Bryncalid. The distance of five miles was
completed in just under seven minutes, something of a
record when one considered the narrow winding roads.

Then, just as he reached the outskirts of Turbury, his
headlights picked out the group of men clustered in the
road. Drunks. He cursed, braked hard and came to a
standstill with a squealing of tyres. He sighed, and opened
the door. John Lewis had radioed that there was a riot of
some kind. More likely it was a drunken spree. This lot
could barely stand. Even as he walked towards them one
keeled over and sprawled on his face in the road.

'Now then,' Price snapped, 'what's going on, eh?'

The others stared at him. Wide blank eyes, mouths
open. No reaction at all.

'Oi!' The policeman was angry at having been fetched
from his own sleepy little beat to deal with a situation like
this. There were too many of them to arrest and not
enough cells to hold them. The town force, twenty miles
away, wouldn't appreciate being called out to cart them
away. 'Get out of the road before somebody runs you
over.'

'Uh.' Tom Blakely was slobbering spittle into his red
beard. 'Uh.'

Just meaningless grunts. Like some animated cartoon
monsters, they stared ahead of them, some not even aware
of the policeman's presence. He was reaching out for the
nearest, intending to shake him into realisation, when Bill
Price noticed something that froze him into immobility.
He stepped back a pace. Blood was seeping out of the

man's ears – a slow, steady trickle. He shone his torch on the next. On a third. On all of them. Oh, Jesus Christ, they were all bleeding from the ears!

He backed away. They weren't just drunk. Something had happened to them, some serious misadventure. He reached inside his car and picked up his pocket radio, which lay on the seat. Watching the grotesque scene around him, he struggled to find the right wavelength.

'Foxfire Seven to Abel Eight.' He licked his lips. His throat was dry, he found difficulty in speaking. 'Assistance needed at Turbury village. Some . . . oh, my God!'

Price saw the bearded man lose his balance and pitch forward. No protecting arms were thrown up. A kind of dead faint, the heavy body striking the front of the police car. There was a sickening thud as the skull hit the front bumper, a loud crack as it split open. Blood gushed out, obscuring the upturned face.

None of the others seemed aware of the fate of their comrade. They shambled to and fro, bumping into each other, mouthing and grunting. It was like a weird puppet ballet where the strings had become entwined.

The bizarre scene was illuminated by the headlights. The sergeant stared, his radio forgotten. He saw them sink down into a heap, limbs moving faintly, faces smeared with blood.

'Foxfire Seven . . . Foxfire Seven. Can you hear me?' He spoke into his radio, his voice unrecognisable, unable to tear his eyes from what was happening in front of the car.

'Foxfire Seven . . . Some men, about a dozen of them. I . . . *I think they've all had . . . had a stroke!*'

8

THE DEAD AND THE DYING

'How long before you return south?' Vicki Mason tried to make the question appear casual but there was a note of urgency in her tone which she could not disguise. It was stupid, illogical. A man she had never spoken to before the meeting tonight, and now he was drinking coffee with her in her living-room and she was worrying how long it might be before he disappeared from her life. Crazy.

'It all depends.' He regarded her steadily.

'On what?'

'A lot of things. This bell mostly. It killed my mother and I want to get to the bottom of it.'

'Killed her! That's going a bit far. It knocks you about, gives you a thumping headache, but . . .'

'It brought on a cerebral attack. I don't understand it any more than you or the other people of Turbury do, but there's a reason for the bell being rung and I want to find out what it is.'

'I'm worried about it, too.' She lit a cigarette. 'It upsets the children. It could have serious consequences if it continues.'

'Which it looks like doing.'

'Regrettably, yes. There's going to be a lot of trouble in the village. It's a pity. It wasn't like this when I came here.' She talked on, scarcely aware of what she was

94

saying. Idle chatter, her thoughts centred on the man who was seated by her side. It was like fencing, looking for an opening, trying to say something which just couldn't be put into words.

Then they heard the Caelogy bell. They tensed, thoughts disrupted. There was no way of concentrating or shutting it out. It was compulsory to listen. Tonight it was faster, more mind-jarring than ever before. Vicki closed her eyes and leaned back on the sofa. She felt Julian's arm come around her, holding her, and thought she heard him say, 'Maybe it'll stop in a moment.' She couldn't be sure.

Finally it ceased, but for a long time they could hear it echoing inside their brains, a dull throbbing of the nerves that speeded up the pulses and heartbeat like a powerful drug.

'Phew!' Julian Dane was sweating. 'That was some noise. Are you all right, Vicki?'

She thrilled at his use of her first name. She smiled feebly.

'I think so. I feel as if I'd been through a combine harvester, but I guess I'm okay. My ears are singing. By the way, thanks.'

'For what?'

'For' – she hesitated, his arm was still around her – 'for holding me close. I needed that, and not just because the bell was ringing.'

He raised his eyebrows. She smiled up at him, and moved an inch or two nearer to him. A few minutes ago she had been fighting to dispel the depression that Hedley Chesterton had brought on last night, desperately clinging to this man, a stranger. Inexplicably, her feelings were reversed. Euphoria, almost. Certainly a boosting of her confidence. Words were gathering in her brain like a flock of migrating starlings all wanting to take off at once.

'I had a lover,' she said. 'Up until last night, anyway. It's all over now. He phoned me today and I told him I didn't want to see him again. I don't. But it still hurt.'

'I see.' Julian didn't, but this sudden confession intrigued him. Either she was a liar with some ulterior scheme in mind or else she was remarkably honest, telling him things she didn't have to.

'I'm a hypocrite.' She stared up at the ceiling as though unable to meet his gaze. 'I'm headmistress of a Church of England school. In effect I should not believe in sex before marriage, adultery or virtually everything that makes me tick. I lost my virginity when I was sixteen, I've had numerous affairs with married men and I've got no intention of settling down. Apart from that, I suppose I fill the requirements for the post. Oh, and I don't believe that Christ was the Son of God. I think he was just a prophet. I'm sceptical about the Resurrection, and I don't believe in life after death. See, I'm a fraud.'

'I'm much the same myself,' he grinned. 'Only I don't have to keep up a pretext. And I never could settle to one girl.'

They laughed. Next second they were kissing for the first time. It seemed natural, the right place and the right time to do it.

'I was telling you about my lover. My *ex*-lover,' she said.

'You don't have to.'

'I want to. He's an estate agent. He negotiated the Caelogy Hall deal for Hamilton. There are rumours of a cash hand-out. The point is, he's been up there since they moved in. I think he knows more than he lets on.'

'Maybe, but we're unlikely to get anything out ⸱ .im. There must be other ways.' He fell silent, his thoughts suddenly switching to Karamaneh. It was the Chinese girl he ought to be with right now. Maybe tomorrow he'd try to contact her. He almost told Vicki about her, but checked himself in time. Women were funny. He couldn't take chances.

'I don't like the sound of that Jones girl going missing.' She furrowed her forehead. 'Now that *is* odd. Her old man's a real Victorian. Won't trust her out with a boy on her own. Has to be home sharp on ten every night. She isn't the kind to go missing unless there's something seriously wrong. And those hotheads who've gone up to the Hall; they're really asking for trouble. This village is like a keg of powder with the fuse lit. Soon there's going to be one helluva blow.'

She closed her eyes. In her mind she could still hear the bell. It was taking over her mind, her body, her actions. It was as though she were a spectator from afar, looking down on herself, seeing her hand sliding along the thigh of the man who held her, slyly creeping inwards. She tried to check herself. It was impossible. Oh, God, you didn't do those sort of things to a man you'd only known a few hours. Her fingers traced the outline of the hardness inside his trousers and began to rub it gently.

Sergeant Price waited inside the car, with the door closed. The engine was still running and the headlights showed up the awful scene on the road in front of him; the bodies sprawled in an untidy pile, occasionally an arm or a leg moving, lips baring, silent screams. Blood everywhere. It flowed in steady streams from every ear. They were bleeding to death, but the policeman couldn't do a thing about it. There was nothing to do but wait until reinforcements arrived; that could take anything up to half-an-hour, and until then he was forced to remain alone with a dozen ghouls who might have come from hell itself. The groans, the grunts, the feeble struggles. Oh, Jesus God!

He prayed that somebody would come. Not just the police. It was too early yet. Another motorist, a pedestrian. Anybody! Anybody to help him hang on to his sanity.

The heap of bodies was stirring. Some were trying to get up. Others were clutching at them as though trying to drag them back. Bloodied hate-filled faces, mindless staring eyes, fingernails raking and clawing. More blood.

Price felt his sanity going, tottering on the edge of a black abyss. He tried to hold on to it, tried to find a reason for all this. There was none. Unless . . . of course, it had to be! *He was dead!* His body was lying at the bottom of a black pit. Hades. These were his companions, writhing helplessly, sightlessly, condemned to everlasting damnation. Just as he was!

He struggled with the door of the car and it burst open. He rolled into the road, screamed as his head hit the hard surface. Blood. He could feel its sticky warmth, its cloying smell in his nostrils. Grovelling, scratching, fighting desperately to claw his way out of this black grave with his fingernails.

Grunts. All around him. He lay there gibbering, watching them coming for him, mis-shapen forms that reached out for him, grinning, lusting, spittle and blood frothing on their lips. *No! I'm not dead. Let me alone!*

Bloody lips moved, mutely threatening, eyes bulging. *But we are. We're dead. Join us in purgatory!*

The sergeant was screaming, grabbing at the open car door, trying to haul himself inside to safety. His efforts failed him. There were too many of them, dragging him back, hands tearing at his uniform, steel-like fingers encircling his throat, choking him. Ghoulish silhouettes, burying him beneath a mountain of living death. His crazed mind pleaded for oblivion. Unconsciousness. Death! All to no avail.

They jostled and fought each other, ripping the thick material of his uniform as though it were flimsy nylon, baring his body, pawing at it, digging deep with their fingernails. Lusting. God, they'd go down for this. Ten years apiece. Found guilty of gross indecency. He felt hands closing over his genitals, squeezing, crushing. His body jerked, writhed. He was screaming in agony, but no sound came, only a gurgle that was stifled by the throttling fingers on his neck.

A terrible thought in the midst of his pain. *If you're dead then they can't kill you!* There can be no blessed relief. This was hell, he was condemned to everlasting torture, not by fire but by inhuman creatures. Maybe he would become one of them, and do this to the next newcomer to this underworld of eternal anguish.

Then everything was slipping away from him. The pain eased to a dull ache. He was floating, drifting in total blackness. He had escaped somehow. He did not even hear the approaching vehicles. Two panda cars came to a halt ten yards behind the Allegro, headlights blazing, blue lights flashing. Four hardened police officers stared in utter disbelief at the scene in the road.

'Fucking hell!' The first constable got out and stood looking at the heap of bodies. 'Price said . . . a stroke. It looks like bloody mass murder. Where's Pricey, anyway . . . *Oh, God!*' He jerked his head away.

There was no mistaking the elderly sergeant who lay on the roadway, bloody hands still clawing at him, throttling him, moving like a mass of eels.

'They've . . . they've ripped his . . .' Another policeman couldn't stop himself from vomiting.

Ashen-faced the officers stared, transfixed. All of them were used to violence, to horrific road accidents. But never had they seen anything which compared with this. If all of the men had been dead it would not have been so terrible. Or if they had simply been badly injured. Neither was the case. They resembled zombies, grunting and groaning as though they had scratched their way to freedom from their graves.

'What are we going to do?' a young sergeant asked. Usually capable and efficient, quick to make a decision, the officer was suddenly willing to step down, to obey the orders of one from a lower rank. But nobody was coming forward. They looked at one another, their eyes reflecting their terror.

'What . . . what happened?' one of the constables asked weakly. Somebody had to say something. 'Maybe it was a road accident . . . they got run over.'

'No. Murder! Christ, most of 'em are half dead. Looks like they set on each other like a pack of wolves. Pricey tried to part 'em, and got . . . killed! What made him say they'd had a stroke, though?'

Nobody could answer that.

'We'll need the meat wagon.' The sergeant pulled himself together with an effort. 'An ambulance, too. Just in case there's any left alive by the time they get here. Bob, put some warning cones out, before some mad bastard comes speeding along this road. That would just make our night! Pete, Wilf, see what you can do to sort 'em out whilst I radio.'

The two constables grimaced. They didn't relish going anywhere near that heap of pulsing flesh, separating the corpses from the near-corpses. They glanced at each other, seeking to boost each other's morale, trying not to heave.

The two men worked in the lights from Sergeant Price's car, grabbing limbs, trying to relate them to a specific body. Some were lifeless, others twitched and clutched at them. Moans floated on the night air from souls in torment. Lips were drawn back in hideous grins.

'Four still alive.' The other nine corpses were laid out in a row on the grass verge.

'I wouldn't say they were *alive*.' The sergeant had taken his time radioing, giving a detailed report, delaying his return to the carnage until the two young rookies had sorted it all out. 'Just the nerves twitching. Nothing to worry about.'

By the time the ambulance and the mortuary van arrived there was no sign of movement in any of the bodies.

Reluctantly, Julian Dane extricated himself from the embrace of Vicki Mason. She sat up with him, rubbing her naked breasts against his bare chest, her pouted lips demanding a kiss. He obliged, closing his eyes. It was like a dream. He couldn't keep up with it. The horror of the bell, and now this. He had known this woman just a few hours. They had made love. More than that, they were involved. It was not merely an opportunist sexual encounter.

'You don't have to go, do you?' she murmured.

'Fred will be worrying himself stiff.' He felt schoolboyish, telling his girlfriend that he had to be in by a certain time. 'What I mean is, in normal circumstances it wouldn't matter, but with all that's happening in the village at present . . .'

'There's a phone in the hall.' She smiled coyly. 'Give him a ring. Then stop the night with me. *Please!*'

'All right,' he nodded. His body ached. Not just from sex. It was as though the bell had ingrained itself into his system like a kind of rheumatism, eating into his bones. It had affected Vicki, too. He could tell, even though they were comparative strangers. He felt sure that it was responsible for the seduction. Maybe she just needed an outlet, something to shake the bell out of her. Or Hedley Chesterton. Maybe both.

'Hurry up.' She regarded him from beneath half-closed eyes. 'Then we can go to bed.'

Julian had hardly reached the door when he heard a car drawing up in the short drive which led to the school house. His uneasiness mounted as the engine died away, a door opened and slammed shut. Footsteps crunched on the gravel. The heavy knocker echoed through the hall impatiently.

'Who the hell's this?' He glanced at Vicki but she was hurriedly pulling on her sweater and jeans.

'Stop in here.' There was concern on her face. 'I'll see to it.'

She brushed past him, closing the door behind her, and he listened to her bare feet padding down the uncarpeted hall. There was something wrong, he could tell. His body tensed, and he looked at his clothes strewn on the floor. Naked, he felt at a disadvantage. Helpless. Like knocking a bird off and then having her husband suddenly arrive home in the middle of the night. You stood there, guilty, embarrassed. His eyes reflected his innermost thoughts,

101

and you thought Oh, Jesus, if only I'd been dressed it wouldn't be half so bad. He's looking at my prick and laughing to himself.

But it wasn't like that. Vicki was single. No man had a hold over her. Except perhaps . . .

'*Hedley!*' He heard her shout the name angrily, and flinched. But the guy had no right here. He wasn't her husband. All the same, Julian concluded, it would be better to get dressed. He looked around for his underpants. They seemed to have gone missing.

'You don't think you can get rid of me as easily as that, do you, you bitch?' The male voice in the hall was rasping, angry. Dane began to hunt for his pants feverishly. There was going to be trouble. Outside in the hall voices were raised in anger.

'You don't own me, Hedley,' Vicki yelled. 'I told you over the phone, we're finished. For good. Now get out and leave me alone.'

'I'm coming inside. I want to talk to you, not hold a shouting match on the doorstep so that half this interfering village can hear.'

'You've been drinking!'

'I haven't touched a drop all night, not that it's any business of yours.'

There were sounds of a scuffle, and then the front door slammed shut. Julian knew that the estate agent was inside the house. And Hedley Chesterton wouldn't be persuaded to leave in a hurry.

'Don't you dare go in there!' Vicki was screaming, and Julian tensed, standing there stark naked, his search for his underwear having failed. He thought about pulling his trousers on without them, but there wasn't time. The door was already opening.

Hedley Chesterton walked into the room, Vicki Mason close behind him, an anguished expression on her face. He paused, his hands thrust deep into the pockets of his raincoat, eyes narrowing when he saw Julian, lips curling into a sneer.

'So there *was* another man, after all,' he jibed, his face flushed with anger. 'I thought as much. A big guy with a little prick.'

Julian knew that he was blushing. He couldn't help it. Fully clothed he would have met the challenge with his usual nonchalance. Hell, it wasn't fair, particularly as this guy wasn't even married to Vicki. A law unto himself, money buying everything, including his women. Hedley Chesterton ended affairs when he wanted to. And not before.

'I think you'd better get the hell out of here.' Julian put his hands on his hips in an attempt to appear casual. It didn't work. It didn't feel right in the nude.

'I'm staying.' The estate agent stepped forward a pace. He was two or three inches shorter than Julian, his slight paunch hidden under his clothing. 'Get dressed, laddie. Miss Mason and I have a lot of things to talk over.'

Their eyes met. It was then that Julian noticed the glint, a kind of slyness like a wild animal that creeps upon an unwary victim, anticipating the kill with relish. It went further than that. Anger that had soared beyond its safety limit. *Madness!*

Julian could hear his heart pounding. He wasn't breathing easily. He knew that he was going to be attacked. No outward sign. Only the eyes . . .

His clenched fist had buried itself in Chesterton's solar plexus almost before Julian realised what he had done. An instinctive act of self-preservation, a heritage from his ancestors who wore animal clothing and lived in caves. Possibly his nakedness had sharpened his reflexes, made him aware of danger. The other gave a cry and doubled up, hands trapped in his pockets. He was falling anyway, but the neurologist gave him a push just to make sure.

Hedley Chesterton sprawled forward on the carpet, writhing in agony. Vicki Mason shrank back, giving a little cry of horror. Julian stood there, towering over the man who had threatened him, and suddenly his nudity was no longer a disadvantage. He was primitive man in

103

a scene that might have taken place thousands of years ago, quarrelling over a woman. The winner takes all.

'You stupid bugger!' Chesterton raised his head, grimacing with pain, almost vomiting. 'I'll have you for that. Grievous . . . bodily harm. Just you . . . wait.'

'Get out!' Julian pointed to the door.

Chesterton made as if to get up, then clutched at his head. He was white and shaking, eyes closing momentarily, almost as though he was going to faint.

'My head,' he groaned. 'Oh, God, my bloody head is splitting!'

Julian glanced at Vicki. The same thought occurred to both of them. The estate agent had been hit in the solar plexus. Even when he had fallen to the floor his head had not been struck. Now his eyes were glazed. He did not seem able to focus.

'What's the matter with your head?' Julian asked softly, curiosity replacing his sudden burst of anger.

'I . . . I can hear it ringing. Oh, God, I can't get it out of my head!'

'*The bell?*'

Silence. He appeared not to have heard, to be unaware that there were others in the room. His quarrel with Julian was forgotten as he pressed the palms of his hands hard against his ears. He dropped back on to all fours, staring down at the carpet. His breath came in rasps and he shook in every limb.

'The bell,' Julian repeated. 'It's the bell, isn't it? It's ringing. Why?'

'They're ringing it for . . . for . . .' Hedley Chesterton shook his head, a determined effort to jerk himself back into reality, to overcome his pain and terror, as though he realised that it was all in his mind.

'*Why do they ring the bell?*' Julian repeated, leaning forward, fists clenched, almost afraid of the answer.

Suddenly Chesterton looked up, and his expression was that of a man who had awoken from a feverish nightmare. He shook himself and slowly, unsteadily, rose to his feet.

'How should I know why they ring the bloody bell?' His reply was defiant, sending Julian's hopes crashing. So near the truth, and now as far away as ever. The madness had gone from the man's eyes. He rubbed his stomach tenderly.

'Damn you!' he looked Julian in the eye. 'You didn't have to do that.'

'You were going to hit me. I saw it in your eyes. It was the bell that did it, wasn't it? You already had the thought of revenge in your mind and the bell stoked it up to boiling point. Now, why don't you tell us about it?'

'You're mad,' Chesterton snapped, and turned towards the door. 'And you're welcome to her. I hope I don't ever set eyes on either of you again.'

The two of them stood and listened to the estate agent's departure, the slamming of the door, the car's engine revving, gears crashing, pulling away, speeding.

'Well, that's that.' Julian spotted his elusive briefs and stooped to retrieve them from beneath a chair.

'I've never known him act like that before.' She sat down, trembling. 'He's always arrogant, pompous, but I've never detected a streak of violence in him.'

'It was the bell. It affects us all in different ways. Even you, Vicki.'

'Me?' Her eyebrows rose.

'You did things tonight you wouldn't have done otherwise. Well, not on a first meeting. Would you?'

'No.' She lowered her eyes, and smiled faintly. 'I hadn't any intention of seducing you when I asked you back for coffee. I'd done it before I realised it, and . . . and my sensations were electrified much more than they usually are. I don't regret it, though. I . . . I hope you don't, Julian.'

'I don't.' He leaned over and kissed her. 'But it's worrying. Frightening. You don't know what it's going to do to you. One occasion you just get a thumping head-ache, the next you're acting totally out of character. Those men who went off to storm the Hall. Hell, they've every right to be angry and frightened, but I'd bet a tenner that if it was an everyday nuisance complaint they'd sit down calmly and write to their MPs. It's turned them into animals. That doctor's daughter. Never been late home in her life before. She is now, and the bell's to blame. And they reckon this village idiot is harmless. He might be in normal circumstances but what's the bell done to him? A deaf-mute that can't hear finds that he can hear the bell. A new experience for him. How will he cope?'

'I'm frightened.' She tried to fight off the sobs which were beginning to shake her body. 'Not just for myself. For you, for everybody, the schoolkids. It can't go on like this, Julian. Oh, God, what's going to happen?'

'I don't know,' he said, 'I just don't know.'

'Don't leave me alone tonight, please.'

'All right.' He crossed towards the hall. 'I'll ring Fred. He'll probably be in bed, but . . .'

The wail of sirens grew louder and louder, like screaming banshees in the night, ambulances and police cars speeding by on some mission of life and death.

'What is it?' Vicki had crossed to the window and was peering out through a chink in the curtains. She was just in time to catch a glimpse of the flashing blue lights before they were lost to sight around a bend in the road.

'I don't know.' Julian was already dialling. 'More trouble, you can bet your life. And you can bet also that the bell is the cause of it. It's not letting up now, almost as though it's mounting a series of attacks, intent on destroying the whole village.'

He heard the phone ringing at the other end.

Brrr–brr–brrr.

'That's funny.'

'What's the matter?' She joined him in the hall, leaning against him.

'Fred's not answering.'

'Maybe he's gone to bed. Or gone out.'

106

'*Nothing* would drag Fred out at night. And he's a light sleeper. He'd hear the phone, all right.'

Julian let it ring for a couple of minutes and then replaced the receiver. His expression was grim.

'I'm afraid I'm going to have to leave you for a while,' he muttered. 'Lock the door after me, and don't open it to *anyone* until I get back. Something's wrong. I can sense it. I just pray to God that my stepfather isn't the latest victim of the bell!'

9

AVALANCHE

Donald Hughes had crouched below the overhanging bank of the wide fast-flowing stream for the last two hours. The icy water had numbed him from the knees downwards. He shivered, tried to change his position and almost fell.

He stared into the darkness. Black meaningless shapes that moved and then were still. Trees, probably. He didn't know for sure. The night held a thousand terrors and he wasn't going to move from here until daylight. Even then, he didn't know where he was going.

His memories of the last few hours were vague. They were also very frightening. It was like a dream, snatches coming back to him. The girl. He hadn't killed her. She had already been dead when he'd found her. Nobody would know what he'd done. He hardly knew himself. Maybe he hadn't actually done it. Like that picture he'd found torn from a magazine in the litter-bin by the post office. A naked girl. Posing. Her legs had been slightly apart, the mound of hair between screening her secrets from his prying eyes. Provocative. He'd kept it beneath the mattress in his room, and when he was all alone he'd pulled it out, smoothed the creases, and then done things to himself. *To himself.* He had never touched *her*. Never. It wouldn't have been right. Her eyes seemed alive, urging him on, but forbidding him contact even with the glossy paper.

That's how it had been with the girl on the edge of the

wood. All covered in blood. He hadn't touched her. He hadn't . . . hadn't . . . *hadn't*!

He almost convinced himself. Then he broke down, sobbing, beating his fists against the squelchy grass of the bank. He knew that he had. He couldn't erase it from his mind. No more than he could shut out the sound of the bell.

It was ringing now, inside his head, jarring his skull, the bone vibrating. The blackness around him seemed denser, closing in on him, invisible hands reaching out for him, alive with things he did not understand.

He clung to the bank, gibbering, crying. This was his punishment for what he had done. The powers of darkness were exacting their own revenge.

Now he could distinguish shapes. People. They seemed to glide rather than walk, grouping together on the opposite side of the stream. They were looking at him, their faces hidden beneath their cowls, pointing, accusing. He twisted round to face them. They commanded his attention.

He knew, even as he watched, that he was on trial. They knew what had happened, what he'd done. They had sought him out, found him, and now they were going to pronounce judgement.

The cowls were thrown back, exposing shaven heads. The features were indistinguishable, in shadow. Just silhouettes. But something was wrong. Even Donald sensed that. Something was missing. *Suddenly, he knew. Oh, God, they had no ears!*

He tried to drag his eyes away from them but it was impossible. He was being forced to look upon their grotesqueness. And the bell was tolling. Louder . . . and louder . . . and *louder*!

His senses were slipping away from him, his hold on the bank lessening. Pointing fingers. They beckoned, calling him across the stretch of dark water. Summoning him to their bizarre court of justice.

Somehow he kept his balance. The water was above his

thighs, intensely cold, threatening to swirl him away. The mud on the bottom sucked at his feet. Movement was slow, almost impossible.

He sensed their anger, their hostility. They would not let him drown. He was not to be spared so easily.

A step at a time. The current was stronger in the middle, above his waist. It was a battle even to remain upright, but he managed it.

Shallower now. A gravel bottom. Another couple of yards and he would be on the other side of this miniature River Styx. No helping hand was proffered. Their arms were folded as he pulled himself up the bank, crawling the last few feet, lying there. He dared not look up, terrified lest he gazed into the terrible countenances of beings that were older than mankind.

Time passed. There was no command. His face was pressed into the mud. The bell had stopped ringing, only its vibrations quivered inside his head. He shuddered. Human sacrifice was on offer. But the forces of evil had not accepted it. Yet.

Still nothing happened. He continued to lie there, eyes tightly closed. The malevolent force seemed less oppressive, the atmosphere was not nearly so cold as it had been earlier.

He raised his head slightly, peeping through half-closed eyelids, ready to jerk his head away, bury his face back in the protecting mud. That was his first realisation that it was no longer dark. Dawn had already broken. The sky in the east was pale, casting a grey twilight over the countryside. And Donald Hughes was alone!

He glanced around him. The stream eddied, carrying with it pieces of vegetation which had come adrift from overhanging trees and bushes. A water vole which had been squatting on a dead branch suddenly dived into the current and disappeared with scarcely a ripple. In the thorn bushes beyond a magpie was chattering incessantly, welcoming the new day. But there was no sign of the

110

sinister cowled monk-like spectres which had dominated the scene.

Donald struggled to his knees, unable to believe that he was still alive and unharmed. His clothing was saturated, plastered with mud. And he was hungry.

Decisions did not come easily to him. He knew that he could not return to the village. Therefore, he had to go elsewhere. But where? Now that the terrors of the night were over, new fears began to assail him. The law would be on his trail, hunting him like a wild animal. Any form of human habitation was unsafe. He glanced towards the western horizon. Jagged mountain peaks stretched as far as the eye could see, some of the slopes thickly planted with coniferous trees, a stronghold for foxes and other beasts of the wild. The landscape looked inviting, shelter from the elements, a place to hide. Food would be scarce. But it would not be impossible to survive. There were rabbits and other creatures of the wild that could be trapped. Donald had often made use of the age-old 'figure-four' trap, a flat slab of rock supported by a slender twig on its point of balance with a trip-wire attachment. Simple, but effective. The gypsies employed this method to catch their hedgehogs. He had lain in the thick undergrowth on several occasions and watched the nomads setting their traps, noting the best killing places. He had even tried it once and caught a leveret. He had sold the carcase to the butcher for twenty pence.

He wished that he had brought his snares with him. That would have been much easier, but it was too risky to go back for them. It would have to be figure-fours, or 'Doctor Deadfalls' as the romanies called them.

He set off westwards, walking quickly, keeping to the hedgerows and woods. The sun came up and he felt its rays warming his back, beginning to dry out his clothing. He chuckled softly to himself. Maybe life wasn't so bad after all.

Only one thing worried him. The nocturnal hours and the terrors they held. Lurking black-robed figures whose

111

ears had been amputated and who commanded him to grovel before him.

Fred Reubens was preparing to go to bed when there came a knock on the front door. He started. It wasn't Julian. His stepson had a key, and even if he had mislaid it he knew that the back door was unlocked.

Hesitantly, the builder went into the hall and opened the door a few inches. He recognised the uniformed figure of John Lewis standing there, a navy blue cape around his shoulders.

'Hallo, Mr Reubens.' The officer seemed ill at ease, unsure of himself. 'I thought maybe you'd gone to bed, but . . . well, I was wondering if I could ask you to help me . . . a bit of trouble . . .'

Trouble. There's always trouble in Turbury, Fred thought.

'Dr Jones' daughter has gone missing,' the constable went on. 'Nothing serious, I don't suppose. You know what young girls are.' He gave a nervous laugh. 'But I've got to go and look for her, and . . . and, well, there's some more trouble brewing. Some of the villagers have gone up to sort Hamilton out, and the reinforcements I've sent for will have to go and deal with that. It's open country all round the village, and . . . one man on his own doesn't stand much chance of finding anyone out there, if you see what I mean.'

Fred Reubens nodded. He understood only too well. It wasn't only a request for help. It was a plea for company out there in the darkness of the wild countryside by a man who did not want to be alone. A man who was more frightened than he had ever been in his life.

'All right,' Fred said. 'I'll give you a hand. Just step inside a moment while I find my wellingtons and overcoat. Any idea where we're going to search?'

'She was last seen at the disco in the Buffalo.' There was obvious relief in John Lewis' voice. 'I think our best bet would be to follow that bridle path from behind the pub which leads out to the woods. We can make a circle of the fields and come back behind the church. Of course, if we don't find her then the lads will organise a search in the morning, using tracker dogs.'

They set off, their torches illuminating the muddy path in front of them. They had barely covered two hundred yards when they heard the Caelogy bell begin to ring, its fast peal vicious and mind-searing. The constable recoiled, clutching at his companion, dragging him back into the hedge.

'God!' he screamed. 'Not again!'

'Easy on.' Fred sensed that the other man was near to breaking point.

They huddled together, wincing at each note, anticipating the next, and the one after that, a battering-ram that was breaking through their mental defences. Thoughts were destroyed instantly, obliterated, until only the bell remained.

And then it stopped. The steel gong inside their heads continued to beat, slowly winding down until at last they were left with throbbing temples and singing ears.

'So much for the deputation of villagers.' Fred Reubens was the first to speak. 'By the sound of it they haven't been successful.'

'And they expect me to bloody well sort it out for them.' Lewis was angry, turning on Fred with wild staring eyes, tapping his chest. 'Me! The copper. Everybody's whipping boy. Got a problem, officer, sort it out will you. All the bloody time. I'm supposed to be off duty tonight. Like last Sunday. I've gone three fucking weeks without a break. Can't even spare the time to go to bed. And what do I get for it? I'll tell you. A kick up the arse from the inspector and a wife who can't take any more so she's gone back to her mother. That's what I get.'

Fred licked his lips nervously, 'Look, I think we'd better go back. You're in no fit state . . .'

'Aren't I? And who the fucking hell are you to decide

113

whether I'm fit for the job or not? There's a girl missing. We've got to find her, whether we like it or not.'

Fred sighed. The constable was in a bad way. On the verge of a nervous breakdown, and he didn't want to return to the village because he was frightened of what he might find there. The builder didn't relish the ensuing hours.

They continued on their way, Lewis in the lead. He was edgy, stopping every few yards, shining his torch in ditch or hedge, peering closely, cursing beneath his breath. The bell had hit him hard this time, caught him when his resistance was at its lowest after long hours of over-work and sleepless nights.

It was sometime after midnight when they found Emma Jones. They saw her legs first, protruding from the undergrowth.

'My God!' Lewis backed away. 'She's . . .'

'Let me look.' Fred stepped closer, peering over a clump of gorse. 'Jesus Christ!'

The policeman was pushing him out of the way, scrambling forward, wanting to see and get it over with. This time he did not even curse. He stood looking down on the bloody corpse, his torch beam focused between the open thighs. That was bad enough, proof in itself of why she had been killed. The worst was to come. Even Fred had not looked higher up her body, seen the ribboned breasts, nipples torn off as though some ferocious wild animal had discovered the human carrion and feasted on it.

'Donald Hughes for a guess,' Lewis muttered. 'The barmy sex-crazed bugger!'

'We don't know for sure.' Fred spoke sharply, resenting the other's hasty conclusion. 'It could've been anybody. You know what the bell does to folks.'

'You're the one who's jumping to conclusions now.' The constable turned away. 'We're all blaming the bell for everything. It's too bloody handy. A ready-made excuse . . .'

His voice died away. The torch dangled from his hand,

the beam dancing on the ground. He was staring open-mouthed into the darkness, backing away.

'What the hell's up?' Fred shone his own light into the blackness of the night. 'What is it?'

'Over there. *Look!*'

Fred peered. He could see nothing except trees gently swaying in the spring breeze.

'There's nothing there,' he grunted. Lewis was really going over the top now. The sooner they got away from here the better.

The policeman was trying to speak but no words came. His torch dropped to the ground and went out. Fred saw his knees start to buckle and caught him just as he started to fall, heaving under the dead weight, lowering him gently to the ground.

'That's all we need.' Fred began to unbutton the constable's tunic, feeling for and finding a heartbeat. The builder sighed with temporary relief. Just a faint. But what had Lewis seen lurking in the shadows?

Fred shone his torch again, licking his lips nervously. A wide arc. All the way back again. Trees and bushes, a rotting gatepost. Nothing else.

He was uncertain what to do. He could go and get help. That meant leaving Lewis. He was safe enough whilst he was unconscious. The danger lay in his revival whilst he was alone. His mind was in a terrible state and there was no knowing what he might do. No, Fred decided, he couldn't leave him. The only course was to wait until he came round.

Fred sat there in the darkness, smoking one cigarette after another. The torch was switched off. There was nothing to be gained by running the battery down. The bulb was smashed in the other one.

He counted the quarters and the hours as the church clock struck, and heard the screaming of sirens in the distance. Then, at last, the policeman began to stir, moving restlessly, mumbling. The incoherent ramblings rose to a pitch. There was no mistaking the terror.

115

'No . . . keep away . . . Jesus Christ! Keep 'em off me. Keep those fucking monks away. No . . . no . . . *no*!'

'Snap out of it.' Fred shook the man on the ground roughly and slapped his face. 'Easy, lad. There's no monks going to get you.'

John Lewis sat up, cringing as he peered into the darkness beyond the light thrown by the torch.

'They were over there,' he whispered hoarsely.

'Who were?'

'The monks. A group of 'em. Wearing cowls, watching us.'

'You've been seeing things.'

'Don't start that again!' Lewis raised a clenched fist. 'I tell you they were there. I saw 'em. Watching us.'

'All right, you saw 'em.' Fred realised that there was no way he was going to convince the other that there had never been any cowled monks. 'I didn't. Now, let's get back and get some help. There's nothing more we can do here.'

Somebody was going to have to break the news to Dr Jones. That wasn't going to be easy.

Donald Hughes lay stretched out on a flat shelf of rock watching the mountain slope below him. A stream cascaded over the rocks, white spume flying, scintillating in the bright sunlight. A few hundred yards further down a block of pines broke up the rugged scenery, proof that man had conquered yet another of nature's wild places. Broom and gorse somehow found a foothold and defied all that the elements could throw at them. A nearby stunted oak had held out for decades but at last it had yielded, roots torn up by the gales, a fallen giant.

He shaded his eyes from the direct sun and squinted into the distance. Movements. Men. And dogs. He licked his lips, tasted again the flavour of partially cooked meat. Grey squirrel. Similar to rabbit but much smaller; not enough meat. He had set the trap again. There was a chance it would catch another before nightfall. But time

116

was running out. They were on his trail already. One day's freedom. It was the dogs, of course, which had led them here.

He looked behind him. There was nowhere else to go. This was the summit of the mountain range, bare rocky crags, a precipice beyond. No cover except one or two scrub bushes.

They knew he was up here somewhere, that there was no escape. He eased back from the edge, taking care not to show himself, and sat with his back to a boulder.

The setting reminded him of those western films on the television. He could never follow the story properly because he couldn't hear the dialogue, but that was of secondary importance. It was the action that mattered, the running gunfights, the Indians, the mountains. Like these. Earlier he had been a trapper with a coonskin cap, removing the squashed body of his victim from the trap, skinning it with a penknife, roasting the carcase over an open fire. That could have been a mistake, he reflected. The posse might have spotted the smoke. Hell, they didn't make mistakes like that on the telly. A sheltered bluff from which the smoke wouldn't be seen. Tinder dry wood that blazed almost as soon as it was lit. But he'd still show 'em.

The night had been an uncomfortable one. There didn't appear to be any caves up here so he'd had to go down to the fir thicket below and huddle there for warmth. He'd slept little, and after a doze just before dawn he'd awoken shivering.

A sudden idea brought a grin to his lips. The boulder, not just the one he was leaning against but those around it and below it. Brief snatches of an old film came back to him, a scout in the hills with Comancheros closing in on him. One against fifty. The guy had waited his chance, let 'em get half-way up the slope and then he'd dislodged a rock. A big round one. It had clattered down the mountainside taking others with it. Clouds of dust. You couldn't see half of what was happening, just bodies being crushed,

117

tossed in the air, bandits trying to get out of the way. And when the dust had settled the scout picked up his rifle, adjusted his hat and walked away over the mountain tops.

Donald Hughes laughed softly to himself. He was cleverer than people gave him credit for. Even if he couldn't read or write. Or speak or hear.

He crawled forward again and peered over the edge. A little thrill ran through his flabby body. The searchers had closed in, were bunching together for the final stretch of the ascent. The dogs, too. The alsatians were being called to heel. The men wouldn't be able to keep up with them if they went too far ahead.

Donald waited patiently. Let them get clear of the fir plantation. Make sure that they didn't have time to run back for cover.

He selected a boulder to his left, perched precariously amidst some loose shale. It was nearly as big as himself but it would only need a slight push. Not yet, though.

Another cautious peep. They were closer than he had expected. A hundred yards. Stooping, he moved across to the boulder and tested it with his shoulder. The point of balance was fine; it rocked. He heaved, felt it leaning, and then it went. It rolled, bounced, rolled again, smaller rocks flying and jumping out of its path.

Donald ran quickly back to his lookout point. Clouds of dust rose from beneath it, partially obscuring his view. Men were panicking, trying to flee, slipping, rolling. The big boulder missed one by inches, but as he grabbed at a silver birch sapling a second one got him, smaller but just as deadly, smashing into his face. Donald tried to work out what was happening. Two boulders careering on down, roughly the same size . . . only the second one was lighter, all sticky and red like a battered tomato. He was just in time to see the headless body being buried beneath an avalanche of shale.

One of the dogs was slithering backwards trying to regain its balance, its hindquarters useless. A piece of rock hit it, and it didn't get up again.

Two more men were being swept away on a tide of shale that was gathering in speed and volume. One caught at a small tree, almost pulled himself clear, and then the tree was uprooted.

The main force of the rock slide had passed on. It hit the forestry thicket like a breaker crashing against a sea-wall, showering rubble high into the air. The bulk of trees checked it, though, once the front line had fallen. Odd rocks and stones bounced on either side, and gradually the moving landscape came to a standstill. A pall of dust hung in the air, slowly dispersing in the breeze.

It was over. Donald saw himself clad in fringed buckskins and a wide-brimmed hat, standing out on the rock shelf, surveying his handiwork. The massacre seemed complete. Most of the pursuers were buried beneath the fall, just the odd limb protruding here and there. An arm was waving feebly. After a few minutes it flopped down, lifeless.

One dog still lived, a black alsatian. It was looking upwards, teeth bared in a vicious snarl as though it scented Donald. He knew that it couldn't have seen him because where its eyes should have been there was a jagged gash that poured blood. It wandered sightlessly, slipping, regaining its balance, slipping again. Finally it lay down, rolled over and stayed still.

Donald turned and climbed towards the last peak. He could almost see the white caption slipping into the picture, super-imposed on him, THE END.

Night. The trapper again, but this time without success. The 'Doctor Deadfall' had been sprung, but it had not caught anything. That meant there was no chance of food before morning.

Donald had deliberated upon his night-time refuge. The thirty acres of firs offered the best shelter, but he could not bring himself to sleep there. The wall of rubble which had spilled into the upper reaches doubtless contained a few bodies. Bodies of men killed by himself. *Murderer!* It was not a pleasant prospect to be alone in there after dark.

It was also too late to make the journey back down to lower ground safely. Therefore, there was just one option open to him; to stay up on the outcrop, huddled against the only boulder which remained at that level.

Sleep would have been impossible without exhaustion. His body ached in every limb, and his eyelids were threatening to close even as dusk approached. He had only pondered briefly on his plans for the following day. At first light he would press on, travelling westwards, keeping on the move. If there were any streams he would walk in the water. Television fugitives always did that. It confused the dogs. And there was sure to be further pursuit. Beyond that, he did not know what he would do. Maybe there was some secluded cave in which he could hide and make his home.

Darkness fell. Even as he drifted into a deep sleep he thought that he could hear the distant strains of the Caelogy bell. But it was impossible. The village was miles away. It had to be his imagination.

It was the bell which jerked him out of a deep sleep, bringing him to his knees, babbling his own peculiar cry of terror. He saw them there in the darkness, standing above him on the slope, the same monks in black robes, their cowls thrown back, gaping holes where their ears should have been. No faces. Not visible, anyway. Just shadows. As silent, as still, and as terrible as before. Arms outstretched. This time they did not beckon. They pointed. *Go, murderer! That way.*

He turned, tried to stand, but his legs would not bear his weight. He fell and began to crawl. Their power, their malevolence, burned into him, driving him, lashing him with the force of a rawhide whip.

Shambling like a crab, the sharp stones slashing his hands and knees, he fled. Trying to vomit, tasting the bile of an empty stomach. Pleading, admitting his guilt.

He was airborne, the wind rushing past his somersaulting body, momentarily cooling the fever of terror. Impact! The breath was knocked from his lungs, a thousand sharp slivers of rock ripping his flesh, gouging deep into the layers of fat, gutting him like a rabbit, spilling out entrails which squelched in his wake, becoming caught up, snapping, rolling, falling. The bell was ringing so furiously that there was no interval between the peals.

A mighty blow snapped every limb. Lying in a huddled heap of flesh and splintered bone, the smell of blood and pines was overpowering. Men arising from their communal grave on all sides, dismembered shapeless forms, shrieking their agony and their cries of vengeance, converged on him, fighting each other to get at him.

Cold dead hands with inhuman strength in their fingers were tearing his shattered arms and legs from his body, spitting on the writhing trunk. *You bastard, this is what you did to the girl!*

One last scream as they tore the soft length of flesh out by the roots. Then the pain was fading, and far away the bell was ringing. Slowly.

10

KARAMANEH

'I must insist on having a look at this bell, Mr Hamilton.'

Martyn Hamilton's expression was impassive as he looked at Chief Inspector Prince. The policeman had a typical TV cop look about him, he decided. Possibly he had even modelled himself on one of the screen heroes. Square-jawed, tight-lipped, eyes that roved everywhere, missing nothing, and liked to let you know who was boss. Arrogant, stocky and powerful.

The owner of Caelogy Hall took his time in lighting a cigar. There was no point in refusing the inspector his enforced request, because then it would simply become an order, backed up by a warrant. Maybe he even wanted it that way.

'Of course.' Hamilton smiled and blew a cloud of smoke up towards the ceiling. 'There's no earthly reason why you shouldn't.'

'I'd like you to ring it for me.'

'All right.'

They left the house and made their way towards the chapel, Hamilton in the lead. His every movement was casual, he took his time unlocking the studded door.

'There you are.' He gestured upwards. 'The bell. A perfectly ordinary harmless bell of Asian origin, as you can see. Fourteenth century, I'm told, although I'm not an expert on these things.'

'What do you ring it for?' The question was direct,

harsh. The inspector's eyes narrowed, watching Hamilton closely.

'For religious reasons.' Mind your own bloody business.

'I see.' The policeman sensed the rebuff. He wasn't used to people being abrupt with him. 'Now, I'd like to hear it.'

'As you wish.' Martyn Hamilton walked towards the bell-pull and let the trailing rope slip loosely through his fingers. 'But I warn you, inspector, it is rather loud in here.'

'*Ring it!*'

Hamilton tensed, took the strain, and pulled. Gently, just enough to swing the clapper once.

Clang.

Prince flinched, his hands instinctively going up to cover his ears. The noise was like a double shotgun blast in the confined space of the chapel, swirling round and finally going out through the open door, leaving tension and vibration behind it.

'Is that all right, inspector?' Hamilton was smiling faintly, still caressing the length of hempen rope, a snake-charmer stroking his pet after an exceptional performance. 'Or would you like me to ring it again?'

'No.' Prince drew a hand across his forehead, feeling the temples pulsing. 'That'll do, Mr Hamilton. I can see what people mean. It's deafening. Hits you like a sledge-hammer.'

'Do you really think so? Personally I am of the opinion that the note is soft and cultured. Loud in here, of course. I understand that the Noise Abatement Society have agreed with my views. The decibels are well below that of a much larger church bell.'

Prince stepped back outside, the sunshine and spring atmosphere a welcome relief. 'Look, there's a lot of unsolved mysteries in this village. And they all started after you began to ring that bell. People have died.'

'People are always dying. In every corner of the world. It is a fact of life, inspector.'

'Is it?' The inspector's features were grim, his eyes

boring into Hamilton. 'Not the way I see it. There have been twenty-two deaths connected with this village in recent weeks. Thirteen men, one of them a sergeant in the police force. He was murdered by a dozen men who died at the same time. Coroner's verdict – cerebral haemorrhage. A dozen all at once, I don't believe it! And hallucinations. A group of deaf children nearly went berserk when they heard the bell. Three of them reported seeing cowled monks in the church nearby, horrific beings with no ears . . .'

'Surely, inspector, you are not going to take any notice of what a bunch of children . . .'

'I haven't finished yet!' Veins stood out on the policeman's forehead and his face darkened. Seldom did he lose his temper. He was having difficulty in controlling it now. 'Not just the kids. I've got a constable on sick leave – Lewis, the Turbury policeman. He saw 'em, too. The bell has been wearing him down. His wife had already left him.'

'Well, that seems to explain it.'

'*Shut up!*' Prince yelled, somehow managing to check his clenched fist from pounding into the other's smirking face. 'You'll damned well hear me out, Hamilton. A sergeant dead, a constable who looks like ending up in a mental institution. Hallucinations. Cerebral attacks widespread. Not to mention seven men killed in a landslide in the mountains, started by a sex-killer, a harmless simpleton who suddenly went on the rampage. Because of *the bell*! It's doing things to people, affecting them all in different ways. This village is terrified out of its wits.'

'Absolute nonsense.' Hamilton thrust his hands into his pockets and regarded the inspector defiantly. 'I have co-operated in every way possible, inspector. A series of most unfortunate incidents are being blamed on my bell simply because you cannot find any other explanations. Witch-hunting, that's what it amounts to. And what are you going to do now? Get a warrant and seize my bell? I assure you that you'll need some proof of its malevolence. Otherwise

124

the matter will end up in the High Court and the police will be made to look extremely foolish, to say the least.'

Prince sucked in his breath. He knew that the owner of Caelogy Hall was right in what he said. There was no proof. Not a shred of evidence which would induce a magistrate to sign a warrant for its seizure. Neither could they stop Hamilton from ringing his bell, not even if the villagers were dropping dead in the street as though bubonic plague was sweeping through the countryside. It could go on until there wasn't a living soul left, and still the man from Tibet could ring his bell.

'Well, inspector, am I now going to be left in peace? I trust that I've satisfied your curiosity in relation to my bell.'

'I shall be staying in the village.' Prince glanced up, thinking he saw a movement at one of the upper storey windows. 'But I may have to come and see you again. A word of advice, though. I wish I could make it an order. Cut out ringing that damned bell for a while!'

Martyn Hamilton smiled, but did not reply. As he watched the car disappearing down the drive his expression hardened. He knew only too well that the inspector would be back.

Life in Turbury became a contrast between activity and inactivity. Police were to be seen daily, making enquiries from door to door and compiling their dossiers on almost every inhabitant. Yet the villagers themselves remained indoors for most of the time, only emerging on essential errands. Everybody was just waiting. The fuse on the powder keg was spluttering.

'I'm going to hang on for another week, if that's all right with you.' Julian Dane looked at his stepfather. 'If it isn't convenient I'll find some other lodgings.'

'Like with the schoolmistress?'

'I didn't say that.'

'You don't have to, lad. I know, and it won't be long before everybody in the village does. The thing that

125

worries me most is that Chesterton feller. He won't let you get away with clobbering him. He's the revengeful type.'

'I'm not bothered about him,' Julian grinned. 'The thing that bothers me most, like everybody else, is this damned bell. Directly or indirectly it's caused over a score of deaths. In some way or other almost everybody has suffered. People are tense, edgy. Petty quarrels have escalated to gigantic proportions. Those suffering with complaints like rheumatism, hernias, things that they've put up with for ages are ten times worse. Jesus, when you stop and think what it's doing to these villagers it's frightening.'

'Dr Jones is in a bad way.' Fred shook his head slowly. 'I hear they've taken him into hospital. He's in the intensive-care unit. Heart attack. Can you wonder at it? God, I saw the girl for myself. It shook me, I can tell you. It doesn't bear thinking about what it'd do to you if it was your own daughter. Mrs Jones has gone to stay with relatives to be near him. So we're left without a doctor in the village, and any day, any minute, there could be another spate of cerebral attacks or serious illness in some form. And John Lewis will end up in the nut-house before the week is out, you mark my words. That bell's just given him the push over to the other side. They say the border between sanity and insanity is pretty narrow, anyway. I'll tell you one thing, not for the biggest cheque that Hamilton can write out will I go and mend that bell again if it busts.'

'Think there's a chance?'

'No. I made too good a job of it last time.'

'That's the trouble with you, Fred,' Julian laughed. 'You don't know how to do a slip-shod job of work.'

'I take it that it's because of this woman you're staying on in Turbury?'

'Not entirely. I haven't given up hope of cracking the bell, to coin a phrase.'

'You take my tip and keep out of it. Let those coppers do the dirty work. The finest police force in the world aren't going to be beaten by a three-hundredweight chunk of copper and tin.'

'There's more to it than just the bloody thing itself,' Dane said. 'It's just a symbol, a link with whatever is going on. And that is what we have to discover. So far the avenues I've tried have all been dead-ends. There's virtually no chance of getting inside either the grounds or the house. So, if I can't get to the mountain, I'm going to do the seemingly impossible and bring it to me. I still haven't renewed my acquaintance with Karamaneh. That's the next step.'

'You watch it.' Fred pushed his chair back from the table and stood up. 'I don't trust these Chinkies. She could be waiting to stick a knife in your back, on Hamilton's instructions.'

'Don't be bloody stupid, Fred. We're not up against a bunch of Triad gangsters. The Hamiltons are up to something, certainly. Something for which they need a big house in a remote village, and a bell that deafens or kills. Find the cause of the cancer and we'll cure it, for sure.'

'Well, I'd better be moving.' The older man reached down a set of overalls which were hanging behind the kitchen door. 'Mrs Evans' blocked drain. That's my first job.'

Julian sat at the table deep in thought for some time after Fred had gone. Eventually his hand strayed to his pocket, pulling out a pack of cigarettes. He opened the flap – empty.

He stood up. A walk down to the village shop would give him a much-needed breath of fresh air. The sun was shining again, a continuation of the dry spell which had followed the hard winter. In all probability the summer would be a wet one. That was often how it went. One had to make the best of things. He slipped on a loose-fitting sweater and went outside.

One or two people were to be seen, mostly women with shopping baskets, hurrying. Furtive glances were cast in the direction of Caelogy Hall. The fuse was still alight and nobody knew how long it would be before the spark ignited the gunpowder. The bell had not rung since the night of Emma Jones' murder. It was unusually silent. Anytime now, day or night . . .

The small shop was crowded and Julian had to squeeze inside, trying to work out which was the back of the queue. It wasn't until he had closed the door that he noticed an unusual air of quiet inside. Mr Nolan, the bald-headed proprietor of the Village Stores was mumbling, totting up some figures on a scrap of paper. The other customers were silent, staring fixedly at the slim girl with long black hair and a green trouser-suit who was busily packing household items into a large raffia shopping basket. All eyes were on her, the hatred burning into her slim shoulders.

Julian Dane tensed. *Karamaneh!* Here, in the village, unchaperoned! His pulses raced. Heads were turned, seeing him, acknowledging him, going back to the oriental. He shifted uneasily. He had been trying to work out ways of bringing about a meeting with her, and now she was standing only a yard away from him. Yet she was as unattainable as if she had been imprisoned behind the high walls and locked gates of Caelogy Hall. This was no place for a clandestine meeting and any approach he made would be spied on, overheard, by these resentful house-wives.

'Seven pounds, fifty-six,' the shopkeeper grunted, hand extended.

Karamaneh opened the small silk purse in her hand and passed over a ten-pound note. Nolan took it and bent down below the counter. Coins chinked in a tin box. He straightened up.

'Fifty-six . . . sixty, seventy, eighty, ninety, eight pounds, nine, ten pounds. Yes, Mrs Williams, what can I get for you?' The resentment towards the Caelogy custom was plain for all to see. I can't stop you coming into my shop but you'll get no favours from me. Not even a please or a thank you.

Nobody moved, not even the frail Mrs Williams who was next to be served. They waited, willing Karamaneh out of the shop. She seemed oblivious of the resentment towards her, taking her time in putting the change back in her purse, shutting it, picking up her laden bag and turning away.

Her eyes met Julian Dane's. For one brief second they flickered recognition, hope. Then she was the impassive silent stranger again, threading her way past the throng of people and going out through the door.

Seconds later a hub-bub of conversation broke out, everybody talking at once, muttering in low tones.

'That's the whore from the Hall. What's she doing in the village?'

'Bloomin' nerve, ain't 'er? Wouldn't think any of 'em would dare to show their faces after what's 'appened.'

'I ain't comin' in 'ere, Bill, if she's in 'ere again, and if she comes in while I'm in, I'll blessed well walk out. You see if I don't.'

'Can't refuse custom.' Bill Nolan dropped his gaze, embarrassed. 'Can't say as I like her, though. Now, Mrs Williams . . .'

Julian waited impatiently. He tried to act casually. A woman enquired after Fred's health, wanting to gossip. A hasty retreat was impossible. He had to think of his stepfather. Fred relied on work locally. It would be easy to alienate people. Rumours would spread that he and Fred were in league with the Hamiltons. After all, Fred *had* rigged up the bell in the first place. It was a quarter of an hour before he managed to purchase his cigarettes and leave.

He stood outside the stores looking up and down the street. There was no sign of Karamaneh. He cursed under his breath, ripped the cellophane from the packet of cigarettes and lit one. It was feasible that the Chinese girl had headed back in the direction of the Hall. There was only one other shop, the butcher's. He would be able to see from the outside whether or not she was in there and it was en route, anyway. He set off at a fast walk, sensing that he was being observed from behind more than one pair of curtains.

The butcher's was empty. Mr Walsh stood in the window, nodding to him, watching him. Everybody was watching everybody else. The village nerves were at full stretch.

Away from the main street he felt easier, quickening his step. The vicarage was on his left. There was no sign of Rawsthorne. That was a relief. An encounter with the clergyman would have used up another valuable ten minutes, possibly more.

Fifty yards past the vicarage a large elm tree spread its branches across the road. As he approached it Julian caught a glimpse of green in the bushes behind, a deeper green than that of the tender new foliage. A figure emerged, stepping out so that he could not fail to spot her, still carrying the heavy shopping basket. He glanced behind him. There was nobody else in sight.

'I hoped I might catch you up,' he smiled. 'It was impossible to talk in the shop.'

'It would have been very unwise.' She was nervous, continually looking about her. 'I waited, hoping. There is not much time.'

'They've let you out at last, then.'

'The shop man has refused to deliver to the Hall any more. There was no alternative. But I must not be long. Mrs Hamilton is ill.'

'I'm sorry. Has the doctor . . . ?'

'There will be no doctor called. Perhaps it is not too serious. Who knows? Mr Hamilton is tending to her himself. He learned to be doctor once, many years ago.'

'And grossly out of touch, no doubt.'

'I beg your pardon?'

'I'm sorry. I mean I don't expect he's acquainted with modern medicine and drugs. What's the matter with her, anyway?'

'The same as is the matter with many others in this place.' Fear flickered in her eyes. 'The bell. In the beginning it causes the head to ache. But after a time the body cannot resist it any longer. Mrs Hamilton has heard it for too long. Here and in Tibet. The same will happen to me eventually. Even to the master, in spite of the special instrument which he wears in his ears.'

'Look,' he snapped, 'I've asked you this before. What's going on? *Why do they ring the bell?*'

She hesitated, averting her gaze, her breathing speeding up.

'I must talk with you. It is the only way. Mrs Hamilton needs your help. So do I. And so does Mr Hamilton.'

'Well, let's hear it, then.'

'Not here.' Her voice had sunk to a whisper. 'It is too dangerous. Even the trees and the bushes see and hear. I shall be betraying the trust my master has placed in me and he has been very good to me. So far I have been loyal. But I cannot see Mrs Hamilton die, nor . . . nor . . .'

'Nor whom?'

'It does not matter now. I will tell you all when we talk. Perhaps I can get out after dark. I cannot say which night. Sometimes my duties are many in the evenings, other times Mr Hamilton retires to his own room and tells me to go to mine. The dog, Sheba, will not hurt me, but she would kill you if you set foot in the grounds after dark. I will try and get out. Tonight. Tomorrow. The night after. As soon as I can. Wait in the churchyard. It is not far from the Hall and I will come. *Please.*'

'All right.' Julian tried to curb his frustration. A few days, even a few hours, could mean the difference between somebody in the village living or dying. The bell had not been rung these last few nights because of Mrs Hamilton's illness. But there was no knowing when it might ring again. 'I'll see you the first night you can get out, and . . .'

'*Karamaneh!*'

They whirled round, like a pair of guilty lovers discovered by an irate Victorian parent defying his orders and incurring his wrath. Martyn Hamilton stood only yards away, the sound of his approach deadened by the thick

131

springy grass. A hand-woven poncho reached to his knees. His face seemed more lined than when the neurologist had last seen him, the eyes appearing to have receded into deep sockets. A tall wizened man. And also a very angry one.

'Karamaneh! What do you think you're doing?'

'I must go.' She turned away, almost running to her master.

'Just a minute.' Julian turned towards Hamilton, his anger getting the better of him. 'Apart from all your other shortcomings, you're bloody rude. I happened to be talking to this young lady and . . .'

'You had no business talking to her.'

'You've got a bloody nerve!' Julian's fists clenched until the knuckles were white. 'This happens to be a free country. I am on a public right-of-way and I'll talk to who the hell I please without your leave. I'll . . .'

Julian stopped. His eyes met Karamaneh's. He read her silent plea, *You will only make it worse for me. Please do not quarrel with him.*

'This is your last warning.' Hamilton shook a forefinger angrily. 'Keep out of my business. Otherwise something very unpleasant might happen to you!'

It required a conscious effort for Julian to stand and watch their departure. Hamilton was in the lead, striding quickly in the direction of the entrance to Caelogy Hall. The Chinese girl was forced to run to keep up with him, struggling with the loaded shopping basket, a dog called to heel and forced to obey under threat of punishment.

They disappeared from sight. Julian turned away and retraced his steps. He feared that his one and only chance of talking with Karamaneh was gone.

And he also feared for her safety.

11

TERROR IN THE PLAYGROUND

The children had been restless all morning. Life was becoming increasingly more difficult for Vicki Mason. It had always been her policy never to mix her private life with her role of schoolmistress, but suddenly the two were merging. She couldn't get Hedley Chesterton off her mind. And she couldn't make up her mind whether she loved him or hated him.

'Please, Miss Mason, it's playtime.'

Vicki looked up from her desk. Twenty-three pupils, their ages ranging from five to eleven, were all fidgeting. Pale faces met her gaze, red-rimmed eyes, listless. She glanced at her watch. 10.40 a.m. They were jumping the gun, as usual. It was pointless continuing like this. Maybe a break, the fresh air, would help, and when they trooped back after playtime they might be able to get down to some work.

'All right, Jeffrey,' she sighed. 'Playtime. And I want you all back in here the moment you hear the bell.' The bell ... Oh, God, was life destined to revolve around bells? The school-bell at nine, playtime, lunch-time, afternoon break, end of school. Eight times a day. And then the Caelogy bell thrown in for good measure. Why didn't someone suggest the use of electronic buzzers, a nice gentle hum, soothing to the nerves?

She watched them file outside, almost in an orderly

133

fashion. A few weeks ago she would have been delighted with their good behaviour. Now she wanted them to jostle and push, shout, play raucous games – anything that would mean that some kind of normality was returning to Turbury School. They were nervy, glancing uneasily about them, fearing those awful chimes that would send them scurrying back inside to crowd around her desk, the younger ones crying, wanting her to nurse them.

Several times she had considered writing a letter to the director of education. It wouldn't be an easy letter. How did one explain the bell, what it did to you? It would be taken as some kind of a joke at the education department. It could also provide them with yet another excuse to try and get the school closed. They'd been trying to close it down for three years now. There weren't sufficient pupils for Turbury to warrant its own school. The children could travel by bus to the larger one at Bryncalid. Their education would benefit as a result. Glib! You almost found yourself believing it. The authorities refused to admit that the village school was a thorn in their sides. It didn't fit into the system. Individuality was a threat to bureaucracy. There should be no black or white. Just grey.

Vicki Mason banged her fist down on the table. Damn them! It was as though they were in league with Hamilton, a kind of communist plot to disrupt a typical example of the British way of life. Drive the kids and the people out of the villages into the towns. Herd 'em all together. They can be controlled easier that way. She almost found herself believing it.

She hadn't seen the vicar for a couple of days. That was unusual for he generally called in during the morning, just peering round the door. 'Everything all right, Miss Mason?' A kind of overseer. A symbol of the Church which controlled the school.

She hoped he was all right. If she got time after school she'd walk across to the vicarage. He was definitely faltering under the strain. No wonder, so were they all. She smiled as she recalled the way he had dealt with that

134

bigoted fellow from the education department at the meeting to decide the future of the school. Rawsthorne had his ammunition lined up, firing shot after shot. Victory was his after the first salvo. That had been eighteen months ago. They hadn't been troubled since, although the threat of closure was always hanging over them.

Rawsthorne was their champion. A match for anybody. Except the likes of Martyn Hamilton.

She consulted her watch again. Eleven o'clock. End of playtime. The handbell rested on her desk. She picked it up gently, almost dreading the sound of the tiny clapper rattling on the brass. One moment of silence first, listening. The children's voices, talking. Only just audible. No shouts or laughter. Subdued.

Vicki walked to the latticed window and gazed out across the playground. Children were huddled in small groups. Some just stood there, staring expressionlessly about them. The older ones conversed in low tones. She knew they were discussing the bell, the recent tragedies. There was no way in which the multiple deaths could have been kept from them.

Death was something her pupils often asked her about. It was a phase that six-year-olds went through. Fear, their first realisation that there is no immortality. Mostly their concern was for their parents. 'Please, Miss Mason, what will happen to me if my mummy and daddy die?' She always did her best to assure them that it was unlikely in the forseeable future. Conning them in a way. Death could happen at any time. One moment everybody is happy, the next they're arranging a funeral. Enjoy life whilst you can. You might be in your grave three days hence. Of course, she didn't tell the children that. It was something they had to grow up with, live with . . . until they died.

There was one question she hated most, and hardly a week passed without it being asked, usually during playtime. One of the youngsters would come back into the classroom, sidle up to her desk, wait for her to look up. 'Please, Miss Mason, what happens to you after you die?'

You go to a much better place, where everything is lovely, and there are green fields and sunshine. Vicki's description of heaven varied according to the age of the child. She tried to make it sound believable. That wasn't easy when you didn't believe it yourself. When you're dead, that's it. Finis.

She wanted to believe – really, she did. She'd tried everything. Listened to Rawsthorne. He was genuine, but, like most clergymen, he conformed with the Church's ideas. He had to, if he wanted the job. In a way she was doing the same. Unless she conned everybody successfully she would be forced back into secondary schools. The system. It would be hard, doing something which she didn't believe in.

Hedley Chesterton was everything a Christian should not be – selfish, greedy. Yet she was attracted to him. He was the type who would survive anywhere. Not just survive; *live*. He would willingly have donned the robes of priesthood if it had been to his advantage, and made a first-class job of it, converting the unbelievers, laughing at them. And yet . . . it was the role which he played in the drama of Turbury which frightened her. He *knew*. But he kept his knowledge from her. The children did not matter to him. Nothing mattered except himself, not even her. You could always buy a mistress if you had the money. For him that was what it was all about. Like cars, you ran the best models and changed them regularly.

Julian Dane was different. He was genuine. Not flashy. Ordinary. But sexually he was superb. Better even than Hedley Chesterton.

The choice ought to have been a simple one. It wasn't. Whichever way she made it, there would always be regrets.

She glanced down at her watch again. 11.10. Strewth, she'd been day-dreaming. The children were still out there in the playground. Not that it mattered. An extra ten minutes was neither here nor there. They looked miserable. And frightened.

She raised the handbell. Winced.

136

Clang.

The noise swept down like a sudden gust of autumn wind, icy cold, scattering the children in the playground as though they were dead leaves, driving them into the corners. Vicki dropped the handbell. She never even heard it hit the floor. Hardly had the first Caelogy peal died away than the second followed in its wake. More devastating. Vicious. Evil!

Vicki ran to the door. It was an effort to move her legs. Her whole body had to be driven by sheer willpower. The ringing bell was numbing her brain. She couldn't think properly. Uppermost was her concern for the children's safety. They had to be brought back into the classroom, where she could control them, comfort them.

Out into the open air, stumbling, shouting, dimly aware that she wasn't making herself heard. She still held the handbell. She shook it frantically, but whether or not it rang she had no idea. It was impossible to hear anything except the Caelogy bell.

She stumbled amongst the children, grabbing them, attracting their attention, pointing back towards the school building. They nodded dazedly, began to move slowly in the direction Vicki indicated. They were sobbing, clinging to one another. She was shouting, screeching, waving her arms.

'Terry, get those girls into the school. Sandra, go with the boys. No, you can't stay out here.'

It was like fighting her way through an arctic blizzard, her head bowed, turning away from the driving snow in order to draw breath. Success spurred her on. It was working. Somehow she had made herself understood and the children were obeying her. Except one. A crumpled pitiful heap over by the far railings. A red-checked dress billowed in the breeze, corn coloured golden hair fell across the tiny face and obscured its features. A rag-doll, cast off, lying forgotten in a school playground.

Clang-clang-clang. There was no let-up from the bell.

Vicki Mason knelt beside the still form of the six-year-

137

old girl. Tenderly she brushed the hair away, saw the tortured face screwed up in agony, the mouth moving. She lip-read the words. 'Mummy. I want my mummy.'

Oh, God, it was pathetic. Vicki felt the hate for Martyn Hamilton welling up in her. The bastard! He showed no mercy. Not even to innocent children. And there was something seriously wrong with Marion Mitchell!

If only the bell would stop for a few minutes, just enough time for Vicki to herd all the children back inside. But it didn't. There was a persistence about it this time, an enemy army charging through the ranks of the fallen, ignoring the surrender, intent on a complete victory. Annihilation.

She didn't know whether it was wise to try and move Marion. The girl's eyes were rolling, the lips forming a silent scream, frothing. Hell, she was having a fit of some kind.

Vicki drew her hand across her forehead. It was damp with sweat. Her vision was blurred. The ground seemed to be moving, undulating like gentle ocean waves. She thought for a moment that she was going to faint but the sensation passed. A migraine coming on? God, she had to get this kid to safety.

Somehow she managed to pick the child up. Tiny legs and arms were beating at her. The schoolmistress turned, began to fight her way back towards the single-storey ivy-covered building. It wasn't easy. She found herself veering off towards the left, her sense of direction disturbed. It took a mammoth effort of mind and body to get back on course, each yard a struggle. Tottering. Once she almost dropped her burden.

Then she was at the doorway, leaning against a post, and with one last stagger she made it inside.

The children were clustered around her desk, white faces looking to her for help. She found herself avoiding their pleading eyes. There was nothing she could do to help them. She was powerless, a failure.

She laid Marion carefully on the long desk. The girl's

138

eyes were closed. The limbs no longer moved. The small chest rose and fell. At least she was still breathing.

Got to get a doctor. Vicki pulled the phone towards her. Her mind was a blank. The number, oh, Jesus, what number must she ring? She started to dial three digits, 999. All she could hear was the bell. The receiver was vibrating. In the distance, far away, almost inaudible, a monotone. *The phone was dead!* She dropped the receiver back on to its cradle and swayed on her feet.

Only then did she realise that the Caelogy bell had stopped ringing. She still heard it pounding inside her head, the children continued to cower and whimper. But it had ceased to ring.

It was some time before she could gather her thoughts and pour out meaningless comforting words to those around her. She didn't even hear the door opening, and only when the vicar was standing by her side was she aware of his presence.

'Mr Rawsthorne,' she started, vaguely hearing her own words.

'Miss Mason.' He was gripping the edge of the table, anxiously looking down on the still form of Marion Mitchell, 'Oh, my goodness! We must . . .'

'The phone's out of order. Someone will have to go for Dr Jones.'

'He's ill. Heart attack.' Dimly she heard the vicar's words, his lips trembling as he spoke. 'We'll have to get her to hospital. The police. I'll call them . . .'

He broke off and his features froze into a mask of horror. She followed his gaze back down to the child. Seeping slowly from Marion Mitchell's ears were little rivulets of bright scarlet, soaking into the golden hair, congealing, matting the fine strands.

'Stay with her. I'll go for the police!' The clergyman broke into a shambling run, his lean body stooped, snowy white hair awry.

Vicki stood there, trance-like, feeling totally helpless. The children were talking in hushed whispers, many of

139

them weeping. Oh, God, she was inadequate. She ought to have been doing something. But what? She thought about sending them home, but it was not as easy as that. The majority of them were collected by their mothers. School transport catered for those living outside the village. She couldn't just disperse them on their own. Apart from the obvious dangers there was no way of knowing when the Caelogy bell might start to ring again.

'Go back to your desks, all of you.' She tried to speak kindly, to keep the frustration and horror out of her tone. But nobody moved. Perhaps they did not hear her, or perhaps their minds were so dazed that they were incapable of understanding. 'All right, stay where you are, then. But don't crowd me. Marion's poorly. We've got to . . . to get her to the doctor.'

They understood that all right. Or possibly they already knew it. Staring frightened faces. She looked at them, sighing with relief when she failed to detect any more bleeding ears.

She held Marion's hand. It was warm and limp, and for the first time for many years she began to pray, muttering inaudibly, eyes closed, asking just one thing; that this child might be spared. It seemed futile, but there was nothing else she could do.

Rawsthorne returned, accompanied by two policemen. She stood back, letting them crowd round Marion, trying not to listen to their furtive conversation. She didn't want to know. The truth was too awful to contemplate.

'We'll call up an ambulance.' One of the policemen turned to her. 'We haven't the facilities for taking her into hospital ourselves. Mind if we use your phone?'

'It's out of order. I tried to ring a short time ago.'

'Let's just try it. Otherwise we'll use the radio.' The sergeant lifted the receiver. Vicki heard the dial whirring, the connections clicking, the ringing at the other end. It was working now. Now that the bell had stopped. The Caelogy bell became more terrible by the hour. Not just humans, it could disrupt mechanical devices. An omnipotent symbol of evil with unlimited power.

'They'll be here shortly.' The sergeant finished his call and draped a coat over the motionless form of the small girl. 'I think you'd better arrange for the rest of the kids to go home, Miss.'

She nodded. It was the only logical solution but a very temporary one. All it did was to take the immediate responsibility off her own shoulders. They would not be safe in their own homes. And what about tomorrow, and the ensuing days? They couldn't stay off school indefinitely. It could all happen again, the bell clanging out its message of death, children huddling terrified in the playground. Another hospital case. Not just one, several. There was no escape, nowhere in Turbury to hide from the bell.

It was a long wait until the ambulance finally backed into the school grounds. Most of the children had already been collected by anxious, white-faced mothers. Three or four stood about outside waiting for the transport car.

The ambulance men carefully laid Marion Mitchell on a stretcher and negotiated the narrow doorway. Vicki followed them out, saw her being loaded into the back, one of the men climbing in and sitting beside her.

'Shall I . . .' She swallowed and couldn't get the rest of the sentence out.

'Don't you worry, Miss.' The driver closed the doors, dropped the bar across and squeezed her arm lightly. 'She'll be all right with us. Have you notified her parents?'

'No.' Vicki Mason quavered at the thought. 'Not yet. I tried to ring them whilst I was waiting for you, but there was no reply. They must've gone out somewhere. I'll keep trying.'

'All right.' He turned away, heading for the cab, 'I'll get the hospital to give you a ring as soon as they know anything.'

Vicki stood and watched the ambulance move off, noting how it picked up speed once it turned out into the road and the blue light began to flash. They didn't switch the siren on until they were almost clear of the village. That was when she broke down and cried, running back into the classroom, slamming the door behind her, beating her fists against the woodwork until they hurt. An innocent child. And the bastard didn't care. He didn't give a bloody damn!

She remained in the schoolroom, sitting at the desk by the telephone. Every quarter of an hour she tried to ring the Mitchells. Still no reply. A dozen rings and she put the phone back on the hook. She couldn't afford to block the line for longer. There could be news of Marion any time.

Suddenly it rang, a harsh jangling. She stared at it for some seconds, wishing that she didn't have to answer it. Then she stretched out a trembling hand.

'Turbury School. Miss Mason speaking.'

'Hi, Vicki.' Julian Dane's voice.

'Hi.' She let out her breath slowly and tried to get her nerves under control. 'You heard it?'

'Sure, everybody did. I've got a contact.'

'Contact?'

'With the Hall. The Chinese girl. I think I may be on the verge of finding something out after all.'

'*If* there's anything to find out. I think they're just trying to kill us all or drive us out of the village. One of my girls has just gone to hospital. A six-year-old. Unconscious, and bleeding from the ears.'

'Oh, Christ! I'm sorry, really I am. But I still think there's a deeper motive for all this. I want to follow it up. That's why I'm ringing. I may not be able to see you for a few nights. Depends on how soon she can get away to meet me.'

'I see.' Her voice was cold, unfriendly. 'Why don't you just tell the truth, Julian? You've got a date with that Chinese wench. You don't have to make up an elaborate story. I know. I've done it myself.'

'What!' His voice rose, agitated, hurt, angry. 'Damn it. It's nothing like that at all. And you know it.'

'Oh, come off it. I'm not a schoolgirl being stood up. If you want to screw her, good luck to you. Only don't come round and expect to screw me afterwards. I might catch something!'

'Damned well listen, will you. What's come over you?'

'I'll have to ask you to get off the line, Julian.' She spoke harshly, as nastily as she could. 'I've got more important matters to attend to. Good-bye, Julian, I can't say it's been nice knowing you.'

She slammed the instrument back. Her fury was mounting, uncontrollable, a monster inside her that had taken over her body and brain. Her fingers closed over a thick exercise book and she flung it with all her strength at the wall opposite. It hit a large map of the world, tore a gash across western Europe, and dropped to the floor. She looked around the desk for something else to throw. A handful of pencils hit North America with the force of guided missiles, obliterated New York and bounced across the room. More tears. Sobbing her hatred.

'Hedley.' She spoke aloud, fingers drumming on the desk top. 'If you came round right now I'd let you fuck me over this desk. I'd strip right off and you could do anything you wanted!'

She stood up, frightened at the extent of her own rage yet unable to halt it. It was like being caught up in a strong ocean current and swept out to sea. She kicked out viciously at desks until her feet hurt. She cursed Hamilton. And Julian Dane. And that Chinese whore. Finally she sank to the floor, her strength having ebbed from her and taken her anger with it, leaving her weak and helpless, sobbing. Deep in some recess in her brain she could still hear the bell, its peals slowly dying away. And she understood.

Oh, hell, was it too late? She pulled herself up, and staggered across to her desk, pulling a telephone directory out from beneath a pile of text books. The pages flipped annoyingly over in threes and fours. Fingers that trembled didn't help. Eventually, she found the Rs. Rawsthorne, Raybould, Read . . . Reubens. Reubens, F, Turbury 551.

Would Julian understand? She had not only given him the brush off, she had insulted him, gone too far. But he knew what the bell did to people. Would he believe her when she told him? She hardly believed herself. But it was true. It wasn't just an excuse. She almost prayed again for the second time within as many hours.

She was just reaching out for the telephone when it rang, exploding into life, causing her to recoil as though from a physical blow. She snatched at the receiver, dropping it on to the desk, then retrieving it.

'Turbury School.' Breathless, a premonition of bad tidings. 'Miss Mason speaking.'

'Bryncalid Hospital. Sister Walters here.' The voice was flat, giving nothing away. 'I want to contact the parents of a child admitted to this hospital. Perhaps you can help me.'

'I can give you the number.' Vicki closed her eyes. 'But at the moment there doesn't seem to be any reply.'

'Is there no way of contacting them? I suppose you can't give me a number where they work?'

'I . . . I think Mr Mitchell's away. Abroad. Mrs Mitchell must be out. I'll keep on trying.'

'If you would please. And ask them to contact us immediately.'

'How . . .' She paused, mustering up her courage to ask the question. 'How is Marion?'

Silence. As though the sister was debating whether or not to answer. When she spoke her voice had a slight trace of emotion in it as if a temporary relaxation of officialdom was permissible on this occasion.

'I'm afraid she was dead on arrival at the hospital,' she said. '*A brain haemorrhage!*'

12

VENGEANCE

It was only during the last few months that Turbury had boasted a bank. Just a small one, but nevertheless it bore the name of one of the clearing banks above its doorway. It provided a full service, 9.30–3.30 daily, had a staff of three and in due course it would expand – so the manager, Bert Oakley, told his customers. What he did not tell them was that he was not a full bank-manager, just a sub-manager. The 'sub' was something that really hurt. He hadn't even told his wife. Anyway, who was to know that the Turbury branch was under the full-management of the Bryncalid branch? The manager from Bryncalid came out once a month to check the cash reserve and discuss business in general. Overdrafts in excess of one thousand pounds had to be put up for sanction to head office by Mr Timpson of Bryncalid. But if the people of Turbury happened to notice one of Mr Timpson's monthly visits, it could be a social call.

Bert Oakley was thrilled at the prospect of his social status in Turbury. Of course, he and his wife would not move to live in the village. A prophet hath no honour in his own country. They would remain in Bryncalid, where Bert had previously been chief clerk.

Turbury was to be his kingdom, he decided on the day the branch first opened for business. The fact that they saw only one prospective customer on that day, and only opened two accounts in the initial week did not discourage him. There was plenty of time.

Bert Oakley was approaching his fiftieth birthday. The grey hairs, thinning rapidly on the head that seemed almost too large and heavy for the shoulders to support, were a guide to his age. A heavy moustache was yellowed with nicotine from the perpetual cigarette burning in the centre of his lips. Eyes that missed nothing. A straight back necessary for strutting through the village with an air of importance.

He was convinced of his popularity. Even amongst his own staff. Both of them. Gerry Pemberton was twenty-three and still learning. At the moment his capabilities were restricted to cashiering, but there was a lot more to banking than that, Bert pointed out to him. Turbury was the place to gain experience, under his guidance. They could have locked up and gone home at 3.35 each day but that would have looked bad in the eyes of the villagers. If the lights were seen to be on after six in the evenings, then word would spread that banking was flourishing in Turbury. Home-life was nothing compared with the glorification of banking. And as for Debbie, the attractive eighteen-year-old clerk/typist, well he fancied her in a harmless sort of way (as doubtless she fancied him!), but an affair or any misconduct would have been detrimental to Bert's kingdom. Of course, she wouldn't mind working overtime. He decided it would be super-fluous even to ask her. She was part of the team and would share in the ultimate glory.

Bert Oakley was desperate to have some new accounts on the sheet by the time the monthly return went to head office. The trouble with Turbury was that everybody was too conservative; they had banked their savings at the little post office for years, and those with thriving businesses in the city kept their accounts there. They just didn't realise how much it meant to Bert. They weren't *interested*. That fellow Hamilton. He had to be worth a mint even to live at a place like Caelogy Hall. But where did he bank? Bert was offended that the man in question

had not even called in at the branch to make his acquaintance. In that case, Bert would call upon him.

'Keep the flag flying until I get back.' He stood in the
doorway of his office and grinned like a lion which has
just come upon a wounded antelope. 'I'm just going up
to the Hall to pay friend Hamilton a surprise visit. I
expect I'll stay for coffee. Maybe even lunch.'

He walked out, taking his rolled umbrella although
there was no likelihood of any rain in the near future.
The long-range weather-forecast had not even mentioned
any areas of low pressure.

If Bert Oakley was offended that Hamilton had not
called at the bank to see him, he was even more offended
to find a padlock and chain barring the way to Caelogy
Hall. He rattled the gates, shouting 'Hey! Excuse me.
Just a minute.'

Then, in the midst of his efforts to attract some attention, he heard the bell start to ring. Up until now it had
not troubled him unduly. Annoying, certainly, but nowhere
near as terrible as half the people of Turbury were trying
to make out. Anyway, he couldn't afford to get involved
in the feud. Might upset Hamilton, and the owner of
Caelogy Hall might have a big account. One day it would
come to 'Bert's Bank' if he played his cards right.

One of the main reasons that the bell had not troubled
Bert Oakley too much was because he lived away from
Turbury. He had escaped the worst of the nocturnal
ringings and the air-raid atmosphere which they created.
Now he felt the full force of it, even the wrought-iron
gates were vibrating like a taut bowstring.

He found himself backing away, retreating into the
bushes opposite, crouching, skulking like a common
vagrant. The steel plate in his head beneath the zig-zag
scar picked up the notes and hummed until he thought
that he would go mad. That war-wound, the one he was
always showing people, ached abominably. Well, it *was*
a war wound, a battle scar, even if it had not been
collected on the beaches of Dunkirk. A daylight raid on

Merseyside, where Bert had commanded a munitions stores, had brought him the plate and the disfigurement. An unlucky piece of flying shrapnel. Or a lucky one! It was as good as an MC. And that Nazi sword he'd picked up for a song in a souvenir shop. 'I killed the damned Jerry who carried that,' he'd once told an audience in a crowded bar.

'The only Jerry you were ever likely to kill,' a coarse cockney voice had called out from the back of the room, 'was the one under the bed!'

Guffaws all round. The sword hadn't been out of the wardrobe since. One never knew. Old wartime associates were scattered around the countryside like dog turds.

Bert Oakley covered his ears. That air-raid was happening all over again. Bursting bombs, the whine of enemy aircraft, a lone ack-ack that started to retaliate until it jammed. Exploding munitions. The pain! He'd been hit again, in exactly the same place, reeling back, screaming for help. Never mind those silly buggers trapped by the blaze. Help *me*! Oh, Christ! He knew he'd black out.

'Oh, well, at least we've got him out of the way for an hour or so,' Gerry Pemberton grinned to Debbie. She was standing on tip-toe, peering over the lower panes of frosted glass at the front of the bank, sniggering as she watched Oakley's duck-like walk up the main street.

'I can't stand much more of him,' she sighed. 'Ever heard anything like it, Gerry? On all day long. *I* did this. *I* did that. Take your time. Rule a red line under everything. Don't just stand there doing nothing even if there's nothing to do. Straighten the telephone cord; those rubber stamps in the holder are out of alignment. I can't let you have a lunch-hour today because I shall be at least two hours at the Buffalo, that's the place to get business. Then he comes back reeking like a brewery, all patronising. The worst thing of all is when he puts his arm round me when he's dictating. I do believe that if I

148

hadn't stopped him the other afternoon he'd've had a feel up my skirt. Dirty old man! He didn't even take the huff when I knocked his hand away!'

'They gave him this place to get him out of the way.' Gerry counted a bundle of fivers for the third time; you certainly had time to make sure things were right in this place. 'You can be as rude to him as you like. Talk about water off a duck's back. That's nothing on him. And he even thinks we like him! God, there are times when I could kill the swine. Murders have been done for a lot less provocation than you get from Dirty Bertie.'

'If I was to tell my boyfriend half the things that happen . . .' Debbie leaned back against a radiator, 'he'd come over and punch old Bertie. Give him a *real* war-wound.'

Gerry got out his newspaper. Oakley's *Financial Times* had accompanied the manager on his proposed visit, blatantly protruding from the pocket of his pin-striped trousers. A hallmark. That was its main purpose most of the time.

'I'm waiting to read something about the bell in here.' He tapped the front page. 'You'd think they'd jump on a story like that. The deaths have been mentioned, but nothing about the bell.'

'Probably the idea is so incredible that they think nobody would believe it. Anyway, nobody's really interested in what goes on in a dead-alive hole like Turbury.'

'I guess you're right.' He turned the pages, browsing idly. Debbie opened a drawer and pulled out a fashion magazine.

They enjoyed about five minutes of tranquillity before the Caelogy bell blasted the silence. The large glass windows rattled, and on the counter where Gerry had been sorting some coins, piles of tenpence pieces cascaded into a heap.

'Oh, Jesus!' He covered his ears. 'I thought it was too good to last.'

'I'm frightened.' Debbie moved closer to him. 'Hold me please, Gerry.'

He pulled her to him, felt her head against his chest, her tears starting to dampen his shirt. Oh, hell, I hope she's not going to get hysterical again, he thought. She had on the last occasion, but fortunately the bell had only rung for a short time. Otherwise, he didn't know what he would have done. His head was jarred and a tooth that needed refilling started to ache, a dull throb. The only opportunity he'd had to hold this slip of a wench close and the bell had to go and fuck everything up! On the other hand, without it she wouldn't be snuggling up to him like this. He half wondered if he'd get a hard-on. If he did, then she'd be bound to feel it pushing against her. It would be interesting to see what she'd do. A strange girl, moody. Sometimes she'd go for days and hardly say a word; other times she'd chatter non-stop. He supposed it all revolved around this feller of hers, Terry. He sounded a bit of a swine, got his own way, no matter what. Of course, the bloke had to be shagging her. They'd been going together for long enough. It wouldn't be natural if they weren't having it off. He laughed softly, in spite of the deafening noise made by the bell. He couldn't imagine Debbie on the job. So prim and proper. Spent half an hour each morning putting her make-up on, and most of the morning manicuring her nails. She'd be frightened of getting messed up with a guy on top of her. Spoil her latest perm.

He didn't know whether she liked him or not. It all depended on her moods. She could be a real bitch if she got upset. Jeez, that fucking bell! He closed his eyes. The pain in his head came and went. Like the Chinese water-torture. You waited for the next drip.

It came as a bit of a surprise to Gerry to find that he'd actually got an erection. Okay, he'd thought about Debbie and screwing and all that, but he hadn't been thinking erotic thoughts as such. Only in an abstract sort of way. God, he'd got a hard-on! It was digging right into his companion, stabbing against her. He eased back a few inches. She moved after him, pressing herself hard against him, as if she was trying to screw herself with all her clothes on. He felt the hardness of her nipples, stiff and spiking him through his shirt. And she wasn't crying any more. She'd gone very, very quiet.

Suddenly she looked up at him, and he noticed how flushed she was. There was a strange glazed look in her eyes as though a thin film had been drawn over them. She smiled coyly.

'You're dying to, aren't you?'

'Dying to what?' His heart missed a beat and there was a lump in his throat. The bell seemed more distant.

'To fuck me!'

Oh, bloody hell! He couldn't have heard right. She never even damned or blasted. The tut-tutting type.

'Well?'

'It *had* crossed my mind.' He closed his eyes. This was a dream. In a minute he'd wake up and find that the bell had stopped and she'd fainted or something.

'There's nothing to stop us.' Her tiny fingers located his zip and started to pull it down, groping inside as she did so. 'Nothing at all.'

The bell was slowing down a little.

'Let's go in old Bertie's room.' He inclined his head towards the open door of the adjoining office. 'There's a nice thick carpet in there.'

'No.' She stood on tip-toe to kiss him, still fondling inside his trousers. 'We'll do it up against the radiator. Standing up. I like it that way. So does Terry. He calls it a knee-trembler.'

She led him over to the radiator and positioned her bottom against it. His trousers dropped around his ankles. The bell was virtually forgotten. If anything, it was having a strangely erotic effect on him, like some hitherto unsampled aphrodisiac. Suddenly he couldn't wait, an instant transformation, pulling her underwear down to make room. She was already helping him, guiding him.

151

Otherwise he didn't think he could have penetrated her satisfactorily. He'd never tried it this way before. He made a mental note to look it up in his dog-eared copy of the *Kama Sutra* when he got home.

It was over almost before it started. For Gerry, anyway. Usually he could give the birds a good run for their money. Disappointment registered in her eyes and she began to gyrate her hips frantically, desperate to make it before it was too late. She shuddered and writhed against him, and then they were both pulling their clothes up, deliberately avoiding each other's eyes. The bell had stopped altogether. The ensuing silence brought a flood of embarrassment with it.

'You might be pregnant,' was his first fear.

'No chance.' She adjusted a strand of hair which had flopped across her forehead. 'I'm on the Pill. Have been since I was sixteen.'

'Oh, I see.' Relief. 'I'm sorry. I mean, I ought not to have . . .'

'Oh, forget it.' She turned away, leaning on the nearest desk, pretending to study a computer print-out. 'What's done is done. Nobody need know. I just hope you won't go bragging to your mates about it because if Terry ever found out . . .'

'Don't worry yourself. If my wife ever got to know . . .'

He went back behind the counter and started to gather up the spilled florins. Funny, he felt angry. Not with Debbie. More with himself. As if he wanted to take something out on somebody, like a football hooligan who went to a match just to put the boot in.

'I expect Bertie'll be back soon,' she muttered.

Bertie. The very mention of the sub-manager's name brought a red haze drifting across his eyes. The guy made his blood boil. Arrogant ignorant pig. And he actually thought people liked him!

'I could murder the old bugger!' Gerry Pemberton voiced his thoughts aloud, his hands trembling with rage so that he spilled another batch of coins on to the floor.

'Who? Bertie?' Debbie's usually husky tones sounded somehow different. He looked up. She was kneeling on a stool, looking down at him over the partition at the back of the counter.

'Who else?'

'Why don't you then?'

He froze. Kill the bastard. Why not?

'Because I've never had the guts before.'

'You mean you have now?'

'I . . . I don't know.' He looked down at the floor then up at the girl. Guts. That's what everything in life revolved around. The difference between success and failure. He hadn't screwed her before because he hadn't had the courage to make an approach. But now he'd made it. That was all that was needed to give Oakley his come-uppance. Guts.

'Why don't we *both* do it, a kind of joint affair?' She was looking down at him in the same way that she had when she was unzipping his trousers. It had a hypnotic effect on him. And as he met her gaze he thought that he could hear the Caelogy bell once more. Not harsh and vibrant this time. Soft, seductive, far away.

'Let's have a look round in his room.' She smiled and climbed down. He opened the counter door and went round the back to join her. His anger was under control but it hadn't lessened. It simmered. A lot of things came back to him. Late sessions just because Oakley had kept back work that had come in during the day. Charges to be taken on deeds. Second mortgages. The sarcasm – '*I* never had much difficulty understanding securities in my younger days.' The bastard!

The small room was more luxurious than Gerry's lounge at home. The carpet had cost three times as much. The oak-panelled cocktail-cabinet. He strode across and flung the doors wide. Loaded shelves – spirits on the top, wines on the bottom.

'We'd better drink to this,' he laughed loudly. 'What's yours?'

'Vodka. Neat.'

He found a couple of glasses, filled one with vodka, passed it to her and topped the other up with whisky.

'Here's to Bertie.'

They drained their glasses at one gulp. Her next movement was too quick for him to follow. Cut-glass smashed against the wall and splintered on to the carpet below. He cursed and followed suit.

'Plenty more where those came from.'

'Make mine a whisky this time.' She held on to the ornate desk to steady herself. 'A double.'

Two more glasses shattered. She seemed oblivious of the cut on her arm where a jagged square of glass had caught her. Blood dripped on to the blotter. It matched a couple of red ink stains.

'This'll do.' She was examining a paper-knife with a carved wooden handle. The blade was about seven inches long.

'Just the job.'

'He brought it back from that cruise he went on in the summer. Moroccan, I think. You can pick 'em up in the bazaars for a quid or so. The bloody old liar was trying to make out that he'd paid a tenner for it. Well, are you going to do it or am I? 'Cause we don't want it messed up.'

'*I'm* going to do it.' He snatched the paper-knife from her hands.

'But I'm going to help. Don't think you can cheat me out of this.'

They stood looking at each other. Everything was so unreal. Like a dream when one thought one ought to wake up before it was too late. Perhaps it *was* a dream, following hard on the heels of an earlier erotic one. Sex and violence, in that order. See it through, Gerry. You'll wake up when it's all over.

It was almost three o'clock when Bert Oakley returned to the bank. He seemed to have lost some of his smartness. His suit was torn in two places, there was mud on his trousers and alcoholic fumes on his breath. There was no doubt in Gerry's mind that the sub-manager had spent the last hour or so in the Buffalo. Certainly this was not the hallmark of Caelogy entertaining.

He went straight into his room and slammed the door. Gerry and Debbie looked at each other. The boss was in a bad mood. Things had obviously not gone according to plan.

Bert Oakley sat slumped in the swivel-chair behind his desk. He leaned back, his eyes closed. Hell, it had been awful. Just like that air-raid on the Merseyside munitions dump. The noise. The terror. Crouching with hands pressed to his ears, the fear. Then the pain. The scar on his head throbbed. As though the old wound had been aggravated. Well, it was always tender.

It was like a nightmare. Staggering back, finding his way into the Buffalo, the regulars staring at him, watching him gulp down three double whiskies, plying him with questions which he couldn't answer. Oh, his head! The whisky made it worse. He was glad to get out into the fresh air. A lot of pride and prestige had been lost today. He had failed to meet Martyn Hamilton, kept from the grounds by a locked gate as though he were a common tramp. He ought not to have gone to the pub. Not in this state, anyway. His customers, prospective customers too, had seen him like this. They probably thought he was drunk. It would take the village a long time to forget, if they ever did.

That bell was to blame. It was right what the people of Turbury said about it. It did things to you. Took over your mind and body, had you grovelling, pandering to your whims. This was the hangover, the headache, the depression. Maybe for once he ought to go home early.

'Come in,' Bert Oakley mumbled as a knock came on the door. Not that he wanted anybody to come in, but if they didn't they might knock again, and his head couldn't stand that.

'Excuse me, Mr Oakley.'

His eyes opened. Debbie. He stared. This *had* to be another dream. It just couldn't be true! Her blouse was unbuttoned right the way down the front and pulled out of her skirt. Bare white flesh. No bra. Her breasts swayed gently from side to side as she walked, perfectly rounded, the nipples stiff and red like cherries topping a sundae.

'Jesus Christ!'

'Are you ready for your afternoon cup of tea, Mr Oakley?' The same words, the same smile she used day after day. Composed as though she was totally unaware of her state of partial undress. Confident.

'Yes . . . yes, but . . .'

She stood there, watching him carefully as though expecting him to say something else. He didn't. He couldn't. It had to be a figment of his imagination. Someone else came into the room. Oakley recognised Gerry Pemberton. The clerk was moving round the desk, going to the steel filing-cabinet at the rear, opening drawers, shuffling papers.

'We don't seem to have any forms 38-E 2, Mr Oakley. Certificates of Interest Paid.'

'Don't we?' Oh, God, what the hell did it matter? Everybody was mad. The typist standing in front of him displaying her tits as though it were something that she always did at three-thirty in the afternoon. The cashier was more concerned about official forms than anything else, blind to her exposure. Himself . . . oh, God! He couldn't get the ring of that bell out of his head. *Clang . . . clang . . . clang . . .*

He knew that Pemberton was standing directly behind his chair. What the hell was the boy up to? He tried to turn his head and winced at the pain.

'What . . . are you doing, Pemberton?' It wasn't Oakley's own voice, he was sure. More like a drowsy old man who had been disturbed from his afternoon nap by his wife dusting the back of his chair.

'Just *this*, sir!'

The sub-manager sat upright, but he could not prevent

156

the length of rope encircling his body, pinioning him in the chair, being pulled tight. Another circle. Tied. A penknife cutting the surplus. His ankles were grabbed from lower down, pulled back to the stanchion, the rope cutting into his skin.

'What the devil's going on?' He was angry, straining at his bonds. They were tight. He couldn't move. 'Let me go. What's this nonsense?'

'No nonsense, Mr Oakley.' Debbie had an empty cloth coin bag in her hand. 'Don't try talking or you'll choke yourself.'

The linen was crammed into his mouth. Pemberton held Oakley's head so that he could not struggle, Debbie stuffed it in, dislodging his false teeth. He only just managed to prevent himself from swallowing them. He heaved, his face reddening, his collar cutting into the roll of fat on his neck. He managed a few angry gurgles, eyes widening in surprise, horror. He saw what they were up to now. They were conspiring to rob the bank! They'd empty the safe and make off together. Damn it, how long had they been working on this one? He would never have suspected it. Most of the time they hardly passed the time of day with each other.

'You're wondering what's going on, no doubt?' Debbie stood in front of him, arms akimbo, blouse wide open so that he had an unrestricted view of her breasts. 'Well, we want you to know, otherwise there wouldn't be any point in killing you. We could have done you in easy enough, but that would have been too quick, too painless for you.'

The prisoner's eyes bulged, reflecting the terror he felt, and Debbie laughed. Gerry came round and stood by her side.

'That's right,' he grinned. 'Dirty Bertie. You don't think we swallowed all that crap you've been giving us, do you? You're the laughing stock, not only of the bank, but of the whole village. But they don't know you as we know you. They don't know the dirty underhand tricks you get up to. That cheque you returned "mutilated" last

157

week. *You* ripped it through. It staved off bankruptcy for old Kelsey, but you didn't do it for nothing, I'll warrant. A sly backhander, eh? Looking after your customers. Treating your staff like shit. Trying to have a grope up Debbie's skirt. Come on, I can fuck you because I'm the manager. It didn't work then but you'd've tried it again later. Only you won't get the chance. Because you'll be dead!'

Oakley was blubbering his fear into the gag, pleading with his eyes, his face turning from white to grey.

'We've been working out how to do it.' Gerry picked up the paper-knife, which lay on the edge of the desk, 'And we've decided this is the best weapon. A quid's worth of Moroccan junk. But it's sharp enough. At least, I think so. We'll soon find out, anyway. Hold the old bugger's head still, Debbie.'

The girl moved, one hand grasping a tuft of greying hair, the other firmly wedged beneath Oakley's chin. His struggles were futile.

'Now, let me see.' Gerry was smoothing away more of the grey hair around the crown of Bert Oakley's head. 'Ah, here it is. The war-wound, a scar left by an accidental piece of flying shrapnel on Merseyside. Nasty scratch. Let's see if we can open it up a bit!'

The cashier gouged with the point of the paper-knife, tearing and hacking at the skin, blood oozing from the incision. He stabbed. Once. Twice. Oakley was screaming in fear and agony, but the gag was efficient.

'That's made you blubber, all right.' There was grim satisfaction in the cashier's voice. 'But I'm afraid your thick skull's harder than I thought it was. I'll need something to bang this thing with. Now, let me see . . .' His eyes roved around the room and alighted on a heavy glass ash-tray. 'That'll do. keep holding him, Debbie. I don't want to make a slip and bang my thumb.'

The knife was held vertically between Gerry's left forefinger and thumb, the blade positioned in the centre of the bleeding wound. He clasped the heavy object with

158

his right hand, and brought it down sharply on the handle. There was a noise like that of a nail being banged into hard wood. The captive flinched, writhed. The hammering was rapid now, the point being driven home. Blood spurted out, trickling down Oakley's forehead. Bang . . . bang . . . bang. Bone splintered. The blade was disappearing slowly, each blow driving it further and further into the skull.

The sub-manager's struggles had ceased. He sagged into the ropes that held him.

'Hold the bugger steady!' Gerry breathed.

'He's had it.'

'Maybe he has, but *I* haven't finished yet!'

'Oh, all right.' With some reluctance she held the head again, trying to avoid smearing blood on her slender fingers. 'I can't see the point, though.'

'Never leave a job unfinished.' Her companion struck three more times, viciously, and then stood back to survey the results of his efforts. The ornate handle had virtually disappeared through the jagged bloody incision. A grey slimy substance resembling frogspawn welled up and spread slowly over the top of the cranium. 'That was what old Bertie always used to say. So I've taken him at his word. There, that should do it. You can let go now.'

'Ugh!' She turned her head away, swayed and grabbed at the desk to support herself. Her eyes met his, glassy. She shook her head as though trying to clear it. Her eyes brightened, realisation filtering through. Horror. Sheer terror. 'Oh, my God! We must've been mad.'

'No,' he laughed. 'He was. That's why we killed him.'

A mist seemed to be clearing from her brain. The trance that had held her was relinquishing its spell.

'We're . . . murderers!' she whispered.

'Maybe, and maybe not. We've done society a favour. Not to mention our employers.'

'I'm going to tell the police,' she muttered.

'No you're not.' He leaped forward and grabbed her by the arm, twisting it until she cried out. 'The trouble

159

with you is you don't know your own mind. I shouldn't have trusted you.'

'You're mad,' she screamed. 'Stark raving mad. And you raped me!'

'You fucking lying little bitch!' He punched her in the face, sending her reeling back to sprawl in the corner of the room. 'There's only one way to deal with you. I'll stop you opening your vicious little mouth.'

She screamed again as she saw the paper-knife being swung upwards. Warm sticky blood from the blade splattered on to her face. Oakley's blood, the man she had helped to murder. Some went in her mouth and she tasted it, bitter. Yelling. Cowering. Pleading. All to no avail.

The knife sank deep into the soft flesh of her left breast, slicing through the tender flesh, tearing its way into the bone beneath.

Gerry Pemberton knelt astride her, stabbing frenziedly until the weapon was blunted and twisted. With a snarl he dropped it. Clenched fists pummelled on to the finely moulded face, pulping the features into a scarlet morass.

Suddenly he stopped, wiping his forehead with a bloody palm. His brain seemed to be struggling, a trapped animal slowly dragging itself from a sucking quagmire. Oh, Jesus Christ!

He looked around the room. Oakley's eyes were wide and staring. Accusing. Blood was dripping on to the thick carpet, forming into a pool and seeping into the material.

The girl beneath him was unrecognisable. It might have been Debbie. It might not. He knew that it was. The right breast was still intact, the nipple pink and firm, provocative even in death.

He staggered to the outer door, struggled with the security lock, heard it click open. Through the bank, out into the bright sunlight. Dazzling, searing his eyeballs,

160

blinding him. He screamed as a hand gripped his shoulder, holding him, jerking him upright.

Two policemen. A panda car was parked at the kerb, its blue light flashing, hurting his eyes. And somewhere a bell was tolling. Mocking him.

13

EXECUTION IN CHURCH

Evensong. Turbury Church was crowded. Extra chairs had been brought from the village hall to provide seating for late-comers once the pews were filled. A silent congregation; not even the usual whisperings amongst the womenfolk. Faces staring fixedly ahead, mumbling snatches of prayers that had been learnt by heart. The organist played softly, wishing the vicar would hurry up and make an appearance. He was already five minutes overdue, and the choir were glancing apprehensively in the direction of the vestry door. Chalmers, the sexton, had stopped ringing the bell. Thank God!

A sigh of relief as Rawsthorne entered, bowing before the altar, keeping his head down as he took his place on the end of the choir stall.

'Let us pray.' The vicar's voice was husky, barely audible at the back of the building. His lined features showed the strain of the past few weeks. He knelt, flicking over the pages of his prayer book. Let us pray. It wasn't easy, certainly not when one tried to put the mutual thoughts of the congregation into words. He had to try, though. They were expecting it; relying on him.

'Let us pray for the recently departed.' His voice was unsteady. 'Especially the child, Marion Mitchell, snatched from our midst . . .'

'*Murdered, you mean!*'

The words cut into him like a whiplash. He jerked, opened his eyes, then slowly looked round. A woman was on her feet in the third pew, slapping at the restraining arm of her husband. Rawsthorne recognised her although she was not a regular churchgoer. Ann Mitchell, mother of the dead child. She wore a black costume with a veil to match. It did not hide the stark whiteness of her features, the dark-rimmed eyes, the bloodless lips. She swayed unsteadily on her feet, holding on to the polished mahogany woodwork.

The clergyman licked his lips. He sympathised. He knew what she was going through. They'd had to support her at the funeral, to hold her up. She ought not to have been there. Twice smelling-salts had been used to bring her round, but she had insisted on seeing it through. No fuss. Not then, she'd been too dazed. Now it had hit her.

'Let us pray,' Rawsthorne whispered, hoping that she might be persuaded to seek solace in prayer.

'Never mind praying,' she shouted. 'We've been doing that for weeks now. And look where it's got us. A death toll longer than the one on the war memorial. Praying won't do any good. It's action we want. Or are we going to be abandoned to our fate until every one of us is dead?'

A soft murmur of assent from all around. The man by her side succeeded in pulling her back down to her knees and Rawsthorne breathed a deep sigh of relief. Some conventional evensong prayers might help. A return to normality.

He tried to find a suitable passage in the red-covered prayer book, something abstract. A rustling of pages. Ah, this one should suffice.

'Now, if you'll all turn to page one hundred and nine of your prayer books, we'll . . .'

That prayer was destined never to be mumbled by the hundred or so people inside the church. Even as they were fumbling to find the page, the bell started to ring. Books clattered to the floor, faces were upturned. Rawsthorne met their stares, read the pleas, the mute mouthings of their innermost fears.

He looked up, fingertips pressed together, eyes closed. Oh, Lord. Save these, Thy people.

The clergyman groaned as his brain began to pick up the vibrations. He opened his eyes. His vision was blurred. The stone building seemed to be shaking as though the force of the bell had singled out for destruction those who had dared to pray against it. The brass candlesticks on the altar were rattling. He couldn't hear them but he could see them. Or was it his eyes?

Loose objects toppled and fell over. A pile of books cascaded from a shelf in the pulpit, bouncing down the steps and skidding into the aisle. The congregation were cowering, beaten. No fight left in them, fatted beasts resigned to their fate at the slaughterhouse.

He had to pray. He must, for all their sakes. His eyes elevated. The large stained-glass window in the west wall. A crucifixion scene. The agony. The evening sunlight lit it up, every detail. It was an example that they all had to follow.

Even as the vicar's lips began to move he knew that there was something wrong with that majestically painted Calvary. The cross shuddered as though under the weight of its burden. It was falling. *Falling!* The vicar saw it. They all saw it. Screaming, throwing themselves down as the oblong sheet of glass caved inwards, splintering into a kaleidoscope of brilliant scintillating slivers of death, hurtling downwards. The enemy was pouring its arrows on those crouched behind the ramparts of the besieged castle.

Men, women and children stampeded in all directions, the pews and the chairs obstructing their flight. Bodies sprawled. Profanity replaced prayers. Glass everywhere, ricocheting from wall to wall. Faces were cut and bleeding. A man was frantically tugging at something embedded in his throat. It came free, lacerating his fingers as it did so, jetting a fountain of scarlet fluid over those around him.

Suddenly, as if it realised that its work was done, the Caelogy bell slowed and stopped. The writing blood-stained congregation were not aware of it, for they still heard it, the echoes torturing their crazed minds. Those nearest the door had fled out into the open. Others had become caught up in the crush. A twelve-year-old boy was writhing and crying on the floor, his left leg bent at an unnatural angle where it had been trodden on and kicked.

Only a few had the presence of mind to go to the aid of the injured. Rawsthorne, the organist, the verger and Beddoes, the ageing church-warden, stepped over the fallen, muttering soothing words but aware that they were totally inadequate.

The bald-headed man with the gashed throat was still jettisoning his life's blood, fingers crammed in the gaping hole in an attempt to stem the flow. He sank slowly to his knees and then slumped forward with a dull splash into the scarlet pool he had made.

The black clad woman rose up like an angry wraith from a huddle of bodies, her face lacerated, streaming blood, the veil saturated and dripping.

'The devil is amongst us.' She pointed an accusing finger, singling out the vicar, her lips bubbling blood as she screeched her hate. 'He has punished us for coming here to pray. *Your* words, vicar, have brought death upon us!'

Rawsthorne closed his eyes and when he opened them again she had fainted. He saw her body sprawled across that of her husband, and for one fleeting moment he thought that perhaps she was right. No, of course she wasn't. He pulled himself together with a conscious effort. He must have faith. They must all have faith.

People were coming into the church, uniformed police-men, trying to help. Rawsthorne sank down on the altar steps, watching, dazed. The comings and goings barely registered in his mind. Time passed but it meant nothing to him. Ambulancemen. Stretchers for the badly injured. First-aid treatment in the aisle for minor cuts and bruises. The man with the severed jugular vein was carried out wrapped in a blanket but the material was saturated before they reached the door. The boy with the broken leg had gone, too.

'I think you ought to come to hospital for a check-up, sir.' Rawsthorne looked up, suddenly aware that a couple of policemen were standing in front of him.

'No, thank you all the same.' Somehow he made it into an upright position without being helped. 'I'm all right, officer.'

'It'd be best, sir. You're pretty shaken. You've been through an awful lot.'

'My place is here in Turbury, with my people. They need me.'

'We'll be making some investigations into how that window fell in, sir. Rotten putty, maybe. Or else the frames had woodworm in them.'

'Rotten putty! Woodworm!' Rawsthorne stared at the policemen, anger and amazement in his expression. 'But surely you *know* why the window splintered?'

'Not until we've checked it, sir.'

'But it was the bell. The Caelogy bell! Everybody knows that.'

'All right, it was the bell, then.' The two men glanced at each other, exchanging winks. There was no point in arguing with a frail old man. 'Now, sir, if you won't go to hospital, I suggest you go home and take it easy. We'll organise the clearing up here. By tomorrow you won't know anything's gone amiss.'

Gone amiss! Rawsthorne sighed as he turned and made for the vestry door. So casual, so callous. He supposed it was because they were used to injury and death. To them it was all part of a day's work. Bodies to be carted away, those that still lived taken to hospital. They were trained to treat it as a job, nothing more. But to him the dead and the dying were *people*. His people! And worst of all, he was failing them. He was allowing them to die.

Rawsthorne went into his study but he did not switch on the light. There was no need. He merely wanted to be alone, to sit in the darkness and try to come to terms with himself. The shooting pains in his head made thinking difficult, but somehow he had to work out a plan of action. The people of Turbury must not be let down again.

Time passed but he did not notice it. He explored and discarded every possibility. He thought of going to see Hamilton again. It would be a waste of energy. The man had no compassion. He was doing this deliberately, and nothing would stop him. The inhabitants of Turbury had been singled out for destruction by the bell. There could be many reasons for it. A building consortium which lurked in the background waiting to buy up a whole village; satanic worshippers about to launch a massive attack on Christianity. It didn't matter what was behind it. The end product would be the same unless the bell was stopped.

Hours later, exhausted, the clergyman knew that he had only one weapon. The same one which had so far proved ineffective and yet must be used again and again. Prayer! His own faith had wavered. It was shameful. But now his batteries were recharged and he was ready for battle once more. There must be no let-up. Time was running out. Pray and pray again. In the end the Lord would save them all. Perhaps it was all part of His plan to test these people. Himself, too. Wars, suffering, the death of many innocent people. Who was he, a mere preacher of the Word, to question his Maker?

There was no time to be lost. He felt weary, almost on the point of collapse. But he was determined not to succumb to the temptation to rest. The remainder of the night would be spent in prayer, humbling himself as he had never done before, offering up his own life if necessary so that others might live and retain their sanity.

He heaved himself up out of the chair. Every muscle in his body ached, crying out for rest. He ignored them. It would not be good enough simply to stay here and pray in this room amongst mundane things. The atmosphere would not be right. Also, it would be too easy. It was

167

necessary to return to the church, to the scene of death and injury where the blood had scarcely dried. Here, on the battlefield itself, he would attempt to communicate with God.

Quietly he let himself out of the rear door, taking care not to wake his housekeeper. The good lady would not understand. She might even summon help, thinking that he had taken leave of his senses.

A bright silvery light flooded the lawns of the vicarage garden. Rawsthorne glanced up, and saw the large white orb in the cloudless night sky. A full moon. Well, it would help him to see his way.

The church was unlocked and he stepped inside. The moonlight poured in through the gaping hole where the stained-glass window had been. Broken glass crunched beneath his feet. Nobody had done anything about clearing up the debris yet. Nobody cared, that was the trouble. The House of God was less important than their own paltry homes. It made him angry, but he struggled to throw off the feeling. It was no good blaming others.

He paused to rest half-way up the aisle, holding on to the end of a pew. The woodwork was wet and sticky, and as he pulled his hand away he saw the dark stain in the moonlight; blood that was still in the process of congealing on the polished surface.

He smelled death, a sour odour which seemed to come out of the shadows, a kind of putrefaction. But that was impossible because all the bodies had been removed. Three dead, fifteen injured. Some of the latter might have died by now. It was a terrible thought.

He experienced a moment of fear but it passed. What was there to fear in the House of the Lord? It was as though the shadows had been alive, evil lurking in every corner. But there could be no evil in here.

He moved into the front pew and lowered himself to his knees. It was right and proper that he should remain one of the congregation, rather than kneel at the altar, a privileged priest. Humility to the extreme.

168

It was cold. Of course, it was bound to be, he told himself, with that gaping hole in the wall. He did not want this night to be comfortable or it would make a mockery of his reason for being here. He shivered, closed his eyes, and began to pray as he had never prayed before.

'Oh Lord, save us from this devilish instrument that crazes people's minds, makes them commit acts of depravity and murder, and which brings pain and sometimes death. Help us to drive it from our village. We who are weak need Thy guidance.'

He paused. The cold was intense, eating into his body. He shuddered, turned up the collar of his overcoat and fumbled in his pockets for his gloves. 'We who are weak . . .'

Suddenly, he knew that he was not alone in the church. There was no sound or movement, just a sensation of another presence. He glanced round. The shafts of moonlight made a zebra-crossing out of the aisle. But the shadow was denser, as though it had closed in on him since he had prayed. He began to feel afraid.

'Oh Lord, help us to have faith.'

The blackness seemed to move, shadows converging on the altar. Figures, barely discernible against the dark background, filed from the vestry in a single column. One moving mass, chanting whispered incantations, shuffling silently.

'Oh God!' Rawsthorne clutched at the pew, staring, unable to move.

Then he heard the bell. Not deafening as it had been earlier that evening, but low, almost melodious, as though it were but an echo across the valley. Its rhythm slowed. The death-knell, rung for a funeral.

He could see plainly now, a soft luminous glow lighting up the altar area. But it was not moonlight, for the beams did not penetrate that part of the building. Every detail was made plain before his eyes.

They were either monks or nuns. It was impossible to tell with the voluminous robes and hoods pulled low to hide their faces. They stood back in a row, looking upwards. Rawsthorne followed their gaze, and the sight which greeted him almost robbed him of any power of reasoning. He could only watch, a prisoner in his own church as surely as if chains bound him to the pew.

A bell hung over the altar, a huge ornate object, its exterior a mass of intricate design, supported by a rope from the oak beams above. He had never set eyes on the Caelogy bell but he recognised it instantly. It swung gently to and fro, the clapper now silent.

The line of figures had their backs to him, kneeling, heads bowed. Their voices were only just audible, that same chant, a foreign language which he did not understand.

More shapes were gliding on to the scene, similarly attired with the exception of one young man, completely naked, every vestige of hair removed from his body. Two of the monks were carrying him, for it was impossible for him to walk; his wrists and ankles were securely bound with ropes. Whatever fate awaited him, he seemed to have resigned himself to it, making no attempt to struggle as he was gently laid down on the floor. It was then that the clergyman had a full view of the prisoner's face. Angular features, the mouth a narrow slit, the eyes dull like those of a dead fish. *And he had no ears!* On either side of the skull were two dark cavities!

The bell was being slowly lowered by two of the robed shapes. There was no sound, not even the rustling of material. The clapper was removed and laid on the altar. The group turned, and as if at a given signal, their cowls were thrown back.

The vicar's mind refused to accept what his eyes saw. Every head was shaven, and there was not a single ear to be seen. Somehow their features remained in shadow. Only those of the young man were revealed. Rawsthorne recognised him. It was impossible! *It was Hamilton, and yet it was not the man as he had seen him up at the Hall. He was younger by at least twenty-five years!*

Rawsthorne's sanity faltered on the brink of a dark

abyss. It was a struggle to hold on. It would have been so much easier to have fallen and drifted. Oh Lord, help us in our darkest hour.

The monks appeared to be oblivious of their audience, going about their task with a grim efficiency. The prisoner was dragged to his feet and the top half of his body held inside the bell. Another length of rope was produced and two of them busied themselves. Rawsthorne had no idea what they were doing. It was totally illogical.

They were hauling on the bell-rope again. The others moved forward to lend a hand. It was heavier this time, and with the bile rising into his mouth, Rawsthorne saw why. *The body of the young man was being dragged up with it, hanged by the neck, his head where previously the clapper had been!*

The bell was stationary now, some ten feet in the air, the victim's feet dangling a few inches above the altar. The body twitched and spun, clockwise and anti-clockwise, until eventually it steadied itself. Horrified, the clergyman realised that the man was dead, barbarically hanged like a common murderer.

Two of the executioners took the bell-rope, leaning on it, pulling. The bell began to move, the momentum gathering.

Thud . . . crack . . . thud . . . crack.

Rawsthorne's hands were over his ears, but he could not shut out the noise, a sound which was far worse than anything the Caelogy bell had ever made before. *Thud . . . crack.* The head of the hanged man was being slowly and methodically cracked against the interior of the bell.

Thud . . . crack . . . thud. It became more liquid in sound as the rhythm speeded up. Something was dripping steadily from within the bell, plopping on to the altar cloth and trickling down. Some of it splashed into a silver goblet. Blood!

There was no relaxation on the part of the silent sextons. They tolled vigorously, sadistically. And then the incan-

171

tations began again, whispers of strange blasphemies that echoed in every corner of the church.

The sound of the human clapper changed in tone. No longer was brittle bone splintering. Soggy blood-and-brain-saturated flesh was pulped. The altar cloth oozed and dripped as though some careless server had knocked over a goblet of communion wine.

Rawsthorne felt the black whirlwind tearing at his mind, dragging him into a void where he floated effortlessly. Faces all around, hideous apparitions whose fetid breath stank of an ancient evil, leering, whispering, chanting. And still that skull was pounded into a bloody paste.

The vicar sat in the pew staring fixedly ahead of him. Daylight was creeping in through the broken window, flooding the church with the dim grey light of reality. Reality!

The altar was only a few yards away from him. He saw its cloth, neat and unstained. There was no sign of the Caelogy bell.

His head ached. He tried to remember. Hamilton. They had killed Hamilton! Those black-cloaked murderers, their earless shaven heads, their obscene chanting. His church had been taken over by the disciples of evil.

He tried to get up out of the pew but fell into the aisle. He began to crawl, painfully dragging his sparse body in the direction of the altar. Some form of exorcism had to be carried out.

It took him several minutes to reach the altar steps. It was getting lighter now. He could see. The bell, the body – they *had* to be here. There was nothing. Not even bloodstains!

The door was opening at the other end. He looked round. Somebody was coming in, screened by the early morning shadows. Shapeless forms that moved and muttered.

He struggled up, finding strength in desperation, and snatched up the silver crucifix which rested on the altar.

172

Holding it aloft, he turned, fear and defiance in his posture. The Lord's Prayer would suffice, surely.

'Our Father which art in heaven ... Hallowed be Thy Name ...'

'Good morning, vicar,' Chief Inspector Prince, two constables close behind him, advanced down the aisle.

'You are too late,' Rawsthorne shouted. 'Too late. They have gone.'

'Who've gone?' Prince regarded the clergyman carefully.

'The disciples of Satan. They have murdered and flown.'

'Who've they murdered, eh?' Prince spoke genially, signalling to his companions.

'Mr Hamilton from the Hall. But a younger Mr Hamilton. They hung him in the bell and crushed his head when they rang it!'

'I see.' Prince mounted the altar steps. 'And which bell did they hang him on?'

'The Caelogy bell. They brought it with them. Here. This is where they performed their foul deed.'

'Well, you come with us, vicar.' The two uniformed men closed in on Rawsthorne and grasped him firmly by the arms. 'You come along with us to somewhere nice and warm, and then you can tell us all about it.'

'No!' Rawsthorne's struggles were weak and he found himself being borne along. 'You think I'm mad, but I'm not. I can prove it. There's blood all over the altar.'

Chief Inspector Prince glanced behind him and shook his head sadly. It was only to be expected after what had happened at evensong the previous evening. There were younger and stronger men in Turbury than the vicar who were already on their way to mental hospitals.

He watched Rawsthorne being taken out to the police car and shrugged his shoulders. Everybody blamed the bell. He had heard it for himself and maybe it did have something to do with all that had happened in the village. That double murder at the bank had been the worst. Last

173

night, well, that was just a case of an insecure window falling on the congregation.

It was all too much, though. Like some strange contagious mental disease spreading through the place. And the vicar was its latest victim. The thing which worried him most was who might be next. It could be any one of them. Even himself. He preferred not to think about it.

14

MOONLIT MADNESS

The tramp had been to Turbury once before, some years ago, he couldn't remember exactly when. That summer when it had been as hot as hell and it hadn't rained for weeks. He'd stayed there for almost two months. Well, he'd've been a fool not to have done. Lived like a lord. Bloody big house and grounds all to himself. Tumbledown, of course. It wouldn't have been any use if it wasn't because then somebody would have been living there, and they wouldn't't've tolerated his kind. Sod 'em. Sod who? Well, whoever might have been living there.

His memories went back to those idyllic weeks. Six bedrooms. One even had an old iron bedstead left in it. It was the first time he'd slept in a bed since he took to the road in the 'fifties. Christ, he was a fool to move on. He'd regretted it many times since, particularly last winter when he'd had to move from barn to barn, and some of those fucking farmers up north even had a last look round with their dogs at night to make sure there was nobody trying to steal a kip in their hay. Mean bastards!

It was on the night when he'd been evicted from a cosy shelter made from straw bales that he'd vowed to return to Turbury. Two hundred and thirty miles. He could make it by the spring. And if that old mansion was still vacant then it was going to have a new tenant. Squatter's rights. He'd heard about them. Hippies, layabouts, not *real* men of the road, were taking over empty houses and the law couldn't shift 'em. He didn't know whether the law had changed or not, but one thing was sure – he was going to test it! Hell, he might even become the lord of the manor in course of time. They'd have to touch their caps to him then. But he wouldn't change. No sir! These clothes were quite good enough. He stroked his unkempt grey beard and pushed the lining back inside his trilby hat. This green corduroy jacket was made for a real gent. It had belonged to one, anyway. He'd watched the gentleman in question hang it on the front gate whilst he trimmed the long privet hedge. It had just been a matter of patience, hanging about until the old boy had clipped his way out of sight round the corner. The grey flannel trousers, well, they had been thrown out, but that was just one more instance of wastefulness on the part of the wealthy. There was a good couple of years' wear left in 'em yet, even roughing it along the roads.

It was after dark when Cyril (he had called himself Sidney last time) arrived in Turbury. He could have made it before dusk but he had preferred to skulk on the outskirts of the village and wait for the moon to rise. The fewer people who saw him at this stage, the better. Once he was fully settled in the big house they'd know all about him, all right. He'd see to that!

He sloped along the main street, squeezing back into the shadows when he heard approaching vehicles. Two police panda cars. He watched them until they were out of sight. That was ominous. Now what the blazes were *two* cop cars doing in Turbury? He moved on, more furtively this time.

At last he was standing outside the huge wrought-iron gates, staring with disbelief at the shiny new padlock and chain which barred his entrance. It shone in the moonlight, mocking him. Hard luck, Cyril. Back to the hedges and haybarns.

He peered through the bars. Part of the house was clearly visible above a mass of rhododendron bushes, gaunt and forbidding. It didn't look any different from when he had seen it before.

'Shit!' he muttered. 'Don't look like no fucker's livin' in, so what's they locked the gates for?'

It was a mystery. One that he meant to solve. Maybe some agents or trustees were just keeping the place empty. A tax fiddle. Not that Cyril was worried by tax problems. At least, not since he had taken to the open life, and what he had owed the Inland Revenue then, they were still whistling for – and, as far as he was concerned, they could go on whistling until they blew their teeth out.

He moved away from the gate, following the high stone wall until he came to a place where a young beech tree spread its branches over into the grounds on the other side. He was remarkably agile for his indeterminable age. Most people judged him to be in his sixties. Somerset House, with much diligent research, could have knocked ten years off that – not that they were ever likely to have cause to look. First they would have to establish his identity. He swung himself up on to an overhead branch and edged his way along until he was straddling the stonework.

He landed on the opposite side with a soft thud, rolled over, and picked himself up. Got to tread carefully. Christ, so long as there are no fucking man-traps set in the undergrowth . . .

He was in sight of the rear of the house when his foot kicked against something in the long grass, something that was soft and heavy, and . . . He looked down and as his gaze alighted on the still hairy shape stretched out on the ground, he stepped back a pace.

'Fuckin' hell!' he grunted. 'A bloody dog. Alsatian by the looks of it.'

It did not move, and after a few seconds he was confident enough that it was dead to approach it. He dropped down on his knees and parted the grass so that he could see it more plainly.

'Bugger's bin shot. In both ears, or else the bullet has gone in one side and come out the other.'

The alsatian's head was a matt of clotted blood, the

177

majority of it appearing to have come from the ears. The jaws were wide, the parted fangs frozen in death, as though the animal had been writhing in agony when life had finally ebbed from its body.

Cyril straightened up, peering about him. All was still. Not a sound, not a movement.

'Mebbe the dog sneaked in 'ere to die,' he tried to reassure himself.

As he approached the house it was soon evident to him that Caelogy Hall was no longer deserted. The broken window panes had been replaced with new glass, and a Mercedes was parked on the mossy forecourt.

'Toffs.' The tramp spat on the ground. 'Fuck 'em!'

He licked his cracked lips with indecision. His plans for taking up residence in Caelogy Hall had suffered a severe set-back. Nevertheless, there were plenty of outbuildings which offered a night's accommodation to one who was used to sleeping rough. He crossed a stretch of open ground, glancing nervously about him all the time. But nobody came out of the shadows to apprehend him.

Beside a pile of rubble and broken glass stood a wooden structure. Some of the side timbers had rotted and fallen off, but the sloping felt roof was still intact. The door hung on one hinge, and he had to lift it to get it to open. A shaft of moonlight streamed in through the doorway, showing him a straw-covered floor, some empty wooden boxes and a heap of mouldy leather riding impedimenta. He sniffed. There was a musty odour about the place. Downright unhealthy, but he could leave the door ajar. It wasn't cold.

He busied himself making up a crude bed. A mildewed saddle served as a pillow, and the straw was dry. He stretched himself out and sighed deeply. Bloody rotten luck, this. Worse still, he'd have to be up and away early in the morning before he was discovered. Apart from that, he had no plans. He never made any, anyway.

He lay there looking up at the moon through the partly open door. An old friend of his, almost like having electric lighting. You could move about whilst everybody else slept, go where you wanted. Sort of warmed you on a cold night, made you feel that you weren't alone in the world. Not that Cyril didn't like being on his own, of course. He began to feel drowsy. It was warm and comfortable in here, even better than the Hall had been that summer. Fuck those toffs, taking a man's home off him. He drifted off to sleep.

It was several hours later that something awoke him. He always slept lightly, stirring uneasily at the presence of nocturnal animals. This time it was something bigger, something that crouched over him, shutting out the moonlight.

'Uh!' he grunted, sitting up, alarmed. 'Sorry, guv, only sheltering from the cold . . .'

His voice died away to a whisper. He could only see the man in silhouette, a massive naked figure with bulging muscles, the head as round and as bare as a football, and there did not appear to be any ears protruding. There was a strong, sour odour about the nocturnal stranger. The smell of urine and sweat.

'What's goin' on?' Cyril was shuffling backwards until a bale of straw impeded his retreat. 'Who . . . who are you?'

There was no reply. He stared into the flat expressionless face. The head was shaven, and the cheeks scarred with many deep cuts that had healed into grotesque zig-zags. 'Oh, fuckin' hell! I didn't mean no 'arm. Just let me go, will yer?'

Massive hands reached out, closed over one of Cyril's ankles and dragged him forward. His attacker grunted with satisfaction. The horrific scarred face moved closer, grinning maliciously.

'God!' The tramp swallowed, his eyes widening, the whites rolling. 'Let me go . . . will yer? I ain't done no 'arm, honest.'

The naked man transferred his grip. Fingers as thick and as large as bananas closed around Cyril's neck. He felt the breath being squeezed out of him, choking him. A red

179

haze swam before his eyes. He tried to scream but it was impossible.

His neck was being forced further and further back. It would either snap or he would be asphyxiated. Maybe both. He was helpless and he knew that he was going to die.

Then, just as the blackness was about to claim him, the strangulating grip suddenly lessened. There was a roaring noise in his ears. He opened his eyes, tried to focus.

The big man was turning away, grunting, leaping for the open door like a fox that has been surprised at its kill by a pack of hounds. The tramp rubbed his neck and tried to sit up. As he did so he was aware that somewhere close by a bell was ringing, becoming louder by the second.

'Jesus!' He covered his ears, closed his eyes.

The air was vibrating, sound waves hitting him like a force field to the exclusion of all else. Even the memory of his attack was erased as he staggered to the door of the hut. He had to get away. Anywhere. So long as he couldn't hear that bell.

He stumbled blindly out into the moonlit night, following the course of the drive. Once he fell, grazed his face, picked himself up again. Ahead of him he saw the gates. He'd have to climb them. It didn't matter if anybody saw him. Nothing mattered.

Somehow he made it to the top of the iron gates before he lost his footing. He knew that he was going to fall and pushed himself outwards. So long as he didn't fall back in *there*!

He hit the ground with a thump that knocked the breath from his body. Every nerve cried out for rest but there was no stopping the pounding in his skull. His ankle was twisted. He couldn't stand. He began to drag himself along the ground.

Oh God, he couldn't stand it any longer. He lay in the middle of the road holding his ears. It made no difference. Dimly he was aware of a warm stickiness on his fingers. He snatched them away, staring at them in the bright moonlight. *Blood!* Frantically he pawed at his ears, scratching like a dog with an infection. Blood began to pour out steadily.

Desperation and sheer terror enabled him to cover another fifteen yards along the road, and then he collapsed. The bell rang, faster, louder. Then stopped.

Cyril began to sob. It was the end, he knew it. He had trespassed in a Garden of Death. A naked shaven-headed man with no ears had virtually strangled him. The bell had come to his rescue, briefly. Toying with him, paralysing his brain. He couldn't think properly. He tried to crawl again but all the use had gone from his limbs.

He lay there on his back, looking up at the moon. A steel piston was thrusting into his chest, making his head judder. Thick warm blood was spreading across his face, trickling into his eyes. Now he couldn't even lie and look up at the moon. Whoever those folks inside the big house were, *they'd* killed him. Like the dog, the alsatian. He realised now that it hadn't been shot.

Cyril, the tramp, smelled death. It was suffocating him; the stench of urine and sweat, and blood.

He heard the engine of an approaching car, coming fast from the direction of Turbury, and a squealing of brakes as the driver, travelling on side-lights, saw the sprawled body in his path too late.

The end was quick for Cyril. A front wheel went over his head, crushing the skull. Blood gushed freely and formed a scarlet pool in the middle of the road. Somehow his body became caught up in the rear bumper, and dragged along with the slewing vehicle, before being flung to the side of the road.

The driver of the car slumped unconscious over the wheel. The engine stalled. Silence.

A pair of ravens were first on the scene, shortly after daybreak. They circled warily, made sure that no human was lying in ambush for them, and alighted beside the crushed skull. Their powerful beaks probed, casting out

181

splinters of bone until they uncovered the eyes. They croaked their pleasure and hopped a few yards further on to where the rest of the body lay. Some of the entrails had already spilled out and they began to rip at them greedily, now breakfasting in earnest.

15

GRAVEYARD
RENDEZVOUS

Julian Dane stirred. He knew by the spotless white sheets, the low pillow, that he was in bed. His head ached and when he tried to open his eyes the fluorescent strip-lighting stabbed into him like thousands of minute spears. He groaned and rested. A few minutes later he tried another look around. This time it wasn't so bad. His vision was distorted; it was like looking out from an aquarium, everything wavy and uncertain, no positive formations.

There were people all dressed in white, busying themselves in various parts of the large room. He groaned. A woman came across to him. She was older than the others, plump. Her uniform was navy blue. Only then did he realise that he was in hospital.

'So you've finally come round.' The sister smiled, shaking her head.

'What happened?'

'You crashed your car.'

'I . . .' Suddenly it all came back to him. The moonlight, driving on side-lights, that figure sprawled across the middle of the road. 'Oh, God! I ran over somebody didn't I?'

'Afraid so.'

'Is . . . is he?'

'Afraid so. He's dead.'

Julian winced and closed his eyes again. Oh Christ!

With everything else, he had to go and run somebody down. As if he hadn't got enough complications.

'It was a tramp,' she went on. 'The police think he was probably drunk, anyway.'

'How . . . how long have I been in here?'

'Since this morning. Not to worry. There's nothing broken. Just concussion. You'll be out in a day or two. Chief Inspector Prince asked me to let him know as soon as you came round. He wants to have a word with you.'

Julian nodded and closed his eyes again. It had been the bell. Nobody would believe it, except the Turbury villagers, but that's the way it was. He'd been driving along at a steady thirty m.p.h. Then the bell had started to ring. It had been like a shot of adrenalin. His foot jammed hard down on the accelerator, the speedo needle soared up to sixty, the guy in the road. With headlights, he might have picked him up in time. As it was, there was no chance. Exhilaration turned to shock, then blackout.

'How long am I likely to be kept in here?' he called after the sister.

'Don't you worry yourself about that.' She half-turned, frowning now.

'I need to know. It's urgent.'

'A few days. Unless there are any complications.' She was already out of the room. Nobody else seemed interested in him.

'Welcome back.' Fred Reubens grinned as Julian walked into the bungalow. 'That's a right shiner you've got.'

'Yes.' The younger man rubbed his eye tenderly. 'I was lucky. In that respect, anyway. Unlucky in others. For instance, tests have proved that that tramp hadn't been drinking. So what the hell *was* he doing? Having a kip in the middle of the road? They've only got my word for it. Prince says he doesn't know whether they'll be preferring charges or not. I mentioned the bell. He was bloody rude about it. Everybody round here's blaming the bell, he said. That bank murder is the only thing that's holding him here

184

at present. Once that's cleared up coppers are going to be a rare sight in Turbury. By the way, how's John Lewis?'

'In the head farm,' Fred grimaced. 'Rawsthorne too!'

'Rawsthorne!'

'Aye. After that do last Sunday night the silly old bugger went back and spent the rest of the night in his church. Enough to send anybody round the twist. When the police arrived early in the morning he was blathering about monks with no ears killing a guy, who he swore was Hamilton, by tying his head inside the bell and using it as a clapper. Almost like John Lewis saw . . .'

'My God!' Julian's eyes narrowed. 'I wouldn't say the vicar was exactly round the twist, although an experience like that is enough to make anybody . . .'

'Blimey, you don't believe that, do you?' Fred grinned. 'I know you've had a knock on the head, but . . .'

'Those schoolchildren, the deaf ones who ran into the church,' Julian snapped. 'That was what *they* saw. Well, cowled figures, anyway. Now, d'you remember what I discovered inside the bell that morning when we both went up to Caelogy Hall?'

'You said it was blood, but I reckon it was rust.'

'It was dried blood. Old, but it was blood right enough. Things are beginning to tie up.'

'Yeah, but the vicar claimed they killed this bloke *in the church*. He reckoned the Caelogy bell was tied to the rafters above the altar. That's nonsense.'

'No, it isn't.' Julian banged on the table with a clenched fist. '*Because what the vicar saw was happening in his own mind. An hallucination.*'

'Then it's right what they say. He's off his rocker.'

'You don't see what I'm driving at, Fred. The vision Rawsthorne had was of earless monks, the same as those deaf children. Therefore, the bell is capable of producing the same vision in different people's minds. It's uncanny. A kind of video-tape recording. Something that happened once, probably in Tibet. The bell has a psychic force within it, and it is capable of transmitting that scene of death to

185

others. God knows how many more people have seen it. People who have never lived to tell the tale.'

'It's certainly strange.' Fred Reubens wasn't entirely convinced.

'And why should the vicar see a *younger* Hamilton? Okay, that may be something to do with his fear and the knowledge that Martyn Hamilton is the "Keeper of the Bell", so to speak. But I think there's more to it than that. Don't forget I've studied the brain for over ten years. It's the most complicated piece of equipment imaginable. Rawsthorne could have picked up some kind of force waves that had been dormant in the bell for years. Had friend Hamilton been earless then I'd say that was what it was, but we both know he's in full possession of both ears. So that rules that out. Anyway, it's imperative that I see Karamaneh as soon as possible. Hell, I would have to go and put myself in hospital just at a vital time. She could have gone to the churchyard on any of the last three nights. I'm going to try again tonight. By the way, is there any news of Mrs Hamilton?'

'Not a dickey.'

'I see. Well, we can't assume that she's recovered. From the tricks our friend gets up to he'd be quite capable of holding his own funeral service in the chapel and burying her in the grounds! I've got to see Karamaneh. Hell, there's lives at risk every day.'

'The bell hasn't rung whilst you've been away.'

'No, but that's no guarantee that it's going to be silent for very long. We both know how it sometimes goes quiet for a spell and then hits you like a pile-driver when it starts up again. Maybe we're getting somewhere at last. I pray for all our sakes that we are!'

Julian Dane arrived at the churchyard shortly before nine o'clock. It was much colder than it had been on previous evenings, and his sheepskin overcoat was buttoned up to his neck. His hands were thrust deep in his pockets. The moon would not be rising until the early hours of the morning and by then he would be back at the bungalow. If there was no sign of Karamaneh by midnight, then she wouldn't be coming and there was very little he could do about it. The whole of his plans rested on the Chinese girl.

It was pitch dark. He found his way across to the line of trees which separated the graveyard from the road, and lit a cigarette. In all probability it would be a long fruitless wait.

His thoughts switched to Vicki Mason. He wondered if she knew about his accident. She must. You couldn't sneeze in Turbury without everybody knowing. But she hadn't telephoned the hospital. There had been, and there still was, an ominous silence from her. Of course, the bell was the culprit. It ruined people's lives in different ways. Probably tomorrow he would try and contact her. He might be too late. Hedley Chesterton could be back there in spite of what had happened. Chesterton was that type. Rather than lose face he'd pick up the threads and await his opportunity to throw Vicki over. Then he would find himself another woman.

Julian dropped the butt of his fourth cigarette on to the ground and extinguished it with the sole of his shoe. He was restless, uneasy. A graveyard was hardly the place to relax, anyway.

An owl hooted from somewhere close by, and he jumped. His nerves were unsteady. The accident hadn't helped. He was depressed, too. That stemmed from the possibility of prosecution by the police. Dangerous driving. Even manslaughter. He didn't trust Prince. The man was a trophy hunter. He'd have made his name in the States, where police chiefs earned their reputations by pulling in scapegoats.

But it all went back to the bell; it was wearing them down. Survival of the fittest. The old and the weak had gone. The rest had given up the fight, their resistance smashed. The initial anger had been quenched – all that was left was fear. If the bell wasn't stopped soon, Turbury would become a ghost village. Hamilton had it in the palm

187

of his hand. *If* that was what he was trying to do. It didn't make sense, but Julian couldn't think of any other reason.

He tried to work out a plan of action if Karamaneh didn't show up, which was quite likely. Another visit to Caelogy Hall in daylight? Waste of time. If only there was *proof* of the bell's power. But there wasn't, and there wasn't likely to be.

He was jerked out of his reverie as something glided between the rows of tombstones. A flitting shape, soundless. He tensed. Oh God, it was like one of those vampire movies! He half expected to see gruesome creatures rising from their graves, converging on him with lusting smiles, oversize fangs jutting from cherry red lips. Silence. It could have been a cat or a fox, or any creature of the nocturnal hours.

'Julian!' The voice was soft and feminine, only yards away from where he stood.

'Yes,' he breathed, and clutched at the trunk of the nearest tree.

She came towards him, a slim shape moving quickly and silently, materialising out of the darkness until she stood by his side.

'I could not get away before.'

'I'm glad you didn't. I crashed my car. I've been in hospital.'

'Oh!' Genuine concern. 'You are not badly hurt?'

'No. Just a few bruises. It was the bell that did it.'

'Yes,' she nodded. 'The bell is a terrible instrument. It makes people do things against their will, destroys their minds. Turns them into animals.'

'I know.' He pulled her close and she made no move to resist him. Her breath was warm and sweet, and some kind of strange exotic perfume wafted up from beneath the dark cape she wore. 'Now, we'd better get a few things ironed out. First, I want to know about the bell, why it does these things and then maybe I'll have an idea of how to fight it.'

'I cannot stop long.' She looked behind her as though

188

fearing to see an irate Martyn Hamilton reaching out to pull her away. 'The dog Sheba was found dead yesterday morning.'

'Oh.' Dane wasn't exactly sorry. 'What happened to it?'

'For some reason the bell destroyed its brain. It is most strange. Usually animals are not affected unduly.'

'That's interesting. Something I hadn't thought of, although I should have. The village pets haven't been unusually disturbed, come to think of it.'

'Terrible things have happened.' She spoke quickly, breathlessly. '*Mrs Hamilton has died!*'

'Oh Jesus! When?'

'Earlier tonight. She went into a coma when the bell was rung the other night. Mr Hamilton has been at her bedside constantly since then. But he could not save her.'

'Why the devil didn't he call in a doctor or have her taken to hospital?'

'Nobody is allowed into the Hall. You know that.'

'Well, they'll have to arrange a funeral now. He'll have to come out of hiding.'

'No.' She stiffened. 'I thought that perhaps now we are in England he would conform with the English way of life. But it is not to be so. *The funeral will be taking place at the chapel tonight!*'

'Good God! Then we can get the police in now.'

'*No!*' Her reply was a low whimper. 'I beg you not to. I . . . I would suffer.'

'But you don't have to go back.'

'I must. I am bound by my vows.'

'That's nonsense. You're away from him now, and . . .'

'I am not freed from him, Julian. Only he can set me free. Even now he might be looking for me. I must return. I need your help but I don't know how you can help me. It is impossible. Please try to forget that I asked you.'

'Now listen.' He sensed the girl's rising panic. 'Just calm down. We've got to think carefully. But what I want to know is this . . . *why do they ring the bell?*'

'I have no right to tell you. I should be breaking my vows and a terrible fate would befall me.'

'Christ Almighty.' He had to control his annoyance. The very reason he had kept this meeting was in an attempt to discover the reason for the bell being rung. And now Karamaneh was refusing to tell him. He felt like shaking her, but he knew it would be useless. If she didn't want to tell him anything then there was no way she was going to be made to.

'There are lives at stake,' he said. 'The sanity of a whole village hangs in the balance.'

'I know.' He thought he detected a sob in her answer. 'But it would not make any difference even if I told you. You would be powerless to stop the bell ringing.'

He felt her edging away, frightened. Guilty at having kept this clandestine appointment. Then, as he opened his mouth in yet another attempt to persuade her to reveal the secret of the Caelogy bell, a loud peal rang out from the direction of the Hall. Another, and a third as the clapper picked up momentum.

'Good God!' He couldn't prevent his hands from going up to cover his ears. 'They've started to ring it. Or rather, Hamilton has, now that his wife's dead.'

'*The funeral has started,*' she gasped. 'I must go back!'

'Hey, hold on.' He made a grab at her but she was leaping away, running quickly into the darkness. 'Come back!'

The bell drowned his words. There was nothing but darkness all around him. Karamaneh had gone!

Julian Dane's mind was made up instantly in spite of the over-powering force of the tolling bell. There was no time to be lost. Only one course lay open to him. He must go to the Hall. This time there would be no half-wild alsatian guard-dog prowling the grounds.

Sylvia Hamilton's weird and illicit funeral ceremony was about to begin. And Julian had every intention of attending it!

16

THE SEEKERS OF SILENCE

He ran on blindly in the darkness. Several times he fell, sprawling over protruding tree roots. Once he cannoned into a tombstone, but he ignored the blow. This time the Caelogy bell was spurring him on. It hammered and vibrated inside his head but it did not deter him from his object. If anything, it angered him. It hurt like hell, and somebody was going to pay for that! Hamilton.

He found the wall and began to grope his way along it, the rough stonework grazing his hands. Somewhere it had crumbled, and that was where he would enter. Five minutes later he found the gap he was seeking. He clawed his way up, and jumped down the other side.

He paused for a few moments to regain his breath. And then the bell slowed and stopped. His head throbbed, but he knew that was the only place he could hear the terrifying clangs. For some reason Hamilton had stopped ringing his devilish instrument of death and madness. In all probability the funeral rites were commencing, black unholy deeds that were a profanity in the sight of God.

Julian's progress was slower now. He realised the need for caution. They would not hesitate to kill him in order to protect their secret. He wished that he had a weapon of some kind. It was too late to go back, though. And, anyway, he could expect no help from the villagers. Win or lose, he was on his own.

He crossed the open stretch of ground in front of the Hall and made his way around the perimeter, keeping close to the shambles of outbuildings. His foot kicked against something. He bent down, groped to see what it was. A small wood-chopper. A pile of logs spilled out of the doorway of the nearest shed. He held the axe by the handle. It was better than nothing.

When he reached the end of the row of stables and sheds he saw the outline of the chapel. A sliver of light from the partly closed door pierced the darkness. And there was total silence.

Julian stood watching. He was damp with sweat, and a sudden breeze chilled him. He shivered. What the hell was going on? It seemed as though everything had come to a sudden standstill. But Hamilton was in there. And so was Karamaneh! The thought of what the Chinese girl might be going through brought the pounding in his head back. Oh, Jesus Christ!

The deathly stillness was shattered by voices. Hamilton's. Another, in a language which Julian did not understand. Shouts. Karamaneh was screaming.

'In the name of God, stop it!' Hamilton was yelling. 'I beg of you. *Adrian!*'

Dane broke into a run. Whatever was going on inside that derelict chapel was now beyond even Martyn Hamilton's control. Not that he was worried about the owner of Caelogy Hall. Karamaneh's safety was uppermost in his mind. He had to save her before it was too late.

He slewed to a halt outside the door, gulping for breath, trying to steady himself. One moment of terror, but he brushed it off. The voices had died away. There was another sound, a dull sort of thudding like a bag of sand being beaten against a sheet of corrugated iron.

Thud . . . thud . . . thud . . . Becoming faster.

He pushed open the door. The sight which greeted him was sufficient to rob any man of his sanity. He thought that he was going to faint. It couldn't be. It had to be a feverish nightmare! He was still in the hospital. He had never been discharged. *Oh God, but it was real. It was happening!*

Hamilton was sitting on the floor, his posture as though he had been forcibly thrown there. Twin streams of blood gushed from his nose. His bloody mouth gaped open. Eyes that reflected mortal terror and sheer helplessness. He was trying to speak, the words inaudible, scarlet bubbles forming and bursting on his lips.

Karamaneh cowered against the small altar, hands covering her face, moaning loudly. The black cloak which she had worn in the churchyard lay crumpled at her feet and her green trouser-suit was splashed with crimson. Julian noted with some relief that she appeared to be unhurt. Probably the blood had splashed on to her when Hamilton had been struck down by . . . *Oh, merciful God!*

The naked man in the centre of the chapel was gazing upwards at the bell, huge thick fingers toying with the rope, savouring what he was doing. The head was completely shaven. The sight of the holes where the ears should have been made Julian recoil with horror. Shreds of the lobes still remained like some unsightly cancerous growths on the large skull, the flesh having grown over the wounds since the amputations. The features bore a striking resemblance to Martyn Hamilton beneath the mass of scars. The body was powerful, muscular. Thick lips moved in an utterance of some strange unholy incantation in a foreign tongue. *Oh, Jesus God, it was barely human!*

It was totally unaware of Julian's presence, gripping the bell-rope, tugging it, swinging the . . . He almost vomited as his eyes elevated to the bell above. *From it a body dangled!* It was a woman. At least, the corpse wore female clothing, a long silken blood-stained nightdress. Julian knew that it was Mrs Hamilton simply because it could not be anybody else. A noose encircled the stretched and emaciated neck, the flesh already scraped from the bone. The head swung and hit the casing of the bell. *Thud . . . thud . . . crunch!* Wrists and ankles were roped securely. Back and forth. Bone cracking, splintering, blood and brains oozing out, a steady drip forming a pool on the floor beneath.

'Stop him!' Hamilton's bloody mouth formed the words soundlessly. His eyes rested on Julian, and there was a faint glimmer of hope in them.

The deaf creature turned suddenly, the huge grimy fingers releasing the bell-pull. It was aware that there was an intruder. Possibly Hamilton's glance towards the door had warned it.

The cloudy eyes moved from side to side, wide nostrils flared like an angry bull. Powerful arms reached out, muscles rippling. Julian acted impulsively, his arm going back above his head, gripping the wooden handle of the chopper. He struck, lurching forward, with all the strength he could muster, closing his eyes as he did so. A prayer. *Impact!* A jarring of his body as the blade sank deep into the wide skull, embedded as though in the trunk of a mighty oak tree.

He was falling. The stench was overpowering, the roar of terror and rage that of a trapped water-buffalo. The other toppled backwards, taking Julian with him, an arm encircling the younger man's body, attempting to crush the life from it.

Julian opened his eyes. A brief view of the agonised inhuman face of his adversary, and then jetting blood hit him full in the face, thick and warm. He was vomiting on to the bare belly, almost suffocating, his ribs threatening to crack at any second, squeezed harder and harder . . . and then, slowly, the death-hold was relinquished.

He rolled over, landing on the floor beside the grotesque twitching body. He turned his head. He dared not look again. His sanity, perhaps even his soul, was in danger.

The steady dripping continued, the only sound in the small chapel, as the body above swung gently to and fro.

'Julian.' Karamaneh was by his side, ashen-faced, helping him up to his knees. 'I am afraid Adrian is dead.'

'And a bloody good job.' He attempted to wipe some of the blood and vomit from his face with a piece of torn silk which she handed him. 'Otherwise we'd all be dead. My God, just what *is* all this about?'

194

'That is . . . *was* my son.' Martyn Hamilton was on his feet, the flow of blood from his broken nose lessening. 'And that . . . that poor woman up there,' he couldn't control the sobs, 'is my wife. I thank God that she was already dead before she was subjected to this foul heathen death ritual.'

Julian looked at the owner of Caelogy Hall steadily. 'Now suppose *you* tell me what this is all about, Hamilton? You can't hide your bell or your secrets any longer.'

'No.' Hamilton stooped and picked up a long bladed dagger from the floor. The hilt was studded with jewels. 'There is nothing more to hide now. It is all over. As you know, my wife and I spent many years in Tibet. Our only son, Adrian,' he glanced briefly at the hideous lifeless shape on the ground, 'was born out there. However, when he was eighteen he became involved with a religious sect known as the Seekers of Silence. They believe that only the deaf are pure, and the initiation ceremony involves sharp needles being thrust into the ear-drums to destroy every vestige of hearing. Then, as an outward sign of their belief, the ears are amputated. Their activities are against the law, naturally, and most of these secret temples are hidden in the mountains. Adrian disappeared. He was missing for a month, and when he returned we were aghast at what had happened to him. But it was too late to do anything about it. His hearing was gone forever. The only thing he could hear was,' Hamilton gestured upwards, 'this accursed bell!

'These religious fanatics worshipped what is known as the *Deathbell*. It is the only sound they can hear, its frequency is such that the noise vibrates in the brain. It can be heard for miles. Indeed, it used to summon our son into the mountains for those long and terrible sessions of worship. It is not surprising, therefore, that he underwent a personality change. He became sullen and vicious, and we had no control over him. All the time these Seekers of Silence were exerting their influence over him, and Sylvia and I knew only too well that one day he would leave us

195

and never return. We should never hear from him again. He was totally alien to us. Indeed, I think he had ceased to regard us as parents.

'The thing we feared most of all was the death ceremony carried out by these maniacs on any who offended them, even their own members. The condemned is tied to the clapper of one of the big bells and hanged. During the process of strangulation the bell is tolled and the skull is smashed to a pulp. There were rumours in the village in Tibet, where we lived for twenty years, of those who had been marked down for death being snatched from their homes. We could not chance it happening to Adrian so we fled one night, and by devious routes and means came back to England, smuggling our son into the country.

'Of course, we had to find a remote place where we could hide our son, otherwise he would have been committed to an asylum. I must add that he was brought here as a prisoner, mentally deranged. At times he became violent, and on more than one occasion has broken out of the room where he was kept locked in, day and night, and roamed the grounds.

'We had only one means of controlling him. The Deathbell! However violent he had become, we had only to ring it and he would at once revert to the subdued mindless creature which he was for most of the time. If he had escaped, then he would come shuffling meekly back to his room.

'However, his troublesome periods were getting more frequent, hence the necessity for tolling the bell almost daily. This bell is an original one belonging to the Seekers of Silence. I stole it myself from one of their temples outside Lhasa. We feared lest they might follow us back to England to retrieve it, so it was necessary to keep the grounds closed to outsiders. The alsatian, Sheba, served her purpose well, but for some reason she became receptive to the bell and it killed her.'

'In the same way that you have killed a lot of other

196

people in Turbury,' Julian interrupted bitterly, 'including my mother.'

'Every death is on my conscience.' Hamilton groaned, every trace of his former arrogance had disappeared. 'The Deathbell was murdering, driving people to acts of madness, but what else could I do?'

'You could have stopped ringing it.'

'Blood is thicker than water as they say, Mr Dane. My wife and I were determined to keep our son as long as possible, whatever the consequences. But it has ended as we feared that it might one day, although never in our wildest dreams did we envisage anything as terrible as this.'

'What happened?'

'My wife fell ill. I have had some medical training in my early days and I thought that I could treat her. But it was the Deathbell which was killing her. I was faced with a terrible alternative; my son or my wife. I tried to keep both, but I was fighting a losing battle. In the end poor Sylvia died, only a matter of hours ago. I decided to bury her myself. I believe that if you go back far enough in the history of Turbury you will find that the ground around this chapel is consecrated. I saw no harm in it. It was to be a simple service, attended by myself and my faithful Karamaneh. But, as though guided by those fiends in the Tibetan mountains, Adrian chose his moment to escape. I am almost inclined to believe that some psychic force was guiding him.

'He burst in here, felled me with a single blow, and seized the body of his mother. I am sure that he did not recognise her, although in those fiendish moods I doubt whether even that would have stopped him. We were forced to watch as he . . . as he . . .' The owner of Caelogy Hall turned away, burying his face in his hands.

'I'm sorry,' Julian said. 'Sorry for all of us. But I'm afraid the police will have to take over now, Mr Hamilton. One thing I'd like to know, though. Some deaf children, and the vicar, who has now been driven out of his mind, had

197

visions of these cowled monks, the Seekers of Silence. Rawsthorne even claims to have witnessed the . . . the death ceremony.'

'Even I do not understand the full powers of the Deathbell,' Hamilton sighed, and wiped some more blood from his face. 'I have had visions myself. Terrible nightmares. Legend has it that every bell records the deaths at which it officiates and can reproduce the illusions centuries later. Who knows? Oh, the foolishness of youth, Mr Dane. Adrian had the world at his feet, and was engaged to a beautiful girl . . . *Karamaneh* . . .'

'What!' Julian gasped. 'You mean to say that . . .?'

'Yes,' Martyn Hamilton smiled. 'They were to be married at the end of that fateful summer, and had that been so then I doubt whether any of us would ever have set foot in England again. But he was lured away by their false promises of everlasting life and peace amongst the realms of silence. Too late, he realised what he had let himself in for. His hearing was taken, and the disfigurements which you see followed. They cut his face, leaving a mass of terrible scars because they were jealous of his looks. I will never forget the first time Karamaneh looked upon him.'

'It was awful.' The Chinese girl clung to Julian and he thought for a moment that the very memory of it was going to cause her to faint. 'But I had made vows to him and I wasn't going to desert the man I loved simply because of . . . of that. But worse was to follow. Deafness I could tolerate, but when they took his mind . . .'

'But you were faithful to the end,' Hamilton smiled. 'To him, and to Sylvia and me. You gave up everything. And now . . . now . . .'

'I will stand by you,' Karamaneh said.

'I would sooner have ended his life myself.' Hamilton glanced at the dagger which he was still holding. 'I surely would have done had he not been too quick and too strong for me. Nevertheless, it is all over. He is at peace, and we should be grateful, Mr Dane, if you would kindly go and call the authorities. Karamaneh and I will wait here.'

Julian Dane turned away. He didn't look back. He couldn't. Thousands of miles away, in the remote mountains of Tibet, a group of religious fanatics had brought all this about. They were the murderers, not Martyn Hamilton. They had taken the boy, Adrian, first and moulded him into a mindless deaf creature. Then, into their vile cesspool they had sucked the parents and the fiancée. Even then they were not content. They had cast the mark of death over Turbury, his mother, old Williamson and many others. Madness had spread like a disease. And in that far country the Deathbells of the Seekers of Silence still tolled, calling their disciples of evil to worship.

Julian walked slowly. His body ached and the stench of that foul creature still clung to his clothing. There was no hurry. Chief Inspector Prince could attend to the details. Julian did not want to set foot in the grounds of Caelogy Hall again.

He was almost at the gates when he heard the crackling of flames. He turned. Columns of fire were leaping high into the sky, throwing up a myriad of sparks. The deep fiery glow lit up the entire scene, the belfry gushing orange tongues, an angry dragon consuming its prey, a red hot bell from which dangled a smouldering blackened human shape. The funeral was over. The cremation had begun.

Julian broke into a run, urging his exhausted body to make one more last effort. Acrid clouds of smoke billowed from the chapel door, and he knew that there was no hope of going inside. He stood there, watching, praying.

The burning door creaked backwards, the curtain rising on the last act of a macabre play. Julian peered through smarting, streaming eyes. The chapel was an inferno. So much dry wood, most of it rotten and riddled with woodworm, the perfect kindling for a mighty blaze.

The grotesque blackened shape lay on the floor. Two more bodies were nearby – Karamaneh, face downwards, her death-wound screened from view, a scarlet stream

trickling out from beneath her, and Hamilton, still writhing, the jewelled handle of the dagger protruding from his
stomach, hands clasped over the hilt, still living, trying to
push the blade in deeper.

For one fleeting moment Julian's eyes met his. The
dying man nodded, tried to smile. Then, with a rumbling,
creaking sound, the roof began to cave inwards. Burning
rafters hurtled downwards and showered the interior with
sparks. Thickening smoke.

Julian backed away. The bell . . . it was leaning at a
precarious angle. Almost contemptuously it shed its load,
the remains of Mrs Hamilton plummeting downwards,
striking her son with a sickening thud as though bent on a
last reunion with the thing that she had spawned.

Total collapse. The Deathbell brought everything down
with it, smashing into the furnace. One last sound: a deep
resonant clang that rushed up into the night air, appeared
to hang suspended, and then slowly died away.

Julian moved towards the Hall, his eyes fixed on the
blazing funeral pyre. The blackness beyond seemed to be
waiting to roll back once the fire had died down. Pregnant
with menace, unseen forces gathering, the Seekers of
Silence waiting to reclaim their Deathbell.

FICTION

GENERAL

☐ The Patriarch	Chaim Bermant	£1.75
☐ The Free Fishers	John Buchan	£1.50
☐ Midwinter	John Buchan	£1.50
☐ A Prince of the Captivity	John Buchan	£1.50
☐ The Eve of Saint Venus	Anthony Burgess	£1.10
☐ Nothing Like the Sun	Anthony Burgess	£1.50
☐ The Wanting Seed	Anthony Burgess	£1.50
☐ The Other Woman	Colette	£1.50
☐ Retreat From Love	Colette	£1.60
☐ Prizzi's Honour	Richard Condon	£1.75
☐ The Whisper of the Axe	Richard Condon	£1.75
☐ King Hereafter	Dorothy Dunnett	£2.95
☐ Pope Joan	Lawrence Durrell	£1.35
☐ The Country of her Dreams	Janice Elliott	£1.35
☐ Secret Places	Janice Elliott	£1.35
☐ Letter to a Child Never Born	Oriana Fallaci	£1.00
☐ A Man	Oriana Fallaci	£1.95
☐ Rich Little Poor Girl	Terence Feely	£1.75
☐ Marital Rites	Margaret Forster	£1.50
☐ Grimalkin's Tales	Gardiner, Ronson, Whitelaw	£1.60
☐ Who Was Sylvia?	Judy Gardiner	£1.50
☐ Lost and Found	Julian Gloag	£1.95
☐ La Presidenta	Lois Gould	£1.75
☐ A Sea-Change	Lois Gould	£1.50
☐ Black Summer	Julian Hale	£1.75
☐ Duncton Wood	William Horwood	£2.50
☐ The Stonor Eagles	William Horwood	£2.95
☐ The Man Who Lived at the Ritz	A.E. Hotchner	£1.65
☐ The Fame Game	Rona Jaffe	£1.50
☐ A Bonfire	Pamela Hansford Johnson	£1.50
☐ The Good Husband	Pamela Hansford Johnson	£1.50
☐ The Good Listener	Pamela Hansford Johnson	£1.50
☐ The Honours Board	Pamela Hansford Johnson	£1.50
☐ The Unspeakable Skipton	Pamela Hansford Johnson	£1.50
☐ Kine	A.R. Lloyd	£1.50
☐ Christmas Pudding	Nancy Mitford	£1.50
☐ Highland Fling	Nancy Mitford	£1.50
☐ Pigeon Pie	Nancy Mitford	£1.50
☐ Gossip	Marc Olden	£1.25
☐ Night Music	Lilli Palmer	£1.95
☐ Admiral	Dudley Pope	£1.75
☐ Buccaneer	Dudley Pope	£1.75
☐ Glory B.	Alexander Stuart	£1.65
☐ Wild Strawberries	Angela Thirkell	£1.50
☐ The Housewife and the Assassin	Susan Trott	£1.50
☐ When Your Lover Leaves	Susan Trott	£1.50

FICTION

HORROR/OCCULT/NASTY

☐ Death Walkers	Gary Brandner	£1.50
☐ The Howling	Gary Brandner	£1.50
☐ Return of the Howling	Gary Brandner	£1.50
☐ The Sanctuary	Glenn Chandler	£1.50
☐ The Tribe	Glenn Chandler	£1.10
☐ The Black Castle	Leslie Daniels	£1.25
☐ The Big Goodnight	Judy Gardiner	£1.25
☐ Rattlers	Joseph L. Gilmore	£1.25
☐ The Nestling	Charles L. Grant	£1.75
☐ Slither	John Halkin	£1.25
☐ The Unholy	John Halkin	£1.25
☐ The Skull	Shaun Hutson	£1.25
☐ Pestilence	Edward Jarvis	£1.50
☐ The Beast Within	Edward Levy	£1.25
☐ Night Killers	Richard Lewis	£1.25
☐ Spiders	Richard Lewis	£1.25
☐ The Web	Richard Lewis	£1.10
☐ Bloodthirst	Mark Ronson	£1.00
☐ Ghoul	Mark Ronson	95p
☐ Ogre	Mark Ronson	95p
☐ Deathbell	Guy N. Smith	£1.00
☐ Doomflight	Guy N. Smith	£1.10
☐ The Lurkers	Guy N. Smith	£1.25
☐ Manitou Doll	Guy N. Smith	£1.25
☐ Satan's Snowdrop	Guy N. Smith	£1.00
☐ The Beast of Kane	Cliff Twemlow	£1.50
☐ The Pike	Cliff Twemlow	£1.25

SCIENCE FICTION

☐ More Things in Heaven	John Brunner	£1.50
☐ The Proud Robot	Henry Kuttner	£1.50
☐ Death's Master	Tanith Lee	£1.50
☐ Electric Forest	Tanith Lee	£1.25
☐ The Dancers of Arun	Elizabeth A. Lynn	£1.50
☐ A Different Light	Elizabeth A. Lynn	£1.50
☐ The Northern Girl	Elizabeth A. Lynn	£1.50
☐ Balance of Power	Brian M. Stableford	£1.75

WESTERNS – Blade Series – Matt Chisholm

☐ No. 5 The Colorado Virgins		85p
☐ No. 6 The Mexican Proposition		85p
☐ No. 8 The Nevada Mustang		85p
☐ No. 9 The Montana Deadlock		85p
☐ No. 10 The Cheyenne Trap		95p
☐ No. 11 The Navaho Trail		95p
☐ No. 12 The Last Act		95p

FICTION

ADVENTURE/SUSPENSE

☐ The Midas Deep	John Brosnan	£2.25
☐ Temple Kent	D.G. Devon	£1.95
☐ The Flowers of the Forest	Joseph Hone	£1.75
☐ Styx	Christopher Hyde	£1.50
☐ Hot Rain	Colin Lewis	£1.65
☐ The Buck Passes Flynn	Gregory Mcdonald	£1.60
☐ Confess, Fletch	Gregory Mcdonald	£1.50
☐ Fletch	Gregory Mcdonald	£1.50
☐ Fletch and the Widow Bradley	Gregory Mcdonald	£1.50
☐ Flynn	Gregory Mcdonald	£1.75
☐ In the Face of the Enemy	Douglas Scott	£1.95

CRIME THRILLER

☐ The Cool Cottontail	John Ball	£1.00
☐ Five Pieces of Jade	John Ball	£1.50
☐ In the Heat of the Night	John Ball	£1.00
☐ Johnny Get Your Gun	John Ball	£1.00
☐ Then Came Violence	John Ball	£1.50
☐ The Floating Admiral	The Detection Club	£1.50
☐ The Blunderer	Patricia Highsmith	£1.50
☐ A Game for the Living	Patricia Highsmith	£1.50
☐ Those Who Walk Away	Patricia Highsmith	£1.50
☐ The Tremor of Forgery	Patricia Highsmith	£1.50
☐ The Two Faces of January	Patricia Highsmith	£1.50

WESTERNS – Blade Series – Matt Chisholm

☐ No. 5 The Colorado Virgins		85p
☐ No. 6 The Mexican Proposition		85p
☐ No. 8 The Nevada Mustang		85p
☐ No. 9 The Montana Deadlock		85p
☐ No. 10 The Cheyenne Trap		95p
☐ No. 11 The Navaho Trail		95p
☐ No. 12 The Last Act		95p

McAllister Series – Matt Chisholm

☐ No. 3 McAllister Never Surrenders		95p
☐ No. 4 McAllister and the Cheyenne Death		95p
☐ No. 6 McAllister – Die-hard		95p
☐ No. 7 McAllister – Wolf-Bait		95p
☐ No. 8 McAllister – Fire Brand		£1.25

NON-FICTION

WAR

☐ The Battle of Malta	Joseph Attard	£1.50
☐ The Black Angels	Rupert Butler	£1.50
☐ Gestapo	Rupert Butler	£1.50
☐ Hand of Steel	Rupert Butler	£1.35
☐ Legions of Death	Rupert Butler	£1.75
☐ The Air Battle for Malta	Lord James Douglas-Hamilton MP	£1.50
☐ Auschwitz and the Allies	Martin Gilbert	£4.95
☐ Sigh for a Merlin	Alex Henshaw	£1.50
☐ Hitler's Secret Life	Glen B. Infield	£1.50
☐ Spitfire into Battle	Group Captain Duncan Smith	£1.75
☐ Women Beyond the Wire	Lavinia Warner and John Sandilands	£1.95

FICTION

CRIME – WHODUNNIT

☐ Thou Shell of Death	Nicholas Blake	£1.25
☐ The Widow's Cruise	Nicholas Blake	£1.25
☐ The Worm of Death	Nicholas Blake	95p
☐ The Long Divorce	Edmund Crispin	£1.50
☐ King and Joker	Peter Dickinson	£1.25
☐ The Last House-Party	Peter Dickinson	£1.50
☐ A Pride of Heroes	Peter Dickinson	£1.50
☐ The Seals	Peter Dickinson	£1.50
☐ Sleep and His Brother	Peter Dickinson	£1.50
☐ Firefly Gadroon	Jonathan Gash	£1.50
☐ The Vatican Rip	Jonathan Gash	£1.50
☐ Blood and Judgment	Michael Gilbert	£1.10
☐ Close Quarters	Michael Gilbert	£1.10
☐ Death of a Favourite Girl	Michael Gilbert	£1.50
☐ The Etruscan Net	Michael Gilbert	£1.25
☐ The Night of the Twelfth	Michael Gilbert	£1.25
☐ Silence Observed	Michael Innes	£1.00
☐ There Came Both Mist and Snow	Michael Innes	95p
☐ Go West, Inspector Ghote	H.R.F. Keating	£1.50
☐ Inspector Ghote Draws a Line	H.R.F. Keating	£1.50
☐ Inspector Ghote Plays a Joker	H.R.F. Keating	£1.50
☐ The Murder of the Maharajah	H.R.F. Keating	£1.50
☐ The Perfect Murder	H.R.F. Keating	£1.50
☐ The Dutch Shoe Mystery	Ellery Queen	£1.60
☐ The French Powder Mystery	Ellery Queen	£1.25
☐ The Siamese Twin Mystery	Ellery Queen	95p
☐ The Spanish Cape Mystery	Ellery Queen	£1.10
☐ Copper, Gold and Treasure	David Williams	£1.75
☐ Treasure by Degrees	David Williams	£1.75
☐ Unholy Writ	David Williams	£1.60

NAME ....

ADDRESS ....

....

Write to Hamlyn Paperbacks Cash Sales, PO Box 11, Falmouth, Cornwall TR10 9EN.

Please indicate order and enclose remittance to the value of the cover price plus:

U.K.: Please allow 45p for the first book plus 20p for the second book and 14p for each additional book ordered, to a maximum charge of £1.63.

B.F.P.O. & EIRE: Please allow 45p for the first book plus 20p for the second book and 14p per copy for the next 7 books, thereafter 8p per book.

OVERSEAS: Please allow 75p for the first book and 21p per copy for each additional book.

Whilst every effort is made to keep prices low it is sometimes necessary to increase cover prices and also postage and packing rates at short notice. Hamlyn Paperbacks reserve the right to show new retail prices on covers which may differ from those previously advertised in the text or elsewhere.